TAKE ME HOME

CARRIE ELKS

CHAPTER ONE

*T*he auditorium resounded with cheers, whistles, and catcalls. The thump of feet on the sticky tiled floor echoed with the sound of blood rushing through Gray Hartson's ears. He stood for a moment, his guitar hanging from his shoulder, his hands wrapped around the microphone, and let himself take it in.

This was the high. The rush that never lasted. But he'd take it while it did. For as long as it did.

"Sydney, you were awesome. Thank you and good night." Even with ear monitors in, he couldn't hear his own voice over the crowd. It didn't seem like they would be stopping any time soon. He lifted his hand and turned to go, but the noise increased, wrapping him like a blanket as he strolled off the stage.

In the wings, one roadie removed Gray's ear monitors, the other lifted his guitar over his head to carefully place it on a stand. Gray took a towel from somebody's hands and wiped the sweat from his face, then grabbed a bottle of water and swallowed the whole thing in one go.

"They're gonna have to turn the lights on if they want

them to go home," his manager, Marco, said, grinning at Gray as they walked down the hallway toward the dressing rooms. "Three encores. Three! Thank god we rehearsed them all. They're in love with you out there." Once upon a time that would have made him feel ten feet tall. Now he was just exhausted.

Gray pushed the dressing room door open, frowning at all the people inside. The guys from *Fast Rush*, the up-and-coming band that played his opener for the last leg of his world tour, were already on their third – or possibly fourth – drink, surrounded by a group of women who were giggling with them. He recognized the A&R guys from his record label, and a whole other bunch of groupies who were turning the dressing room into a party. He tried not to sigh.

It wasn't their fault the low was already hitting.

"Oh my god! It's Gray Hartson!" One of the girls surrounding *Fast Rush* had noticed him. All of a sudden, the support band was forgotten as the women surged forward.

"Is the other dressing room empty?" Gray asked Marco, his voice low.

"Yep."

"Okay, I'll use that one."

The second dressing room was used by the local musicians who'd supported the final part of the tour. He turned to leave, but one of the girls grabbed his arm. She slid something into his jeans pocket, and he found himself recoiling at the pressure of her fingers against his hip.

"Something to make you happy," she whispered, her eyes sparkling. "And my number. Call me."

Marco closed the door to the first dressing room and rolled his eyes. "I told them not to invite people back. I'm sorry, man."

"It's okay. It's their first major tour." Gray shrugged as they walked down the hallway. "Can you make sure some-

2

body stays sober to look after them? And to make sure they get back to the hotel safely?"

Marco nodded. "Of course."

"If there's any damage, put it on my bill."

They'd made it to the second dressing room, and as Gray pushed open the door, Marco walked off to take care of the support band, muttering something about calling for a car. Unlike the first room, this one was almost empty, save for one of Gray's session guitarists drinking a glass of orange juice.

"You not partying with the others?" Gray asked the older man as he grabbed himself another bottle of water.

"Nope. I'm heading back to the hotel shortly. My bed is calling me." Paul's eyes crinkled. "How about you? I didn't expect to see you back here."

Touring created strange allies. The only thing Gray had in common with this fifty-something, grizzled Australian was the fact they both played guitar. And yet, for the past two weeks they had hit it off, talking quietly at the back of buses and airplanes while the rest of the entourage shouted and laughed at the front.

"I'm too old to party."

Paul chuckled. "You're thirty-one. Just a baby."

"Tell my muscles that. And my bones." Gray rotated his head to iron out the kinks in his neck. "Anyway, I've got a flight to catch tomorrow. I don't want to miss it."

"You're heading to see your family, right?"

"Yeah." Gray sat back on the leather sofa and crossed his feet on the coffee table in front of him. "That's right."

"Funny place. Hartson's something…" Paul grinned. "Not many people I know have a whole town named after them."

"Hartson's Creek. And it's not named after me. Probably my great-great-great grandpa or something." Gray's brows scrunched together thinking about the small town in

3

Virginia where he'd grown up. The same place he hadn't been back to since he left more than a decade earlier.

"What is it they used to call you and your brothers?" Paul asked, a grin pulling at his lips. *The Heartbreak Brothers?* He'd overheard one of Gray's interviews while on the bus and hadn't let him live his past down since.

"Don't remind me." Gray shook his head. He couldn't remember who'd invented the damn name, but it had stuck to them like superglue. He and his three brothers – Logan, Cam, and Tanner, had rolled their eyes every time they'd heard it while they were growing up. Yeah, they were four strong, attractive teenage boys growing up in a small town, but that stupid nickname always drove them crazy.

Not as crazy as it drove their little sister, Becca, though. She hated hearing her female friends describing her brothers as 'hot'.

Something was digging into Gray's thigh. He frowned and pushed his hand into his pocket, finding what the woman had slid in there earlier. Pulling it out, he could see it was a clear plastic baggie, with white powder inside. She'd written her name and number in blue pen on the outside.

"That what I think it is?"

"Yup." Gray threw it in the trash can and leaned his head back against the wall. There was a time when he would have been partying like crazy after a gig. As his stardom rose up, he'd been like a kid in a candy store for a while, feeding on the fruits of his fame like there was a famine right around the corner.

But after the rise had come the crash. Waking in one strange bed too many, his head thumping with pain, his body filled with so many chemicals he could have set up his own lab. All followed by a three-day hangover that cost the record company thousands of dollars in unused studio time, and a missed performance on Jimmy Kimmel that had made him feel like a piece of shit.

It hadn't taken much to clean up his act. He was an idiot, not an addict. Marco had arranged for him to rent a studio in a secluded spot in Colorado, and he'd put his head down until he'd finished his second album. The record that raised him up from being a little famous to being a star.

God, he was tired. It wasn't just the tour – though that was draining on its own. It was everything. Trying to work on songs for the next album, talking with Marco about what kind of tour he wanted to promote it, and dealing with the calls from his sister about his dad being in the hospital with pneumonia.

It felt like all the energy had been sucked out of him. He wanted to sleep for months.

"Your car is here," Marco said, pushing the dressing room door open. "You just need to say goodbye to a few people first." He frowned at Gray, slumped on the bench. "Hey, you okay? You haven't showered."

"I'll do it back at the hotel." Gray stood and rolled his shoulders.

Paul walked over to shake his hand. "It was a pleasure working with you."

"And with you. Take it easy. Enjoy that family of yours." Gray had seen all the photographs of Paul's wife, three children, and six grandchildren.

"I intend to. I hope your father's feeling better soon."

"That reminds me," Marco said, steering Gray out of the room. "I spoke to your sister earlier. Your father was discharged and is recuperating at home. She wanted your flight details so they know when to expect you."

"She could have called me."

Marco laughed. "Do you know when your flight gets into Dulles?"

Gray frowned. "No."

"Which is why she called me. I also told her you'd be staying for a while, like we talked about. Give you a chance to write some songs in peace. There's no place like home, right?"

Home. Gray swallowed hard at the thought of the imposing Victorian building with the pristine lawn that led down to the creek that gave the town it's name. His father's house. The one he'd left as soon as he could and had sworn he'd never return to.

And yet here he was, about to return for the first time in more than ten years. To the place where his father still lived, along with his Aunt Gina and his sister, Becca.

After a quick talk with the people from his record label, they made it to the exit. Cool air was wafting through the open doors, reminding him that although it was spring in the US, Australia was slowly slipping from fall into winter. A security guard was waiting for them at the door, and he talked into his headset as soon as he saw Gray approaching. "Mr. Hartson," he said, turning to greet him. "If you'll follow me, I'll make sure you get to your car safely."

The tour was over. It was time to begin the long journey home. From the arena to the hotel to the airport, and onward to the US. His final stop being Hartson's Creek.

As he followed the guard through the doors, and into the dark Sydney night, he felt his stomach contract at the thought of where he was headed.

The crowd of fans gathered at the back of the arena roared as he stepped out, their voices loud as they began to chant his name. Gray lifted his hand to wave goodbye to them.

It was time to go home.

∼

"A<small>CCORDING TO THE</small> GPS, we should be there in five minutes," his driver said as they passed into the Hartson's Creek town limits. According to the weather-beaten sign, the town's population was still 9,872, the exact same number it had been when he left.

Gray turned his head to look out of the window. His stomach clenched at how familiar it all looked. The painted Victorian houses, the long lawns, and the wide, weatherworn roads. Had the town stood still for the last decade? Even the shops looked the same. As they stopped at a red light, he stared into the window of Bella's Bakery, taking in the iced cinnamon swirls and donuts he used to adore as a kid. He could almost taste that buttery, sugary goodness on his tongue. And next door, as always, was Murphy's Diner, the scene of his first gig – the one that led to the infamous Homecoming Brawl of 2005. His lips twitched at the memory of the carnage. At the way Ashleigh Clark had rubbed ointment onto his cut eye and split lip, telling him he looked hotter than hell after he'd been in a brawl.

He hadn't felt so hot the next morning when his dad received the bill for the damage done to the diner. Nor when he'd spent the following summer cleaning every inch of Murphy's greasy kitchen. He shuddered at the memory.

"We're here." The driver pulled the car to a stop.

Gray looked out of the window again. They were about a hundred yards short of the driveway to his family home, and he was okay with that. "Can we wait here for a minute?" he asked.

The driver shrugged. "You're the boss." He turned off the engine and leaned back in his seat as Gray looked toward the green hedges that bordered his father's land. He couldn't see the driveway but he knew it was there. Gray-and-red gravel that made a hell of a noise when you were trying to sneak home after curfew. It led to what he remembered as an imposing house. Tall red roof, white boarded walls, and a cupola in the center you could only reach via a rickety staircase.

The climb was always worth it. Because when you got to the top, the lantern windows gave you a three-sixty view over Hartson's Creek. To the west you could see the fields that stretched out in a green carpet to the Shenandoah Mountains far beyond. To the east was the sparkling blue of the creek, leading to the wheat farms that would be colored a burnished gold come fall.

The house didn't look so white anymore. The boards were peeling and decayed, down to the base wood in places. Even from here he could see where some shingles had slipped from the roof. But more than that, it looked small. So much smaller than he remembered. Like a miniature version of its real self.

He shook his head, his lip quirking up. Houses didn't shrink. Maybe he'd grown.

Two minutes later, Gray was standing at the base of the driveway, lifting a hand in goodbye as the black sedan made the turn out of Lawson Lane. Even the air smelled different. Cool, with a hint of corn coming up from the fields. And something else. Something old. As though every molecule of oxygen held memories of the past centuries since Hartson's Creek was founded.

"Gray. You made it!" The front door flew open and a blur of pink and blue rushed toward him. He had just enough time to put his guitar and suitcase down before Becca was jumping into his arms, her dark hair flowing out wildly behind her. "I thought that was you," she told him right as he caught her. "I saw a car stopped down the road. Aunt Gina owes me five dollars."

"You bet on that?" Gray's smile was broad. It always was when he saw his little sister. Gina had brought her out a few times to watch his shows, and he was always pleased to see her.

"The Wi-Fi's out again. We have to keep ourselves entertained somehow." Becca shrugged as though it wasn't a big deal. "Why didn't you get that big ol' car to drive up to the house? That would have given us something to gawk at."

"And that's why I didn't have it drive up to the house," Gray told her, deadpan.

Becca pulled herself out of his hug and grabbed his hand. "Come on, everybody's waiting inside."

"*Everybody?*" He ignored the pulling at his gut.

"Well, there's me and Aunt Gina. And Tanner's here for a couple of days," she said, referring to Gray's youngest brother. "Logan and Cam couldn't make it now, but they're coming in for Tanner's birthday." She grinned broadly. "All the Hartsons in one place. People won't know what's hit them."

"And Dad? Is he in there?"

"He's in bed." Her voice dropped. "His recovery is slow." She waited for him to pick up his things before she pulled him up the front steps, skipping over the middle one with a gaping hole in the plank. When he got to the top, he saw Tanner standing in the doorway, leaning casually on the doorjamb. At twenty-eight, Tanner was the youngest of the four brothers, but still four years older than Becca.

"The wanderer returns," he drawled as Gray reached the door, and leaned his guitar against the weatherboard wall. "What, no paparazzi? No screaming fans?" He dropped his voice an octave. "No groupies?"

"Sorry to disappoint you." Gray wrapped his brother in a bear hug. "What are you doing here? I thought you were in New York."

Tanner shrugged, lifting his hand to push his sandy hair

from his eyes. "I heard you were coming. I came for the groupies."

Becca wrinkled her nose. "You're disgusting," she said, swatting his arm. "Both of you."

Gray held his hands up straight in front of his chest. "Hey, I didn't say anything."

"He doesn't need to say anything. They flock to him." Tanner grinned. "Hey, Becca, did I tell you about that time I saw Gray in Vegas."

"What's all the noise out here? You trying to drive your father crazy?"

Aunt Gina walked out of the kitchen and down the hallway, her eyes lighting up when she saw Gray on the porch. "Grayson. You're here," she said.

"Yep. And you owe me five bucks," Becca told her.

Aunt Gina shuffled over the threshold and pulled Gray into a hug. "Oh, you're a sight for sore eyes," she whispered into his chest. "I didn't think you'd really come."

"Then why did you get his room ready?" Tanner frowned.

"Because I always have hope." Aunt Gina took a step back and looked Gray up and down. "Is that new?" she asked him, pointing at the edges of a tattoo peaking out from under his sleeve.

"This old thing?" Gray grinned at her, and went to pull his top off to show her more. "You wanna see?"

"No, I don't. You keep your t-shirt right where it is." She shook her head. "We have standards in this house."

"Unlike in Vegas," Tanner drawled, winking at his aunt. "Gray's top was constantly off there."

"You can be quiet," Aunt Gina said, shaking her head at Tanner. "And bring your brother's things in."

Tanner frowned. "He can carry his own stuff."

Gray swallowed down a laugh. Some things never changed. Becca's over enthusiasm, Tanner's bitching, even

Aunt Gina's cluckiness felt so familiar it made his stomach twist. It was like he was straddling two time zones, somewhere between the man he was and the kid he used to be. "I'll carry my bags," he told Tanner. "I wouldn't want you to hurt your back, sweetheart."

Tanner rolled his eyes. "I'll take it," he said, grabbing the handle. "I'd hate for you to hurt those pretty hands of yours. They must be insured for a million dollars."

"Two, actually." Gray shrugged, remembering his own outrage when he'd first discovered that fact.

Tanner reached for the guitar case, but Gray got there first. "I'll bring this one," he said, gently lifting the strap over his shoulder. As he followed his aunt inside, the smell of butter cookies filled his nose, making his mouth water.

He was home. Whatever that meant. Maybe a few weeks here wouldn't be so bad after all.

CHAPTER TWO

*I*n spring and summer, Friday evenings meant
Chairs, the strange name the good folk of Hartson's Creek gave their weekly gatherings. They'd all
congregate in the front yards alongside the creek, bringing
jugs of sweet tea and the odd bottle of something stronger,
along with their own chairs that gave the gathering its
name.

Chairs had been a part of Maddie Clark's life in Hartson's
Creek for as long as she could remember. As a child, she'd
run around playing games while the adults talked, reveling at
the freedom of being able to mess around until dark without
being sent to bed. Then as a teenager, when she'd do
anything to avoid having to go and listen to boring grown up
talk. The kind of small minded gossip that made her grateful
to be offered a scholarship place at The Ansell School of
Performing Arts in New York to study for her Bachelors in
Music.

And yeah, she had no doubt that she was the subject of *a
lot* of petty gossip when she came home less than a year later,
and unwilling to tell anybody why. Not that anybody said a

word to her. Not when she was waitressing at the diner, nor when she was teaching piano to the younger kids in town.

Still, her mom enjoyed being able to catch up with her friends and neighbors, and find out what was going on around town. For her mom, Maddie grinned and bared it, pushing her mom across the road in her wheelchair. She had an old, fold up chair for herself, the legs looped over her shoulders to carry it. A small cooler filled with sweet tea and snickerdoodles rested in her mom's lap.

"There are a lot of people here tonight," Maddie remarked as they reached the creek. "Must be the weather." It was her favorite time of year. Spring and summer were battling it out for dominance, the result already a foregone conclusion. The cold and snow of winter was just a memory, made more hazy by the warmth in the air and the smell of corn in the breeze.

She wheeled her mom over to where her friends had set themselves up, next to the refreshment table, where she unpacked the food they'd brought before pouring her mom a glass to drink from. Then she carried her own chair over to where the younger crowd was gathered. Women she knew from when they were at school gossiped about their husbands and called out to their children to calm down when their voices got too loud. The husbands were standing by the creek, drinking from brown beer bottles and laughing, ignoring everything around them as they dissected that week's football game.

"Did you hear the news?" Jessica Martin called out before Maddie could open her chair and place it on the grass.

"No." Maddie smiled politely. Jessica had been in the same grade as Maddie's sister, Ashleigh. They'd been cheerleaders together for as long as Maddie could remember, though she'd been six years younger than them both.

"You want to guess?" Jessica asked, rubbing her hands together. "Oh, you'll never guess."

"There's been an outbreak of chlamydia among the over fifties?"

Maddie bit down a grin at Laura Bayley's deep voice.

"No. Ewww. Of course not." Jessica wrinkled her nose. Then she looked at Laura. "That's not true, is it?"

Laura shrugged. "Nothing would surprise me around here."

Shaking her head, Jessica turned back to Maddie. "Have you heard from Ashleigh lately?"

"She lives in the next town," Laura pointed out. "It's not exactly Antarctica."

Maddie shot Laura a look of gratitude. Though Laura was a few years older than Maddie, they'd been friends since Laura had opened up her dress shop next to the diner where Maddie worked. Her favorite part of the day was when Laura came in for her morning coffee. "She came over with her kids last week," Maddie told them.

"And did she say anything?" Jessica asked, leaning forward, her blonde hair falling over her face.

Maddie blinked. "Like what?" She could feel her stomach tighten. Was there something wrong with Ashleigh? Or even worse, Grace or Carter? Maddie loved her niece and nephew like they were her own.

Jessica sat back in her chair. "I guess she doesn't know then."

"Know what?" Maddie asked, trying not to sound exasperated.

"That Jessica's the typhoid Mary of the chlamydia outbreak," Laura whispered from the corner of her mouth. Maddie laughed, in spite of herself.

"That Gray Hartson's back." Jessica gave Laura a smug smile. "I guess I'm the only one who knows anything around here."

Maddie felt herself freeze, in spite of the warm air

surrounding her. "Gray Hartson?" she repeated, ignoring the strange drumming in her ears.

"Yep. Carrie Daws told me. The one who works at the grocery store. According to her, he arrived in a black Rolls Royce." Jessica folded her arms across her chest. "I guess that's how the rich and famous travel when they're visiting their hometown."

"Is that why Becca isn't here tonight?" the woman sitting next to Jessica asked. "I was wondering about that."

Along with Laura, Becca Hartson was one of Maddie's closest friends. She enjoyed *Chairs* as much as Maddie did, so her absence wasn't a surprise. Maddie had never considered it could be because Gray was back in town.

The thought of him being here after all this time made her body feel light. She curled her hands around the metal tubing of her chair to stop herself from floating away.

"What will Ashleigh say?" Jessica asked, her voice loud enough to cut through Maddie's thoughts. "Do you think Michael will be jealous?"

"Why would Michael be jealous?" Laura asked. "Ashleigh went out with Gray for a few years during high school. Big deal. It's been more than ten years since then." She grinned at Jessica. "*Some* of us have grown up in the past decade."

Maddie leaned her chin on the palm of her hand and looked out toward the creek. The water was dark, and she could hear its movement rather than see it. On the far side, fireflies lit up the trees like thousands of tiny sparkling lamps.

Gray Hartson was back in town. It felt strange, knowing she was in the same town, watching the same sunset as he was. Once upon a time, she'd had a crush on him. One of those heart wrenchingly intense ones that only a preteen could have. She'd sit and watch him from her window as he brought Ashleigh home from a date, holding her breath as

15

he'd wipe a strand of hair from her sister's face, leaning in to press his lips against hers.

She'd felt a strange mixture of jealousy and wistfulness back then. Even at thirteen, she'd been mature enough to know he was out of her league. Too old, too talented, too good looking. But Ashleigh had been a match for him with her ice-blonde beauty and popularity at school. Together, they'd been the king and queen of senior year.

"You should probably tell Ashleigh before Jessica does," Laura said, leaning in to whisper in Maddie's ear as she walked past. "I know it's been years, but nobody likes seeing their ex unaware. Give her a chance to get to the beauty salon and look like a million dollars." Laura stood and winked at her. "I'm heading to fix me a drink. Anybody else want one?" she called out.

After Jessica's revelation, Maddie felt the urge to drink something much stronger than sweet tea.

And it was all Gray Hartson's fault.

CHAPTER THREE

"*W*ell your secret's out," Becca told Gray as they sat at the dinner table. "I just got a text from Laura Bayley. You're the talk of *Chairs.* By the end of the night, everybody in town will know you're here."

"Sweetheart, you know the rules. No phones at the dinner table," Aunt Gina chided. Becca grinned and slid her iPhone back into her pocket.

"*Chairs?*" Gray frowned. "You guys still do that?"

"This *is* Hartson's Creek we're talking about," Tanner said, scooping a giant spoonful of mashed potatoes onto his plate. "It's barely reached the twentieth century, let alone the twenty-first. What else is there to do except get drunk and gossip?"

"People don't drink at *Chairs,*" Aunt Gina said, taking the bowl of mash from Tanner and passing it to Gray. "And we talk, not gossip."

"Tomayto-tomahto." Tanner grinned at her. "And we all know Rita Dennis spikes the iced tea. That's how the gossip always starts." He swallowed a mouthful of potato. "I tried to

17

explain the concept of *Chairs* to my friends in New York. They looked at me as if I was crazy."

"Grayson, can you make your father a plate of food?" Aunt Gina asked him, passing him an empty plate. "He should be awake by now. Maybe you could take it in and say hello."

"I'll probably ruin his appetite." Gray took the plate anyway, and loaded it up.

"No gravy for him," Becca said.

"I remember." Gray nodded. "It ruins the taste of the meat." Strange how Gray could recall his father stating that so clearly. He stood, leaving his own food half finished. He knew that Aunt Gina would warm it for him when he got back.

The way she always had.

"Gray?" his aunt said.

"Yeah?"

"Go easy on him, he's still not well." Her lips pressed together as her eyes met his.

"I wasn't planning on doing anything else."

"I know." Aunt Gina's smile was tight. "It's just that you two… well, you always knew how to push each others buttons."

"What she means is, don't piss him off," Tanner drawled. "Which is almost impossible in my experience."

"Ignore him," Becca said, raising her eyebrows at Tanner. "He's just annoyed because nobody's talking about *him* at *Chairs*."

"That's because I come home more than once a decade," Tanner pointed out.

It was just like old times. Gray could remember the constant banter at the dinner table as he and his brothers ribbed each other mercilessly. As the eldest, he'd always tried to be the peacemaker. There were days when he expected Cam and Logan to fight each other to the death.

Until their father intervened, that was. One slap of his hands on the table was usually enough to quiet them down. And if for some reason they didn't respond, raising his voice a couple of notches always did the trick. By their teenage years, they'd learned not to push him any further. Not one of them wanted to be told to meet him in his study after dinner.

"If you'll all be quiet, maybe I could hear myself think," Aunt Gina said, shooting them all a dark look. "And show some respect, Tanner. This is your father's house. He deserves it."

"Respect is earned," Tanner said, his voice light in spite of his words.

"I'll take it easy in there," Gray reassured his aunt. She nodded and gave him another smile.

"Good luck," Becca whispered, squeezing his free hand as Gray walked past her.

As far as Gray was concerned, he didn't need it. He wasn't a child anymore. He had his own home, his own car, earned more money in a month than his father had his entire life. That old man in the bedroom at the end of the hallway didn't scare him anymore.

"To hell with it," he whispered to himself, before he rapped his knuckles on the door. His hand remained in a fist when he pulled it away, as though his body was expecting a fight, the other still grasping the plate of food he'd made up.

"Come in."

Gray blinked at the familiarity of that voice. He set his jaw strong, and curled his fingers around the handle, bracing himself as he arranged his features into a smile.

People thought it was strange when he told them he hadn't spoken to his father in more than a decade. They wanted all the details of the fight that must've led to such a cut-off. But there hadn't been a fight – not a single explosive episode of one, anyway. Instead, his relationship with his father had been the victim of a thousand paper cuts.

As a child, he'd dreamed of escaping this place. He'd build a tree house in the woods that bordered his father's land to the north, fill it with comics and sodas and invite his friends over. In his mind, his dad would never find him there.

As he grew older, his plans grew more sophisticated. At first, they were academic. He studied hard, played football, did anything that would help him get into college. But where his grades were good enough for an acceptance, his sports weren't good enough for a scholarship. And his father's income was too much for him to receive any financial assistance without loans.

One thing he knew, he couldn't be beholden to his father any more. So when his one way of relaxing – his music – proved to be his one-way-ticket out of town, he'd jumped at the chance. Left everything – *and everyone* – behind. A necessary sacrifice to gain his freedom.

Of course he saw his family still. His brothers would come to meet him in New York or L.A. when they could. Aunt Gina and Becca would see him play in concert in Virginia and D.C. There was one year when he paid for them all to fly to London to watch him play at a festival there. That had been a great week.

But his father never came. He refused to unless Gray personally called to invite him, but Gray knew that was a trap. His father only wanted the pleasure of rejecting his offer in person.

"I said come in," his father shouted. "What are you doing, playing with the handle?"

Gray shook his head and pushed the door open, squaring his shoulders as he walked inside. The first thing that hit him was the smell. Though the room wasn't a study anymore, the walls were still lined with old books, their musty pages turning the air sickly stale. Then there was the pine of his father's soap – the same soap he'd used for as long as Gray could remember.

"I brought your dinner in."

The old man looked up from his position on the bed. The years Gray had been away hadn't been kind to his father. Grayson Hartson III's hair was sparse, barely covering his shiny red scalp. His skin was wrinkled, almost rubbery in complexion. But it was his body that shocked Gray the most. Even through the sheet he could see how thin his father was. His arms looked like the kind of twigs Aunt Gina used to bring in at Christmas time to make up seasonal displays.

"The food'll be cold with the time you took to come in," his dad grumbled.

Gray swallowed. "You don't want it?"

"I didn't say that. Bring it here." His father nodded at the table in front of him. It was on wheels – the kind you saw in hospital rooms. Gray carried the plate over and set it firmly in the middle.

"So you decided to visit?" his father said, leaning over to look at the plate. "Damn beef again. Your aunt knows I can't eat that. Gets stuck in my throat."

"You want me to get some gravy to help it go down?"

His dad sniffed. "I'll just eat the potato. Get me a fork."

Gray passed him the silverware, and watched as his father scooped a morsel of mashed potato between his lips. Time seemed to pause as he moved his jaw around, his withered throat undulating as he tried to swallow it down. "You want a glass of water?" Gray asked him.

"No," his father rasped out. "Go back to your dinner. I'm fine here."

Gray wasn't sure what to feel as he watched his dad lift another shaky forkful to his mouth. Sympathy fought with resentment, as his mind tried to take in this new reality. His father was old and sick, yet he was still the man who'd made Gray's childhood a misery.

"This isn't a free show," his father said when he'd swallowed the second mouthful. "You can go now." He stared at Gray with the same blue eyes he saw in the mirror every day, and then made a shooing movement with his hands.

Gray shrugged and turned away. He'd done his duty, nobody could say he hadn't. When he returned to L.A., his father would be a hazy memory once again.

MADDIE STARED AT HER PHONE, her fingers hovering over her sister's name on the screen. *Ashleigh Lowe.* She may have slipped down a few letters in Maddie's contacts since getting married, but she'd stepped up a whole lot of social stratas when she said 'I do' to Michael Lowe. A prominent attorney in Stanhope, the city twenty miles north of Hartson's Creek, Michael was also the son of a senator, and was working hard on being his father's replacement in the next election.

The two of them had met when Ashleigh was working in a restaurant in Stanhope and had served Michael and his coworkers. She'd only been twenty when they married a little over a year later, to Michael's thirty-one. Not that anybody raised an eyebrow. They were too busy questioning whether she was still rebounding from Gray Hartson.

Maddie pressed her finger on the screen and waited for her call to connect. She was struggling with her reaction to Gray's name being mentioned at *Chairs.* She'd reacted like the teenage girl she'd been when he was last here, her heart clattering against her chest, her head feeling as light as air.

Thank god nobody else had spotted it. She was usually so cool. When did they say he was leaving again?

"Maddie? Is something wrong?" Ashleigh's voice echoed through Maddie's phone. "Is it Mom?"

Maddie glanced at the old Casio on her wrist. It was almost eleven. "Sorry, I didn't realize it was so late," she told her sister. "Did I wake you?"

"No. I'm waiting for Michael to come home. I'm sitting on the deck drinking a mug of hot chocolate. Are you okay?"

"Yeah. I just wanted to tell you something." Maddie pulled at a loose thread in her comforter. "It's probably nothing, but I wanted you to hear it from me first."

"What gives?"

"Gray's back in town. Jessica Martin told me, and Laura called Becca to make sure it was true. You know what the gossip's like around here."

Ashleigh was silent, save for the rhythm of her breathing. Maddie pulled her lip between her teeth, waiting for her sister to respond. It felt strange, having this conversation. Neither of them had mentioned Gray for years. It was an unspoken agreement. They never talked about his music, his success, or about any of the gossip that seemed to surround him like fireflies in the summer. It was as though Ashleigh had cut him out of her life with a pair of scissors and thrown him in the trash can.

"Ash?" Maddie said, tiny lines furrowing her brow.

Ashleigh cleared her throat. "I'm sorry. I was listening out for the children," she said quickly. "So he's back. I'm guessing it's not for long."

"For a few weeks, according to Becca."

"That's probably for the best." Ashleigh's laugh sounded forced. "Hopefully I won't bump into him while he's here."

"I don't imagine you will. That was all. I just wanted you to know."

"Thank you. Are you still okay to watch Grace and Carter on Sunday?"

"Yeah, I'm looking forward to it. I finish work at three, so any time after works."

"I'll send you a message once I know. Good night, Maddie. Sweet dreams."

"And to you." Maddie ended the call and put her phone on the nightstand next to her bed, falling back until her head hit the soft pillow. It had been a long day, and yet her body was still buzzing like it was filled with a hive full of bees. She was due to work at six in the morning and she needed the sleep, dammit.

But her body felt strange. Electric. Like everything around her was on the edge of something different.

She wasn't sure she liked the sensation.

CHAPTER FOUR

*G*ray lay awake in his too-small childhood bed and looked at the walls closing in on him. They were bare – all the posters he'd put up as a teenager in defiance of his dad's rules were long since gone, leaving behind only dark rectangles of paint and shiny circles where he'd affixed them to the wall.

He sat up, running a hand through his hair. Maybe he should get outside for a few. Breathe some fresh air and let the breeze blow away the dreams that had been haunting his brain all night. He pulled on some fresh clothes from the suitcase he hadn't bothered to unpack and quietly let himself out of the house. As he locked the door behind him, he hoped to hell that somebody was up when he returned to let him back in.

As he made his way down the gravel driveway, he pulled a grey knit beanie over his dark hair, by habit more than need. He was used to making himself look as unremarkable as possible in public. The roads were quiet as he walked through town, only the occasional roar of an engine cutting through the still morning air. Gray felt his muscles loosen, his jaw untense. He'd forgotten how much that house put him on edge.

When he made it to the town square ten minutes later, there was a light on in Murphy's Diner, and his stomach growled as if it knew what that meant. He slapped the pocket of his jeans to make sure he had his wallet and headed in.

The diner was as empty as the streets. He walked up to the counter and took in the glass domes covering freshly baked chocolate chip cookies and generous wedges of lemon cake. The smell made his mouth water.

"I'm sorry, I didn't hear you come in," a woman called from the half-open door to the kitchen. "I'll be right there."

"No rush."

Gray leaned on the counter as the woman backed through the door, pushing it open with her denim-clad behind. He blinked when he realized he was staring. Soft, rounded, and completely inappropriate to be caught looking at. Somehow he managed to tear his gaze away before she turned around and put the tray she was carrying on the counter in front of him.

"Oh." She blinked. "Can I get you some coffee?"

Her expression was unreadable. He had no idea if she knew who he was or not. Becca had said that most of Hartson's Creek knew he was back in town, but his little sister was always known to exaggeration.

He nodded. "Black. No sugar, please."

"Coming right up." The waitress smiled as she poured him a cup. "Are you ready to order?"

"I'll let the caffeine work first." He took the mug from her, the tips of her fingers sliding against his. He frowned at the shock it sent up his arm, the sensation making his hand shake, hot coffee splashing over the rim and onto his fingers.

"Oh my god, I'm sorry." The waitress tore a wad of paper towel from the roll on the wall behind her. "Are you okay? Did I burn you?" She pressed the towel against his hand. "I have a first aid kit here somewhere. We must have some cream in it."

"It's fine," he said, amused. "It was just a few drops. We can probably hold off on the burn kit."

She looked at him through her thick lashes. Christ, she was pretty, in a girl-next-door kind of way. Big hazel eyes and freckles across her high cheekbones that reminded him of a fawn. As she leaned across the counter and dabbed at his hand, he tried not to look down at the curve of her chest.

What the hell was wrong with him? He really wasn't that kind of guy. Bringing his gaze firmly back to her face, he realized she looked familiar.

Not that it was a big surprise. He probably went to school with her, or played football with her brother, or made out with her cousin at a school dance. He only had to ask her name to find out who she was and who her relations were, yet he didn't.

Because then he'd have to tell her who he was.

He lifted the cup to his lips and swallowed a mouthful of coffee, watching as she wiped up the counter. He barely tasted it as it went down.

"You want a top up?" she asked him.

"That'd be good." He held his mug out. She was extra careful this time, pouring slowly and leaving a good inch of space between the coffee and the rim of his cup. "I'll order in a minute. I'm still trying to make up my mind."

"Take your time. Murphy's still half asleep back there, anyway. I always advise customers not to expect anything edible before eight a.m."

Gray laughed. "Is that why this place is so empty?"

She shook her head. "It's empty because everybody's sleeping as long as they can before church starts. We're never busy on Sundays until service lets out."

"Everybody goes to church?" *Still?* Gray hadn't stepped foot in a church in years.

"Pretty much."

"Except you."

She grinned. "I pray at the church of coffee."

"You're going to hell." He winked at her.

"I've been there. Stayed a few years, got a t-shirt, decided not to go back again." She raised an eyebrow as she leaned her elbow on the counter and rested her chin on her palm. "Pretty sure the devil has more important people to concentrate on than me."

Her lips curled up and they did something to him. They were completely devoid of make-up, yet as plump as any he'd seen in L.A.

It had been way too long since he'd gotten laid, that was for sure. And the thought of remedying that in Hartson's Creek made him want to laugh. Gossip flew through this place faster than the speed of light, and he was way more concerned about Aunt Gina finding out than any gossip rag that might pay for that kind of information.

"Okay, I think I'm ready to order. I'll take the pancakes, maple syrup on the side. And do you have strawberries?"

"Sure do."

"I'll take some fresh ones cut up in a bowl on the side."

"You want any eggs?" she asked him.

"Nah."

"Good call. We had a food critic from the *Stanhope Daily* come here once. He called them inedible." She shook her head and leaned a little closer. "That's kind of a lie. What he actually said was *'eating fried eggs at Murphy's Diner reminded me of the first time I gave my boyfriend some deep affection.*

Readers, I advise you to spit, not swallow.' She wrinkled her nose.

Gray burst into laughter. God, she was cute. He really wanted to see if those lips felt as good as they looked. Wanted to run his fingers through that hair and see if it was as silky as he imagined.

"Definitely hold the eggs," he told her. And as she turned to walk into the kitchen, he averted his eyes and stared out of the window onto the square. Yeah, she was pretty, but he was used to pretty girls. The one thing he didn't need was a complication like that.

AFTER HE DEMOLISHED two plates of Murphy's finest pancakes, Gray walked out of the diner, his long, denim-clad legs covering the distance between the counter and the door in a few strides. Maddie's face heated up as soon as the door closed behind him. Through the glass, she saw him adjust the woolen beanie on his head then stuff his hands into his pockets as he headed down the sidewalk. His cheeks were pulled in, his lips pursed as though he was whistling. She grabbed the empty plate and let out a big sigh.

"Murph?" she called out.

"Huh?" He was sitting on the chair in the corner, reading a newspaper, a goofy smile on his face. Which was weird because Murphy never smiled.

"What are you reading?"

"The funnies."

"You look like you're enjoying them."

"They're crap." As though he'd just realized he was smiling, Murphy's brow pulled down and he rolled up the paper and threw it across the room. "Don't know why I buy that rag anyway."

Maddie bit down a grin. Murphy had been cultivating the grumpy-old-man look for years. "I'm going to take a break. There's nobody in the diner, but I'll keep an eye out and come back if we get any customers."

"Huh." He nodded and slid his eyes back to the paper on the floor.

Taking that as a yes, she poured herself a mug of coffee, adding extra cream, before making her way out to the bench set at the center of the town square. It was her favorite place to take a break, especially when there was nobody else here. In the summer, she'd close her eyes and smell the scent of the rose garden carried up in the warm breeze. And in the winter, she'd zip her padded jacket up tightly and huddle around her mug as though it was a warming fire.

"I forgot to ask your name." The smooth, deep sound of his voice made her jump.

Maddie looked up to see Gray standing over her, his tall body blocking out the early morning sun.

"My name?" she repeated, her brows knitting together.

"Yeah, I want to write a Trip Advisor review. Tell all the readers that you told me to avoid the jizz eggs."

Maddie bit down a smile. "In that case, my name's Cora Jean," she told him. "You want me to spell that for you?"

"You don't look like a Cora Jean." He tipped his head to the side, his dark blue eyes catching hers. She'd forgotten how magnetic he was. How he drew everybody toward him. She curled her free hand around the wooden slat of the bench in case her body decided to throw itself at him.

"What does a Cora Jean look like?"

The corner of his lip twitched. "I'm kinda screwed here, aren't I? If I tell you Cora Jean looks about sixty years old with nicotine stained fingers and a better moustache than I could ever grow, and your name really turns out to be Cora Jean then you're going to want to hit me."

"And if my name isn't Cora Jean?"

His voice lowered. "Then I'd say I'm not surprised, because you still have a way to go with that moustache."

"You're a real sweet talker."

"That's the effect you have on me, Cora Jean." He grinned.

Her own lips twitched. It was almost impossible not to smile at him. God, he looked good. His gray long-sleeved t-shirt did nothing to hide the contours of his chest or the size of his biceps, and his dark jeans clung to his ass like they never wanted to let go.

When they'd first locked eyes in the diner, she'd expected him to recognize her right away. She hadn't changed that much since she was a kid – or at least she didn't think so. And yet there was no hint of recognition in his eyes as she'd wiped the coffee from his fingers.

And for some strange reason she liked that. She didn't have to explain why she was still living here in Hartson's Creek, years after she was supposed to have left. Didn't have to tell him that while he was topping the charts in five different countries, she'd been living with her mom and flinging hash to keep a roof over their head.

For a few minutes back there, she'd liked being somebody else. But it was fleeting, she knew that. Somebody only had to walk past and greet her and he'd figure out exactly who she was. Nobody flew under the radar in this town.

"My break's over," she told him, swallowing the last of her coffee. "I need to get back."

He nodded and took a step back. "Well, it was good to meet you, Cora Jean. Thanks for breakfast, and for saving me from scrambled sperm."

She laughed and shook her head, flipping her braid over her shoulder as she stood. "Any time."

Then she turned and walked to the diner without looking back, because her throat felt too tight to look at him again.

31

As soon as she pulled the door open and stepped inside she let out a lungful of air.

Gray Hartson ate breakfast with her. If she told the story at *Chairs* they'd be talking about *her* for weeks.

Which was exactly why she wouldn't tell a soul.

CHAPTER FIVE

"I never thought I'd see the day when you'd come to church willingly," Aunt Gina said as she slid her hand into the crook of his elbow and they walked up the steps to the First Baptist Church right off the town square

"What else is there to do on a Sunday morning?" Gray shrugged.

"Becca and Tanner found things to do."

"They aren't even awake yet." Gray smiled at his aunt. "And I'm all kinds of jetlagged. My body doesn't know if it's yesterday or tomorrow."

"Well, you're a good boy." She pulled her hand from his crook and patted his face. "Though you could have shaved."

"I'm hoping God'll forgive a few hairs."

He pushed open the church door and swallowed hard as everybody turned to look at them. The benches were full-to-bursting with worshippers, and what looked like some non-worshippers, too. He could see a few of the latter tapping furiously on their phones. He swallowed hard, hoping word about him being here wasn't going to get out.

"It's busy today," Aunt Gina murmured, patting his arm.

"A lot of younger folk, too." She tisked as she saw the phones. As they passed one girl who was blatantly recording him, Gina glared at her. "Can you believe that?" she hissed. "They're not even embarrassed about it."

"It's okay. I'm used to it."

"Well I'm not." There was a deep 'v' notched into the skin between her eyes. "It's so rude."

Gray led her to a bench a few rows back from the front, and everybody shuffled across to make room for them. He recognized a few faces there – parents of his old friends and friends of his parents. Their faces a little more worn, their hair whiter than when he'd left, but still the same.

Somebody tapped him on the shoulder and he turned to see a phone held out by a teenage girl. "Can I have a selfie with you?"

"Uh. Yeah. Sure."

Before he could even get the last word out, she was putting her shoulder next to his and angling the phone at their faces. "Hey," she said as she took what seemed like a hundred shots. "Are you going to sing today?"

"Of course he's going to sing," the girl next to her said. From the color of their hair and the similarity of their features, he assumed they were sisters. "It's a church. We have hymns, you idiot."

"I meant up front. A solo. Wouldn't that be amazing? I could record it." The first girl's eyes lit up. "Do you have an Insta account? I'll tag you in the pic. Oh, could you comment on it? That would drive Ella Jackson crazy. She says she's your biggest fan, but she doesn't even know all the words to *Along the River*."

The organ blasted out, its deep notes stifling any possible reply. Not that he had one. Gray turned to face forward as Reverend Maitland walked in, his long white robe fanning out behind him.

He could still feel the burning on the back of his neck. The one that told him he was being watched. Maybe he should have brought some security to town with him, but really, what kind of asshole brought protection into their local church? It was a lose-lose situation. Either he sat here and took it, or he acted like a diva and walked out. As Aunt Gina looked up at him, her concerned expression illuminated by the half-light, he realized he was in for the count.

He just had to get through the next hour. He could do that, couldn't he?

And then he'd avoid church for the next millennium or so.

MADDIE BUSIED herself in the still-quiet diner, wiping down tables that were already clean and rearranging the menus stacked in their holder on top of the counter. She always hated this part of Sunday, the calm before the storm, when church let out and everybody rushed to the diner to try and secure their favorite seats.

Last week there'd almost been a fight between Mary-Ellen Jones and Lucy Davies as they both tried to slide their ample behinds into the booth near the front door. It had taken ten minutes of negotiation and the offer of free pastries before Lucy could be persuaded to take the booth behind it.

The bell above the door rang out and Cora Jean walked in, her glorious silver hair pulled back into a perfect bun. Despite her age, she was sprightly, and still loved to work every Sunday to cover the post-church rush. She also managed to put the fear of god into most of Hartson's Creek's teenage population.

Seeing Cora reminded Maddie of her conversation with

Gray. He wasn't really planning to write a Trip Advisor report, was he? If he did, she'd have to refute it and apologize to Cora Jean. Oh god, what if it went viral?

She shook her head at her own idiocy. It'd seemed so funny pretending to be someone else at the time.

"What are all those folks doing hanging around the church?" Cora Jean asked as she hung her jacket on the row of hooks beside the counter. "I haven't seen so many young'uns up this early since they released the last Harry Potter book."

"That was ten years ago," Maddie said, amused.

"Yeah, well they don't make kids like they used to. They're too busy watching videos on their phones and writing bleats to care about books anymore." Cora Jean pulled her apron over her head, expertly avoiding her hair. "Do you know I miss the days when you were all television addicts?"

"Bleats?" Maddie repeated.

"You know, that twitter thing. Bleats. Don't tell me you don't know what they are?"

"They're *tweets*. As in birds. That's why it's called Twitter." Maddie had to bite down a laugh. "And I'm not sure the kids use that any more. It's all Snapchat and Instagram. Anyway, why are there so many people at the church? Is there a christening or something?"

"Not that I know of." Cora Jean shrugged. "They're all sitting on the steps like they were waiting for a bus. With their phones stuck in their hands, of course."

"I'm going to look." Maddie walked to the door and stared out. The First Baptist Church was at the opposite corner of the big green grass square, partially obscured by the bandstand and oak trees that nestled around it. She craned her head up anyway, but it was no good. She couldn't see a thing.

"You okay here if I leave for a moment?" she asked Cora Jean, who nodded.

Outside, Maddie walked around the square, stopping on the other side where, sure enough, there was a crowd of at least thirty people, all staring up at the whitewashed walls of the First Baptist building. When the oversize wooden doors opened the crowd started to buzz. Those who'd been sitting on the steps stood and surged toward the open door. The others joined them, pushing their way through with elbows, holding their phones up in the air.

"Is Gray Hartson in there?" one of the girls shouted.

"Yeah, we want Gray."

The noise increased, and Maddie stood frozen to the ground, a little appalled and way too entertained.

Was Gray really in there? What the hell was he thinking? Hartson's Creek might have been a sleepy little town, but it wasn't comatose. News spread as quickly here as it did in LA and New York and whatever other city he was used to.

Quicker, probably, because bored people loved gossip.

Reverend Maitland appeared in the doorway. Even from here, Maddie could see the confusion on his face at the sudden interest the local kids were showing in the First Baptist Church. He held out his hands and she half expected the crowd to part like the Red Sea, but instead two girls ducked behind him and ran into the building.

"Young ladies!" Reverend Maitland called out, his brows pinched together. "The service is over."

Maddie stifled a laugh. This was all so preposterous. And so out of the ordinary for a Sunday in Hartson's Creek.

Another teenager bumped into Reverend Maitland and the smile slipped from Maddie's face. Somebody was going to get hurt. Reverend Maitland stepped forward to steady himself, and the space he'd vacated was immediately filled by more people.

Maddie let out a big mouthful of air and walked toward the church, frowning as Reverend Maitland was forced down another couple of steps. "Hey!" she called out, trying to push through all the people. "You guys need to chill. Stop pushing."

It was as though they'd heard nothing. They continued to push against each other and the Reverend. Maddie had to elbow people out of the way to reach him.

She reached for his arm. "Are you all right?"

"I'm okay," he said, a little breathless. "Maybe a little bruised. But there's a young man in there who's a lot worse off than me."

"Is Gray in there?" she asked. Even though her voice was low, the mention of his name made the crowd roar again.

"I'm afraid so. I told them all to remain seated while I went to see what was going on out here. And now I can't get back in."

"Can you let the Reverend back in his church, please?" she called out to the crowd on the steps. "Come on, show a little respect."

Apparently, respect was a scarce commodity around here. But her elbows seemed to work where her request didn't, and somehow she managed to help Reverend Maitland back to the porch. "You should probably close the doors," she told him as they reached the door. "I'll call the police and get these teens cleared."

"The only one on duty is Scott Davis. These kids will eat him for breakfast," Reverend Maitland told her. "We need to get Gray Hartson out of here. That should take the wind out of their sails."

"Where is he?"

"In the third row when I saw him last." Reverend Maitland gestured to the middle of the church. Nobody was sitting down anymore. They were all milling around, talking rapidly, their eyes wide as though nothing like this had ever happened in Hartson's Creek.

"Is the back door open?" she asked.

"Yes. You just need to push the safety bar. But there's nowhere to go except around to the front of the church."

She remembered it well. The rear of the First Baptist was surrounded by the backyards of the road beyond. And in front of those was the river. Whether you were walking or driving, the only way out was around the town square.

"I'll work it out," she muttered. "It's that or feed him to the lions."

CHAPTER SIX

"This is stupid," Gray said to his aunt as she held onto his arm. He was exasperated by all the fuss going on around him. "I'll just go out there and let them take some photos. They'll get bored soon enough." He went to walk away, but she grasped on tighter. He could have easily prized her off, but there was no way he wanted to hurt her.

"Stay here," she said firmly. "Reverend Maitland will deal with it."

"It'll be easier on everyone if I go. I don't want anybody to get hurt." He could imagine the headlines now. He was big enough and bad enough to take care of himself, after all.

"Here comes Reverend Maitland," the woman standing next to them said. "And he doesn't look very happy."

"Is everything okay?" Aunt Gina asked as Reverend Maitland approached them. "Has the crowd gone?"

She loosened her grip and Gray took the opportunity to pull his arm away. "Sorry about this," he said to the reverend. "I'll go out and speak to them and ask them to leave. That way everybody can get on with their day."

"No, I really don't advise that." Reverend Maitland's

cheeks were pink. "They're a little bit… overexcited. I want you to leave through the back door, the one between the pulpit and the organ. Someone's waiting there to help you out."

Gray looked at the door then back at the reverend. "The back door?" he repeated. "You want me to make a run for it? I'm not scared of them, it'll be fine." This was getting crazy. It was Hartson's Creek, not Hollywood.

"You might be, but I'm worried about the girls out there. It's safer if you disappear."

"He's right, Gray," Aunt Gina told him. "It'll be easier if you leave by the back door."

"All right. I'll go. Even if this is all damn crazy. Are you coming?"

She shook her head. "I'll slow you down."

"We'll take care of her," Reverend Maitland told him. "Once you're gone, the crowd will disperse. And then maybe I can have some breakfast."

"Gray! Gray Hartson! Where are you?" somebody called out.

"You should go now!" Reverend Maitland said urgently.

Gray had been hustled out of places before – usually surrounded by his security detail, his head down until he climbed into a waiting car and was driven away. But he'd never had to escape from a church before. And if he was honest, it felt a little emasculating.

He shook his head and kissed his aunt on her cheek. "I'll see you at home, okay?"

She nodded and he followed Reverend Maitland's directions, striding toward the door, yanking it open, and walking through. Another step forward and he walked into something small and warm and… shit… did he knock someone over?

No, not someone. *Her*. Again.

"Cora Jean?" he asked, as she stumbled against the clothes rail on the side of the tiny room. "Did I hurt you?"

"No." She shook her head. "I'm fine." She straightened the robes that were hanging from the rail. "We need to get out of here. Follow me."

"Follow *you*?" His brows knit together. "Where are we going? The diner?"

She grinned at him, and he found his lips curling up in response. She was still wearing her Murphy's Diner apron over her tight jeans and black tank. Even with it covering her body, it was impossible to ignore the curves beneath. She licked her dry lips and he tried not to stare at them. *Honestly.*

"We're not going to the diner," she said, inclining her head at the door on the other side of the robing room. "I hope you go to the gym regularly. We're going to climb through a few backyards."

Gray resisted the urge to smile at the serious expression on her face. She wanted to play the savior and who was he to let her down? And if it meant spending a little more time with her, he could live with that.

"Come on," she said, grabbing his hand, leading him to the emergency exit on the far side of the room.

She tried to push the bar, but it didn't move. "Here, let me," Gray murmured, pressing down on the bar. It gave with a metallic sigh and the door opened into the churchyard.

Grey looked around and saw the yard was empty. *Thank God.* "Where next?" he asked, letting her lead the way.

"Over here." She pointed at the fence. "We climb over the Thorsens' fence, then through the hole in the Carter's wall. You'll be pleased to hear there's a gate between the Carters and the Shortlands." She winked at him. "Rumor has it, old man Shortland was having a tryst with Mamie Carter and the gate made things a little easier."

42

Small towns. He'd forgotten how much they drove him crazy.

The first fence was easy. Gray went in front, lifting himself up easily, his biceps contracting as he swung his body over the ridge. He held a hand out to Cora who took it and scrambled up beside him, the two of them dropping to the lawn on the other side.

"Where's the hole?" he asked.

She blinked. "It was there," she said, pointing at five rows of bricks. "I'm sure it was. Just enough to wriggle through."

"Did you wriggle through it often?"

She pulled her lip between her teeth and *damn.* What was it about this woman? "I wasn't a big fan of church when I was a kid," she confessed. "Whenever the sermon got boring, I'd go to the bathroom and escape for a while. Nobody ever noticed."

"You really are going to hell." He grinned.

"We both will be unless we get out of here." She looked at the big house at the end of the two-hundred foot yard. "Maybe we can knock on the Thorsens' back door. They'll let us through."

Gray shook his head. "Nah. Let's not get them involved. Besides, I want to watch you climb that wall."

She raised an eyebrow and he wanted to smooth it back down. "You think I can't do it?"

"I didn't say that. Just said I wanted to watch."

"Hmm." She walked over to the wall and looked it up and down, as though trying to work out the easiest way over. It was towering over her. Taller than him, too, but with a jump and the strength of his arms he was pretty sure he could scale it.

She tipped her head to the side and flexed her hands. He watched as she rolled on her feet, her body tensing as she readied herself to launch.

"Wish me luck," she muttered. Bending her knees, she pressed down on the grass then jumped up, the tips of her fingers skimming against the top of the wall.

And then she fell back, her legs staggering against the grass. Gray walked forward until her body hit his with some force.

Enough to take his breath away.

"Oof." She leaned her body against his and the warmth of her surged through him. He had to curl his hands into fists to stop himself from sliding them around her and pressing his fingers into her skin.

She tipped her head back against his chest until her eyes met his. They were hot and intense, as though she could read his mind. He swallowed, shocked by how his body responded to hers. If this was another time, another place…

"Who's there?" a voice called out from the house at the far end of the yard. He looked to see a figure standing on the deck, hands on hips.

"That's Della Thorsen," Cora murmured.

Gray lifted his hand in a wave. "Shall we get out of here?" he asked Cora.

"You go. I'll throw myself at Della's feet and beg for forgiveness."

"Save your begging for another time," he said, his voice thick. "I'll help you over the wall."

"And how do you intend to do that?"

"Like this." He threaded his fingers together, palms up, then scooted down in front of the wall.

She sighed. "I'm too heavy. I'll break your fingers."

"It's okay, they're insured."

She gave him a look.

He grinned. "Hey, I figure you know who I am. These fingers are my tools. If I lose them, I lose a lot of money."

"That's a good reason for me not to stand on them," she

told him. "And for the record, I always knew who you were. You were wearing a hat, not a mask."

"Well thank you for not giving me special treatment."

"I warned you off the eggs," she pointed out. "I'd call that special treatment."

"I'm calling the police," Della shouted from her deck. "You're trespassing!"

"Come on," Gray urged Cora. "Let's get out of here."

With a skeptical expression, she slid her foot into the cradle he'd made with his palms and reached her hands forward. Gray stood and flexed his arms to push her upward until her hands curled around the top of the wall.

"What do I do now?" she called out. "I don't think I can swing myself over."

"Just keep holding on. I'll give you another boost." This time, he slid his hands around her warm, denim-clad thighs. "I'm going to push again," he told her. "Try and go with the momentum."

"I'm sending the dogs out," Della Thorsen shouted. "Sic 'em, Dodger."

"Dodger's seventeen years old and incontinent," Cora muttered to him. "Ignore her."

Gray slid his hands until they were right below the swell of her behind, then launched her up, letting go as she swung her legs with the momentum of his thrust. Her foot almost hit his face, and he had to step backward to avoid the collision, but sure enough she made it over the wall. He took a running jump and reached for the top of the stones, easily pulling himself over before he dropped to the other side.

"You make it look simple," she muttered. "That's not fair."

This time, they didn't stop to see if the homeowner was going to let their dogs out. Gray took her hand and they ran to the gate at the back of the yard. It was bolted shut, the lock rusty, but he managed to shimmy it free and opened the gate to let Cora out first.

As soon as it closed behind them, he started to laugh. Not just because his whole morning had been completely absurd, but because the adrenaline pumping through his warm veins was making him feel high. He leaned against the fence, letting his head tip back, as his chest erupted with loud amusement.

"It's not funny," Cora said, though she was laughing, too, enough for her eyes to water and tears to escape. "Imagine the headlines, *Gray Hartson Mauled by Hound of Hell as he Escapes from Church*. You'd never live it down."

"My publicist would love it," he said. "It'd be great for sales."

Another tear rolled down her cheek. Without thinking, he reached out to wipe it with his fingertip, feeling the damp warmth of her skin. She was flushed, her cheeks pink and glowing, and it did something to him.

Something really damn good.

"You're really pretty," he told her, his voice soft. Through heavy eyelids he took her in. High cheekbones, soft lips, a nose so straight he could draw a line with it, and those damn eyes that weren't crying anymore.

They were staring into his instead.

She was only a couple of feet away from him, but it felt too far. A step forward closed the gap. Then he was running his finger from her cheekbone down to her lips, tracing the bow along the top as her warm breath caressed him.

God, she was so warm and soft. He slid his palm around the nape of her neck, angling her face up. And all the time she was silent, her gaze appraising him, as though she was waiting for him to make his next move.

He leaned closer and her chest hitched. Sliding his other hand around her waist, Gray pulled her body against his. The need for her thrummed through him, desire replacing adrenaline in his bloodstream.

She blinked and he swore he could feel her lashes against his skin. His lips were a breath away from hers, *so close*, and he could taste the anticipation of her on the tip of his tongue.

"Cora," he whispered, lowering his mouth to hers. "What are you doing to me?"

It was like a switch had been flicked. She jerked her head back, cutting the connection between them. Running the tip of her tongue along her bottom lip, she shook her head and took a step back.

"I'm sorry. You should be okay now. I need to go…" She glanced at her watch.

It was Gray's turn to blink. *What the hell just happened?* One minute it seemed inevitable that his lips would be on hers. The next? It was like somebody dumped a bucket of ice water over him.

He opened his mouth to thank her, but she was already gone, running toward the town square without a glance back at him. Gray watched her with a sigh. She was intriguing as hell. And if she thought she could escape him, he knew better.

Eating breakfast at the diner might become his new favorite pastime.

CHAPTER SEVEN

"There's no way you ran through peoples' yards and climbed over their fences," Tanner said, shaking his head after Gray recounted his escape from the church.

Gray'd been home for a couple of hours now, and Aunt Gina had served up lunch. He and Tanner were cleaning up the kitchen as she and Becca sat with his dad. "You're making it up."

"I'm not. Go and ask Cora Jean at the diner. She's the one who helped me."

"Cora Jean?" Tanner raised a dark eyebrow. "You're telling me Cora Jean jumped over a seven foot wall?" He grinned. "Now I know you're lying."

"Why would I be lying?" Gray asked, his voice full of confusion.

"Because Cora Jean is seventy-four. You must remember her from when we were kids. She was always hollering at us for making a mess." Tanner frowned. "Come on, you *have* to remember?"

"I really don't recall a Cora Jean." He frowned, willing his brain to work. "Wait... you mean the Battleaxe?"

"Yeah." Tanner nodded. "Tiny old lady. White hair pulled back into a bun." He took a breath. "And apparently really great at vaulting walls."

Gray ran the pad of his thumb along his bottom lip.

"She wasn't old," he told Tanner, who had a shit-eating grin on his face. "She couldn't have been more than twenty-five." And yeah, she was young and pretty and made him want to laugh in a way he hadn't in a long time.

And he'd wanted to kiss the hell out of her until they were both breathless.

"But she said her name's Cora Jean?"

"Yeah. She works in the diner."

"What can I tell you." Tanner shrugged. "The only person under the age of fifty working in the diner is Maddie, and I'm pretty sure you'd know her since you dated her sister for three years."

Gray's mouth turned dry. "Maddie Clark? Ash's sister?"

Tanner laughed. "That's what I said."

That wasn't right. Maddie Clark was fourteen years old and wore braces. Gray shook his head to try and clear his thoughts.

"What about Maddie Clark?" Becca asked as she carried an empty plate into the kitchen.

"Gray's getting confused between Cora Jean Masters and Maddie Clark." Tanner's eyes twinkled. "It's an easy thing to do."

"All this fame's gone to his head." Becca rolled her eyes. "And from what Aunt Gina said, Maddie Clark saved your ass. Those teenage girls wanted to eat you for breakfast."

Gray was still trying to get his head around it. "Maddie Clark," he said again. "I didn't know she was still living in town."

Becca grabbed a fresh towel from the drawer and helped Tanner dry the dishes as Gray placed them on the rack. "She left for a while. Went to Ansell to study music," she told him. "But something happened and she came home again."

"Something happened?" Gray repeated. Curiosity rose up in him. "What was it?" Everybody knew only the best got into Ansell. The performing arts college in New York had one of the most prestigious music programs in the country.

"I assume she came back to look after her mom." Becca shrugged. "It's a shame because I thought we might've had another star on our hands." His sister grinned at him. "It might have shrunk your head a bit."

"Maddie performed?"

"She played piano. Still does."

"I knew she played. I remember her having lessons with her mom when I dated Ash." He frowned, remembering those days. Ash in her cheerleader's outfit, Gray always sporting a bruise or two from football. Little Maddie sitting at the piano, her mom leaning over to point at the sheet music in front of her.

He could almost smell the aroma of pot roast drifting out from the kitchen within his memory.

"But now she works in the diner?"

"And teaches piano." Becca shrugged. "Has for years."

He wanted to ask more, but Becca was already curious as to why he was curious. Another question and she might be asking a few herself. And right now, he wasn't prepared to answer them.

A couple of hours ago, he nearly kissed his ex-girlfriend's little sister. And what a shitstorm that would have released.

Gray finished washing the last dish and placed it in the rack, then emptied the water, frowning as it took forever to drain. "Does anything in this house work the way it's supposed to?" he asked.

"Nope." Becca grinned. And wasn't that the truth. After the morning he'd had, it made him want to hit something.

"I'm going to head up to my room and play some guitar," he said when they finished putting the dishes away. "I'll see you later." A little strumming was what his soul needed. Anything to take his mind off this house and this town and the damn inhabitants who were driving him crazy.

Especially the one who made him laugh and want to kiss her, and lied to his face about her name.

Yeah, especially Maddie Clark.

"COME IN," Maddie called to her niece and nephew, flinging the door wide open with a grin on her face. Little Grace threw herself at Maddie, who just about managed to catch her without getting winded. Carter hung back, a shy smile on his face as he pulled at the collar of his shirt. "Hey bud," Maddie said, ruffling his light brown hair. "You're looking dapper."

"What's dapper?" he asked.

"It means fancy. But old-fashioned fancy. It's how guys used to dress when they knew how to woo a woman."

"What's a woo?" Grace asked as she climbed down from Maddie's hold. "Is it something to do with witches?"

"Are you confusing my children again?" Ashleigh asked as she walked up the steps to where Maddie was standing.

"Mom, what's a woo?" Grace asked her, scratching the top of her blonde hair.

Ashleigh's confused eyes met Maddie's. "I was telling her about wooing," Maddie said. "Like in the old days."

"Wooing is when a man decides to make a woman feel happy," Ashleigh said, rolling her eyes at Maddie. "But it's not a word either of you will need for a long time. Now go inside and see Gramma. I want to talk to Aunt Maddie for a minute."

Maddie stepped aside so Grace and Carter could slip by, their shoes hammering against the wooden floor as they ran to the kitchen. She could hear the deep tones of her mom greeting them, followed by the higher pitch of the childrens' responses.

"Is everything okay?" Maddie asked her sister.

Ashleigh was looking beautiful as always. Her pale blonde hair was pulled into a low chignon, and the simple lines of her navy dress flattered her slim frame. Maddie felt like a mess standing next to her, wearing only a tank and jeans, but what was new about that?

She'd always been in Ashleigh's shadow. It was something she'd come to accept over time. Laugh about, even. And if occasionally she wished people didn't compare them quite so much, well that was okay, wasn't it?

Ashleigh patted the back of her hair. "Any news in town?" she asked with an innocent expression. "Anything I should know about?"

Maddie shrugged. "Like what?"

"I heard Gray was at church today, causing an uproar. I wondered if you saw anything from the diner?"

For a moment, Maddie froze. Did Ashleigh know about their escape? Or even worse about the near-kiss? "Like what?" she said, keeping her voice as even as she could.

"I don't know. I just thought I'd ask." Ashleigh looked pensive. "Do you think I should go to see him?"

Maddie blinked. "Why would you want to do that?" Her stomach felt strange. Like there was liquid heating up inside it.

Ashleigh shrugged. "I was the love of his life once. We dated for three years. It seems rude if I don't at least say hello, doesn't it?" Her voice dropped. "Unless you think it might give him the wrong impression?"

Maddie's fingers curled into her palm. "Wouldn't that

upset Michael?" she asked. Ashleigh's husband didn't seem like the jealous type, but then again, Maddie wasn't sure what type he really was. Whenever she saw him he was always so quiet, as though he didn't want to be at whatever event they were attending. He was ten years older than Ashleigh – which made him sixteen years older than Maddie – and she couldn't think of one thing they had in common apart from Ashleigh and their children.

"What kind of impression would it give?" Ashleigh asked, laughing. "It's not as though I've been pining after him for all this time. I'm married, after all. And I'm hoping he's gotten over me, too. It's been more than ten years since we ended things."

"I don't know," Maddie replied, still feeling off. "The whole thing just feels weird, you know?"

"Why do you feel weird? You hardly knew him. You were still a little kid when he left town." Ashleigh shook her pretty head. "Honestly, Maddie, you don't need to worry about me. I just want to do whatever's right. I don't want everybody talking about me, thinking I was rude if I don't visit. But then, I also don't want them saying I was desperate to see him, either." She let out a sigh.

Appearances were always important to Ashleigh, even as a kid. She'd been the prettiest girl at school, the head cheerleader, and of course, her boyfriend had been the one all the other girls lusted after.

Sometimes it felt that life came so much easier to her big sister than it did to Maddie. Most of the time she found that funny. But occasionally it hurt, like somebody jabbing an old wound.

The same way thinking about her sister going to see Gray Hartson was like a scratch to her heart.

"I should go," Ashleigh said, leaning forward to hug Maddie. "Thanks for looking after the monkeys. We should be back around eight. Are you okay to get them in their pajamas? It'll make bedtime so much easier."

"Of course. I'll get them showered and all ready for bed." Maddie kissed Ashleigh's cheek. "Have a good time."

"Thank you. I'll see you later." She leaned into the house and called out. "Grace, Carter, I'm leaving. Be good for your aunt and Gramma."

"Bye, Mom!" Grace and Carter shouted, not bothering to come out of the kitchen.

Then Ashleigh was walking down the front steps, her high heels clicking on the stone steps as she went.

Maddie watched her and touched the back of her own head, wincing when she felt how loose her braid was and how many hairs had escaped from it. She quickly pulled her hand away, shaking her head at herself.

There was no point in trying to compete with her beautiful sister. She'd learned that lesson long ago.

AFTER DINNER WITH HIS FAMILY, and more jibing from Tanner about climbing over fences, Gray headed back to his room, claiming jetlag, but really he'd wanted to be alone.

He still couldn't get over the fact that it was Maddie Clark who helped him escape from church. When the hell did she grow up? But more importantly, why had she lied about who she was?

She knew who he was. She'd admitted as much, when they were trying to climb over that damn wall.

He'd tried to distract himself by playing his guitar. He had an album of songs to write and a studio booked in four months' time, yet his fingers didn't seem to be working. It was like he'd forgotten how to write music, to lay one note next to each other until it became a melody. Instead, each time he strummed it sounded wrong.

So wrong.

He'd put his guitar away and showered, then lay down in bed, trying to remember why he'd come back here in the first place.

Because you promised your sister. And your father's sick.

Oh yeah, and the fact he hadn't been back to Hartson's Creek in forever. In the end, sleep seemed preferable to over-thinking, but like everything else in his life it was stubborn.

It was a few hours later that the first drip came. It barely registered in his slumbering mind. The second worked its way into his dream as rain. But it was the third that woke him up.

Not that it was only a drip. More of a flood pouring down from the ceiling and drenching everything in its wake – including Gray and his bed.

He sat up, spitting water out of his mouth and blinking it out of his eyes, his brows pulled together as he tried to work out what the hell was going on. The water continued to pour onto the dent in the pillow where his head had been, and he followed it to the source – a hole in the plastered ceiling that revealed half-rotten beams and a rusty pipe.

A rusty pipe with a hole in it.

He jumped out of bed and looked around for a bucket, a bowl, anything he could put under the deluge. "Tanner!" he called out. "There's a leak in the ceiling. Help me out."

"Wha?" Tanner asked, running into his bedroom, clad only in a pair of pajama pants. That was one up on Gray, who was only wearing a pair of boxer shorts, and running around to try to find a goddamned bowl.

"Where is it?" Becca appeared carrying a bucket, thank the Lord. He and Tanner pulled the bed across the room then settled the bucket under the leak.

"Where's the water shut off?" Gray asked.

"Under the kitchen sink."

He ran down to the kitchen, Becca and Tanner following close behind. As they passed Aunt Gina's room, she pulled open the door. "What's going on?" she asked them.

"Another leak. Gray's room this time," Becca told her aunt.

Another? This time?

Gray knelt down in front of the sink, yanking the painted wooden cupboards open and pulling out the cleaning bottles that were stored there, then leaned forward to turn the shut-off valve. It was stubborn and rusted, and his arm ached from reaching at an awkward angle. But eventually it turned, and he sat back with a sigh.

"When did you get that tattoo?" Becca asked, taking in the ink on Gray's body.

He looked down at his chest and the black scrolling tribal tattoos that radiated from his chest to his upper arms. "A while back." The design had taken over a year, intricately planned with his tattoo artist who'd flown into whatever country he'd been touring in at the time. From the moment he'd felt the first needle puncture his skin it had felt right. Like layering up his armor, protecting himself.

"It's pretty," Becca said, following the design around. "But don't let Dad see it. He wasn't keen on your second album cover."

"Yeah, well I kind of had to bleach my eyes myself," Tanner said, grinning. All those billboards in New York with my brother's naked body staring down at me. They gave me nightmares."

"Do you regret them?" Becca asked him, ignoring Tanner.

"Nope. In my list of regrets, they're lingering right at the bottom." Gray shrugged. "Now, do you have a number for the emergency plumber? We need to get these pipes replaced."

CHAPTER EIGHT

"What do you mean he won't get all the pipes replaced?" Gray asked, his voice tight. "It's crazy to replace one piece of pipe when you know the whole thing is rusting. How many leaks have you had in the last year?"

"A few." Aunt Gina shrugged. "But you know your father. He's stubborn. And he didn't like any of the quotes he received for the work."

They were sitting at the breakfast table, Gray sipping hot coffee from an old chipped mug. It was strange how many things needed repairing around here. Not just the roof and the plumbing and the peeling paintwork outside, but the kitchen and the bathrooms were still the same as from when he was growing up. It was as if nothing had been touched for years.

"How much is it?" Gray asked. "I'll get the money wired over. You should have told me before. You know I would have taken care of this. I'll arrange for somewhere for us all to stay while the pipes are being replaced."

It made him mad that they hadn't asked him for help.

"I couldn't," Aunt Gina said, pressing her lips together.

"Dad wouldn't let her," Becca told him as she poured herself a mug of coffee. They'd had to fill the coffee maker from the outside tap, along with the pans on the stove that were boiling, ready to clean up after breakfast.

Gray shook his head at it all. "I've got more money than I know what to do with," he protested. "Let me help."

"Dad's proud. You know that." Becca sighed. "He keeps saying he'll repair everything when he's better. But he's never really better, you know?"

Yeah, Gray knew. Or at least he did now. Much like the state of this house, his father's health had also come as a shock. "I'll talk to him," Gray said, his voice determined.

"And rile him up while he's sick?" Aunt Gina asked. "Why would you do that?"

"Because you shouldn't be living like this," Gray told her. "This is the twenty-first century. We're in the greatest country on Earth. And I can fucking afford it."

"Language." Becca raised an eyebrow at him.

"I'm sorry." He shook his head. "But this makes me so fu... damn mad. Dad's pride is stopping you from living like civilized people." He put his coffee down. "Just let me talk to him, okay? I won't shout or rile him up. I promise."

"That's what you said last time."

Gray half-smiled. "Well this time I mean it."

"Let him go," Tanner said, leaning back on his chair. "Maybe he can persuade the old man. God knows I've tried."

"It's all right for you," Aunt Gina said, her brows knitting together. "You don't have to live with him full time. You'll be leaving soon and Becca and I will be the ones left sweeping up the pieces if you drive him crazy."

"You two don't have to stay either," Gray pointed out. "You know I'd buy you a house anywhere. Just say the word."

"I'd never leave him." Aunt Gina crossed her arms in front of her chest. "You know that."

Gray's heart softened at her loyalty. He knew it wasn't for show, either. Growing up, Aunt Gina had been like their guardian angel, taking care of them when they needed her the most.

She'd arrived at their home the day after their mother – her sister – died, and never left. From that moment on, she'd taken care of them. Wiping their eyes with her handkerchief at their mother's funeral, holding them tight when bad dreams had woken them in the middle of the night. Chided them when they hadn't handed in their assignments on time, or when the principal called to tell her one of the four Hartson brothers was missing from class.

She'd eased their heartbreak and cheered their victories, and every one of them loved her for it.

"Why do you stay?" Gray asked her. "Most of us left long ago. Even Becca will move on soon. You've fulfilled your promise to mom."

From the corner of his eye he could see Becca's face crumple. She'd been so small when their mom died she couldn't even remember her. Aunt Gina was the only mother figure she'd ever known.

"I promised my sister I'd take care of all of you," Aunt Gina said, her voice low. "That *includes* your father. And he needs me." She stood and carried her plate over to the sink. "I'll be here for as long as he does."

"In that case, I'm paying for new plumbing. And a roof," Gray told her. "Thanks for breakfast. I'll go talk to him now."

She shook her head as he stood and walked into the hallway, heading for his father's study. As he lifted his hand to rap on the door, he could hear her response.

"They're both as stubborn as each other. This will all end in tears."

~

WHEN GRAY WAS TWENTY-YEARS-OLD, he'd told his father he was leaving college to move to L.A. and record an album, having been offered a two-album recording contract by one of the country's biggest record labels.

His father had said nothing for a full five minutes. Just stared at Gray through those watery blue eyes, his lips pressed together, the right side of his jaw twitching.

More than a decade had passed since then, but his dad was staring at Gray in exactly the same way. Like Gray was nothing more than the shit on the sole of his shoe and he was waiting for the opportunity to scrape him off.

But there was a problem with that. Gray wasn't scared of the old man anymore. And he had Aunt Gina to think of. He wasn't going to leave her and Becca here in this broken down house while they took care of his dad. She deserved better than that.

They all did.

"No."

The reply was faint enough for Gray to have to lean forward, his strong body towering over his father. "What?"

"I said no. We don't need your help. Never have." His father coughed and his whole body shook. If it had been anybody else in the world, Gray would have asked if he was okay, but he knew better than to do that to his dad. Compassion equaled weakness in Grayson Hartson III's eyes. Any emotion did.

"This house is falling apart. And from what I can tell, there isn't any money left to repair it. You need my help."

"I don't need any help." His dad's eyes were flinty. "You think you're a big man, flashing cash around? Think it makes you better than me? That money you got is tainted. I don't want any part of it."

Gray frowned. "Tainted? How?"

"It's not properly earned."

"I've earned every cent. Wrote songs, recorded them, traveled all over the world promoting them." His father was pulling him in to this, Gray knew it, yet it was impossible to stop. The old man knew how to push every button, and each one of them hurt.

"You prostituted yourself. You think I haven't seen the photographs? You parade yourself around until girls throw money at you." His dad's eyes narrowed. "And now you want me to take that money? No thank you. I don't take the devil's dollar."

Gray wasn't sure whether to laugh or shout. *The devil's dollar?* It was a pretty good name for an album, but a really shitty way to describe your son.

"So you'd rather let Aunt Gina and Becca live in squalor?" Christ, his father was stubborn. But then again, he was, too. The streak ran through the veins of all the Hartsons, and it made for some spectacular clashes.

Maybe he should leave early. Get the hell out of here and on a plane to L.A. He could be sitting on his balcony, strumming his guitar, writing new music as he overlooked the ocean.

"I'll be better soon enough," his old man said, squaring his shoulders even though he was propped up in bed. "I'll fix it up then. The way I always have."

The way he said it, Gray almost believed him. He was pretty sure his dad believed it, too. But you only had to look at him in that bed, his body frail and wasted, his face lined with age to know it wasn't the truth. There was no way he was climbing on the roof or replacing pipes.

Gray swallowed down the compassion that tried to rise up in him. Covered it up with a shrug. "I'll do it," he said.

"Do what?"

"I'll replace the pipes. Mend the roof."

His father coughed out a laugh. "You'll do it? Seriously? You've never done a day of manual work in your life. You know how to cut through pipes? Weld them together?" Another cough. "I'd like to see you try."

"I said I'll do it and I will." Gray took a deep breath, his jaw square, his chest pushed out.

He wasn't sure who was more surprised at his determination – his father or himself. Either way, he had to swallow down the taste of frustration that always seemed to settle on him whenever he spoke to his father.

"Be my guest. I could do with some entertainment around here."

Gray shrugged and walked out of his father's study, the walls pushing in on him as he emerged into the hallway.

He needed to get out of here for a while. This house was making him feel stir crazy.

MADDIE WALKED into the diner through the kitchen door, calling out to Murphy to let him know she was back. He looked up and beckoned her to the door that led to the diner. "Who d'ya think that is?" he asked, pointing at somebody sitting in the corner booth. "He was asking for Cora Jean." He lowered his voice. "You don't think he's one of them gold diggers, do you? After her for her money?"

Maddie tried not to laugh. Cora Jean had a small pension and the money she earned from working at the diner. She wasn't exactly sugar momma material.

Looking across to where Murphy was pointing, Maddie knew exactly who that was with his broad back and brown hair that curled at the top of his neck. He was wearing a dark blue cap, the peak pulled low over his face, and his head was angled down as though he was reading the menu in front of him intently. It allowed her to study him for a moment, to take in the muscles of his back, the tattoos that were almost-but-not-quite covered up by the sleeves of his black tee. She wondered what it would feel like to trace her finger across the ink.

"There's only one way to find out," Maddie told Murphy, sliding her bag into a locker, and grabbing a fresh apron from the hook. "I'll see if he wants coffee."

"Try to sell him some waffles. I made too much mix up."

"How much is too much?" Maddie asked him, curious.

"About five quarts." Murphy shrugged. "It's been quiet in here today."

Maddie grinned and pushed through the metal double doors into the main diner. Murphy was right, it was as quiet as hell in here. That was Tuesdays for you.

"Coffee?" she asked, carrying a full pot over to the only occupied table.

Gray looked up, a slow smile curling his lips. "Cora Jean," he said. "How're you doing?"

His eyes caught hers and she felt her skin tingle. Even with the peak of his cap pulled low he was ridiculously hand-some. She wanted to throw a damn bucket of water over herself. Yeah, he was good looking, but she'd met a lot of good looking guys.

Though, none of them had ever made her body tingle like this.

"Black. No sugar, right?"

"You got it."

She poured out a mugful, then inclined her head at the menu in front of him. "Can I get you something to eat?"

"Pour yourself a cup and sit with me," Gray said, his eyes still on hers. "Maddie."

She'd been expecting it. You didn't stay in town for long

and not find out everything, and Gray wasn't stupid. Yet she still felt her stomach drop as he said her name. Not because he didn't say it beautifully – he did. But because it meant she had to be herself.

Lame old Maddie Clark.

She'd kind of enjoyed being intrepid Cora, leading him astray.

"I have to work," she told him.

He looked around the diner. "You're not exactly rushing around in here. I'll buy you breakfast. Name your poison."

"I hear the waffles are good," she said, her mouth quirking with humor.

"Better than the eggs?"

"Anything's better than the eggs." His eyes caught hers and she found herself blushing. He had an irresistible charm to him. One that made children grin and young girls swoon and older women spend a helluva lot of money on his music.

"Two servings of waffles it is."

She gave Murphy the order, then grabbed herself a mug for coffee. "You're brave sitting by the window," she told him. "After Sunday I thought you might want to lay low."

"I figure most of those girls are at school right now. And I wanted to see you."

Her breath caught in her throat. "You did?"

"Yeah. I got a question for you."

"I might not want to answer it," she told him, tipping her head to the side. He smiled again, a sunshine kind of smile that wrinkled the corners of his eyes.

"I'm getting that feeling when it comes to you." He leaned his chin on his knuckles and leaned forward, his eyes narrow as they caught hers. "But I figure you owe me the truth."

"How'd you figure that?"

He leaned back, sizing her up. "Because we trauma

bonded on Sunday. You don't go through something like that without building a connection with someone."

"We climbed over a couple of fences."

"And nearly got mauled by a ferocious dog." He took a sip of his coffee, raising an eyebrow.

"An incontinent dog who's lost most of his teeth."

"See." A glint of amusement flashed in his eyes. "That's scary shit."

She laughed. Couldn't help it. There was something about him that made it easy to breathe. He was a human oxygen machine, making her feel lighter than air. "Okay, so we've trauma bonded. Surely that means you should go easy on me."

"I'll go really easy on you." His voice was sugary low. She could feel it on her teeth. "So why didn't you tell me who you were?"

"Because you would have asked questions I didn't want to answer."

"Cute." He grinned again. "Let me guess. You thought I'd ask about your sister?"

She tightened her hold on her mug. "Wouldn't you?"

"I don't need to know about Ash. I'm pretty sure she's married with kids. Probably living in a huge house a few miles away from here. She volunteers at her kids' school, maybe for a well-chosen charity or two – nothing controversial. And she spends every Friday at the salon getting ready for date night with her husband."

Maddie frowned. "How do you know? Have you been asking other people about her?"

"Nope." Gray leaned back, folding his arms across his chest. She tried to ignore the way his biceps flexed as he did it. "It's what she always wanted. And Ash always gets what she wants."

Except you. Maddie blinked at the thought. "I guess that's not what you wanted."

He shook his head. "I'm not a small town kind of guy."

There was no arguing with that. Gray Hartson didn't belong around here. He was too talented, too good looking, too... *everything*. He seemed to dwarf everything and everyone he came into contact with.

"So why are you here?" she asked him.

"When dad got sick, Becca asked me to come. So I stopped in on my way home to L.A."

"Will you be leaving soon?"

He shook his head. "Not that soon." He looked down at his cup, ran his finger around the rim. "I'm staying in town for a while."

"How long?" Her chest tightened. She couldn't quite work out why. Was it fear, excitement, nervousness? All of them seemed to rush through her in a heady cocktail.

Fear because him staying here meant change. It meant he and Ashleigh would see one another again and even though Ash was married, she'd probably entrance him.

Excitement because being close to Gray was like hanging upside down on a gravity-defying rollercoaster. It made her heart race and her blood pump in a way she'd never felt before.

And nervousness? Well she didn't like feeling out of control. She'd tried that before and fallen low, low, low.

"For a couple of months. Long enough to work on some new songs and help fix up the old house. It needs new pipes and a new roof. I thought I'd help out."

"Help out how?" Maddie asked. "You gonna supervise the contractors?"

"I'm going to do it myself." He ran the tip of his tongue across his bottom lip, capturing a bead of coffee.

She had to press her lips together not to laugh. "Yourself?"

She tried to imagine it. Grammy award winning Gray Hartson on his childhood home's old broken roof, a tool belt around his waist... If she took that photo she'd make enough money to pay for her mom's medications for the rest of their lives. "Why?"

"Dad won't let anybody else do it. You know what he's like." Gray shrugged.

"Have you ever renovated a house before?" she asked him.

"Kinda." The corner of his mouth quirked up. "I did some work on my first place in L.A. And I have a few friends who can help me out. You know the Johnson brothers?"

"The ones with the TV show?" Maddie asked. "*How To Flip Your House in Thirty Days?*"

"Yeah, that one. They're gonna talk me through anything I can't figure out. I'll video chat them if I need to. How hard can it be?"

"Waffles are ready!" Murphy shouted from the open kitchen door. "I've been ringing for you, Maddie."

"Saved by the bell." She wiggled her eyebrows. "Stay here and I'll bring your breakfast over."

CHAPTER NINE

"*H*ave you seen this?" Becca asked Gray when he made it home from town. She was holding out her phone and he leaned in to look at it.

"An email?" Gray said.

"Yep. From Reverend Maitland. Reminding his flock that we should be respectful to all visitors in town and make them welcome, not take photographs and share them on social media."

Gray frowned. "Does he mention me?"

"No, but we all know it's you he's talking about." Becca's voice was gleeful. "I guess he doesn't want you running through anybody's yard again."

"This is really unnecessary," Gray said, scanning through the missive. "*Just as Jesus welcomed everybody into his flock, we should do the same,*" he read. "*Please do not encroach on anybody's privacy in church or outside of it.*"

"Reverend Maitland's emails are like papal edicts." Becca was still grinning. "His word is law. People will leave you alone now."

"Oh come on." Gray handed back her phone. "This is the twenty-first century."

"This is Hartson's Creek," Becca pointed out. "And as you keep reminding us, it hasn't quite made it past the millennium yet."

Gray's phone buzzed in his pocket. He pulled it out to see his manager's name flashing on the screen. Swiping his finger, he answered it.

"Marco?"

"I got your message. You're not serious about replacing those pipes and fixing the roof, are you?"

"I'm deadly serious." Gray leaned on the kitchen table. "I promised my dad."

"But you have an album to write," Marco reminded him. "The recording studio is booked. Your label's gonna be pissed if we pull out."

"I'll still be writing. You don't have to worry about that."

"Okayyyyyy…" Marco trailed the sound out for four syllables. "But let me talk to the label, let them know what you're doing. Maybe schedule a video conference. And about this construction, I'll have to check your insurance, see what you can and can't do."

Gray laughed. "I'm almost certain they don't mention plumbing in the cover letter."

"It'll come under manual labor. I'll have to talk to the broker." Marco paused as though he was making a note. "And how's the family?"

"Okay. Wet." Gray filled him in on the flood.

"Is your aunt okay? None of her things got ruined, did they?"

"She's fine. Stronger than all of us put together. Can you arrange a truck for me while I'm here. I'm going to need it to pick up supplies."

Marco started to laugh. "You're really doing this, aren't you?"

"Of course I am." Gray frowned. "Why does everybody laugh when I tell them?"

"Because you're Gray Hartson. You earn more in a minute than a plumber earns in a month. There's no sense to what you're doing." Marco cleared his throat. "Did you really call the Johnson brothers for help?"

"They're giving me some advice." Gray knew he sounded defensive. And that it wasn't Marco's fault he was finding it all so strange. Heck, it *was* strange.

"Okay, look, just don't do anything stupid, okay? I don't know why you're doing this, but you are and I'm going with it. But take care of those hands and make sure you write some music. That's all I ask."

The music wasn't the problem. He'd already written two tracks. Raw, gritty, and full of emotion.

The way he felt every time he woke up in Hartson's Creek. Or each time he stepped into the diner and saw a certain brunette behind the counter. He raked his fingers through his hair, trying to work out what it was that drew him to his ex-girlfriend's little sister. Yeah, she was pretty, but he was so over pretty women. Like the drugs and the drink, being surrounded by perfect lost its luster pretty quick for him.

But then Maddie wasn't perfect. She was forthright but cagey, confident yet he could see the vulnerability there, too. Madison Clark was an enigma, and so different to the teenage girl he remembered. And he was fascinated by her.

Marco cleared his throat. "Ah, Gray?"

"Yeah?" He watched as Aunt Gina walked in with a basket full of clothes. Sandwiching his phone between his ear and his shoulder, he took it from her and carried it to the laundry room.

"Are you okay?" Marco lowered his voice. "As in, you know, mentally okay?"

"What?" Gray coughed out a laugh. "Yeah, I am. Why do you ask?"

"Because you're making strange decisions. I've seen it before. A long tour followed by burnout. Shall I arrange a video consultation with Doctor Tennison?"

"I don't need to talk to my shrink. I'm just taking care of my family. Try not to worry so much." Gray shook his head. "Two months and I'll be back in LA, recording the next album. Don't worry."

"I do worry. Don't do anything stupid. And keep your head down. I've no idea how I'm going to spin this. Maybe we can get a film crew in or something..."

"No film crew." Gray shook his head. "We don't need to spin anything. I'm going to repair a few pipes and shingles and spend some time with my family. Nothing could be simpler."

"Famous last words," Marco said quietly.

"I'll speak to you later, Marco." He hung up before Marco could suggest anything else. Because this was fine. He had it under control. He'd spend the next few weeks repairing the house and writing songs.

What could go wrong with that?

"HERE YOU GO," Maddie said, putting her mom's prescriptions on the kitchen table. She'd stopped in to the pharmacy on her way home from work. "Enough to see you through the next month. And Murphy sent some pie over for us to have after dinner."

"What kind?" her mom looked up with a smile. She had that hazy look that she wore after her nap.

"Cherry. Your favorite. I'm going to take a shower and then cook us something tasty. You need anything?"

"I'm good. Rita Foster came over earlier. Helped me with lunch."

"That's good." Maddie leaned down to kiss her mom's cheek. "I stink of grease, I'm sorry."

"Rita said that Gray Hartson had to escape from Church on Sunday. Said you helped him."

Maddie's spine straightened. "Oh did she?" she said, keeping her voice light. "I'd have thought she'd have saved that for *chairs*."

Her mom chuckled. "She couldn't help herself. Said there'd been complaints. Della Thorsen says you almost scared her to death."

"Della Thorsen could barely see us. We were at the end of her yard for about three seconds. I was trying to help. Reverend Maitland asked me to smuggle Gray out of there."

Her mom smiled. "How is he? He was always such a lovely young man. At one point I really thought he and Ashleigh…" her voice trailed off. "Well that's history now," she added hastily. "Ashleigh is so happy with Michael and the kids."

"Yeah." Maddie's throat felt scratchy. "And he's good. I'm sure he'll come by at some point to say hi. He always had a lot of time for you."

"How long is he staying in town?" her mom asked.

Maddie cupped the back of her neck with her palm. Her skin felt clammy and warm. "A couple of months, I think. He's helping his dad repair the house."

"Gina will love that. She's always complaining about that house. And of course she loves it when her boys come home. They don't do it enough." She clucked her tongue.

Maddie gave her mom a smile and headed down the hallway. She didn't want to think about Gray Hartson right now.

It had been a long day and she was beat. Maybe a shower would spruce her up.

~

"I DON'T KNOW what to tell you," Mac Johnson said, his head shaking as he stared at Gray through his cellphone screen. "Those pipes are at least fifty years old. See that corrosion there on the right? That pipe's made of lead. Some of the others look more like galvanized steel from what I can tell. But without seeing it for myself all I can do is make a best guess. Do you know when the pipes were last replaced?"

"I think Dad did it when he and mom first got married." Gray ran his thumb along his jaw. "I guess that was about forty years ago."

"Yeah, that's where the steel pipes come from. The lead ones could be originals. If it was my house, I'd rip 'em all out and start from scratch."

"How long will that take?" That was Tanner. He leaned over the phone, fascinated that Gray was casually taking advice from one of the Johnson brothers.

"If it was me, a week. For amateurs? Your guess is as good as mine." His brows pulled together. "Are you sure you want to do this, Gray? I could understand if you were doing it for publicity or charity. But anything else? Call in a professional."

"Why does everybody keep asking me that?"

"Because you're crazy, bro," Tanner told him. Mac laughed.

"You should listen to him," Mac agreed. "Pay a professional, then go make another million dollar album."

"I'm doing it myself," Gray told him.

"He's stubborn as hell." Tanner shrugged. "We all are.

When he sets his mind on something there's no persuading him otherwise."

"Yeah, well he might need that if he's replacing the pipes." Mac sighed. "I've spoken to a plumber friend of mine and he's going to draw up a plan for you. List out the supplies you need, the timeline for repairs, what tools you'll want, and the sequence to replace it all. But you have to realize, this is a professional job. I wouldn't expect to pick up a guitar and be able to play it right away. You shouldn't expect to be able to do this either. You *will* make mistakes and you *will* cause damage."

"That sounds ominous." Tanner smirked.

"Are you going to be helping him?" Mac asked.

"Not for long. I'm heading back home after next weekend. After that, he's on his own."

"I'll be here," Becca protested. "I can help."

"You look like the most sensible of all of them." Mac nodded. "All right, I'd better go. We've got a meeting on next season in half an hour."

"Okay." Gray nodded. "Thanks, Mac. I appreciate it."

"And I'll appreciate it when you sing at my daughter's wedding," Mac said, winking at him. "Good luck. You're going to need it."

Gray hung up the phone and looked at his brother, who was biting down a smile. "I told you this was crazy," Tanner said.

"Ignore him. You can do this, Gray. You were always working on the house when we were kids. And you fixed my bike when I crashed it into the wall, remember?" Becca grinned.

"You're going to have to record this," Tanner said, ruffling his little sister's hair. "I need to see it in all it's glory."

"Nobody's recording anything," Gray growled. "When are you leaving exactly?"

"The Monday after my birthday. The same time that Cam and Logan will leave." Their brothers were making a quick visit to town for the weekend of Tanner's birthday, to celebrate with him and catch up with Gray, too.

"That reminds me. I spoke to Sam, and the Karaoke Contest is a go," Becca said, her eyes sparkling. "Eight o'clock sharp at the Moonlight Bar."

"Karaoke contest?" Gray shook his head. "Seriously?"

"Karaoke at the Moonlight is the best," Tanner said, his face serious. "You're gonna love it."

Becca clapped her hands together. "It's going to be amazing. All my brothers in one place."

"Are you sure I should go?" Gray felt like he was pissing on her parade. "I don't want to cause any more problems like I did at church."

"It'll be fine," Tanner told him. "They won't let teenage girls in. And Sam who runs it is as straight as they come. He'll have our backs."

"Come on, Gray," Becca urged. "We've never been to a bar together. I want to dance with my big brother."

"He can't dance," Tanner said, grinning. "But it would be good to have you there."

"I don't know…" Gray pressed his lips together.

"Just say yes. We'll look after you. So will Logan and Cam." Becca squeezed his arm.

"Maybe he's scared." Tanner winked. "What if he loses at Karaoke? He'll never live it down."

Gray groaned. "I'll come. But I won't be singing Karaoke." He looked at his sister. "And I won't be dancing, unless I'm full of whiskey."

Becca raised her eyebrows. "That sounds like a challenge." She leaned forward to kiss him on the cheek. "I'm so happy you're here. You're the best."

CHAPTER TEN

*G*ray couldn't remember the last time he'd ached this much. It was only eight in the evening, yet his muscles were begging him to put them to bed and let them sleep for a good twelve hours. And he would've, if he didn't have a damn album to write. While he'd spent the past few days with his body contorted into crazy positions to work on the plumbing, he spent the evenings in his dad's old summerhouse with his guitar and blank sheet music, determined to write at least one song a week and be ready for the recording studio in two months.

He'd almost flooded the kitchen on the first day he'd started. Cue panic from Becca and loud groaning from his father as he mopped up the water and tried to determine where he'd gone wrong. Everything seemed to take twice the time he thought it would.

"Damn, I'll be glad to get home," Tanner said, circling his head as though trying to work out the knots in his neck. "Why did I say I'd help you again?"

"Because otherwise I would've kicked your ass," Gray told

him as he dried a plate and passed it to his younger brother. "And that would've hurt more."

"Yeah, right." Tanner grinned. "You can barely hold that dish towel, let alone inflict bodily damage on me. Besides, I heard what your manager said to you about your hands. Keep the gloves on at all times, no cuts, no nicks. Those pretty fingers are worth too much."

Gray rolled his eyes. "You always had a smart mouth."

"It's only getting smarter." Tanner winked. "Man, I'm pooped. You want to come with me to the Moonlight? You can buy me a beer to thank me for my hard work."

"I'll buy you a beer on Saturday," Gray told him. "We can toast your leaving."

Tanner laughed. "Are you that desperate to get rid of me?"

Nope. Gray was dreading his brother leaving. Not just because he'd been helping him with the remodeling, but because he'd enjoyed having this time to connect with Tanner. At three years younger than him, his little brother had been a pain in his ass for most of their childhood. Yet he'd protected him as best he could – first from the pain of their mom's death, then from the anger their dad could never shake.

Tanner had been almost seventeen when Gray left for L.A. Still a kid, despite his protestations. But now he was a man, and Gray was connecting with him on a new level.

It was going to be quiet here without him.

"I'm going to work on some music tonight," Gray told his brother. "But I'll definitely be there on Saturday."

Tanner's eyes softened. "That means a lot. Thanks, bro."

Gray made a mental note to put his card behind the bar. Saturday night was on him. "And if you get drunk tonight, avoid the third step. Otherwise dad will hear you come home."

"Ah, the old third step trick. Don't worry, Logan taught me that one," Tanner told him. "Good luck with the music."

"Thanks." Gray watched his brother grab his jacket and call goodbye to Aunt Gina and Becca, who were watching an old movie in the living room. Then he walked down the hallway, planning on grabbing his guitar and music before heading out to the summer house.

"That you, Gray?" his father called out as he passed the study. For a moment, Gray considered ignoring him. What could he do, anyway? It wasn't as though he was going to chase him up the stairs the way he'd done when Gray was a kid.

"Yeah, it's me." Compassion won out over disdain. He pushed the study door open, spotting his dad sitting in the wing backed leather chair next to his bed. "How are you feeling?"

"Okay." His dad nodded. "Or as okay as it gets." He cleared his throat, and Gray winced at how much fluid he could hear. "How's the plumbing?"

"It's slow but sure. We managed to replace about six feet today. The worst part is stopping and turning the water on each time. It takes forever to test the seals."

"Hmmm." His dad nodded but said nothing more.

"You need anything?" Gray asked him. "Want me to get you a drink?"

"No thank you."

"Okay then." Gray lingered for a moment, nonplussed by the lack of venom in his father's voice. "I'm going to head out and play some guitar."

"Keep it quiet. Remember the neighbors."

"I've got headphones. Nobody will hear."

His father picked up the book from the table in front of him. "I'll see you tomorrow." He cleared his throat. "Thank you for the work you're doing."

Gray did a double take at his father's words. When was the last time he thanked him for anything? It felt weird and uncomfortable, so he just nodded and went upstairs to grab his guitar.

He couldn't remember a time he didn't resent his old man. And though that feeling was still there, tonight it felt diluted. And he wasn't sure what to do with that knowledge right now.

An hour later, he was sitting on the cushioned wicker chair in the summer house, the glass doors wide open to let in the cool evening air. His headphones were around his neck as he played around with some lyrics, the only sound in his ears the constant buzz of the cicadas. He'd forgotten how loud they were around here. How they'd been the soundtrack to his teenage summer evenings, along with Nirvana, or the Foo Fighters, or whatever band he was playing on repeat that week.

Maybe somewhere a teenage kid was playing Gray's own music on repeat. The corner of his mouth lifted at the thought.

He stood and rolled his shoulders, releasing the tightness in his muscles. He was humming a riff that had come to him when he was playing around with his guitar. He stepped outside of the summerhouse and took in the sweet, heady scents of the lilacs planted around the wooden building.

Like everything else, it was decaying. Could do with a coat of paint, new windowpanes, and the interior being refinished. But he liked the way it made him feel in there. As though he was still sixteen, permanently glued to his guitar, dreaming of being a famous musician one day.

And now he was. He should be happy. And yet...

...that sixteen-year-old kid wasn't content with what he'd achieved. Because that achievement was supposed to bring his father's approval. And it hadn't. Not at all.

He hated that a part of him still yearned for it.

He quietly closed the door to the summerhouse and walked to the front of his father's yard. From here he could see the tall spire of the First Baptist Church, and the red roofs of the shops that clustered around the town's square. Beyond was farmland – the growing corn illuminated by the moonlight.

Apart from the hum of insects, the town was eerily quiet. He checked his watch – it was only nine-thirty, yet it felt as though everybody but him was asleep. Maybe he should head to the bar after all. Tanner was probably still there, a beer or two into a good night. He could order a whiskey, let the strong burn of alcohol take the wistful feelings away.

But instead he found himself heading toward another familiar road. One three blocks down from his own.

It took less than five minutes until he was there. He frowned as he stared at the old bungalow, wondering what the hell he should do next. And then, through the open window at the front of the house he saw her sitting down at the piano.

Madison Clark. *Maddie*. His ex-girlfriend's little sister who was all grown up. He stepped away from the glow of the streetlamp and into the shadows, watching carefully as she lifted the piano lid, then flexed her fingers and rolled her shoulders, sitting up straight as her hands rested on the keys.

She started with a scale. One handed at first, then adding the other. It became more complex, her fingers moving fast as it turned from a scale into a song, the melody sweet and low as it echoed into the night air.

Maddie Clark was good; you didn't need to be a rockstar to tell that. It was in the way the notes flowed effortlessly without a single fault, the tempo rising as she reached the crescendo, her chest rising and falling with the beat. What was it Becca had said? That Maddie had studied at Ansell.

So why the heck was she working in a small town diner for a living?

As the melody tapered off, her fingers slowing as they moved over the last few keys, Gray stepped back into the light, planning on heading back home.

But then she lifted her head and stared out of the window. Their gazes clashed and Gray could hear the beat of his pulse as it rushed through his ears. She walked to the window and pulled the gauzy curtain away so she could lean out.

"Hey," she called out softly. "What are you doing standing there?"

"I was listening to you play." He took a step forward so he didn't have to shout. "You were good."

Her lips curled up. "Thank you. If I'd have known a famous musician was listening, I might have tried a little harder."

"I'd hate to hear how good you are when you try harder." He was only a yard away from the house now. Enough to see the freckles across her nose and the shadows beneath her eyes. "What were you playing?"

"Nothing you'll have heard of."

"I know that. Was it something you've written?"

She opened her mouth then closed it again, her fingers still curved around the open window pane. "You want a beer?" she asked him.

He wasn't sure who was more surprised by her question. Yet his mouth watered at the thought of the ice cold liquid. "Yeah, I'd like that. If I'm not disturbing you."

"Come around to the backyard. I'll bring us a couple out," she said, inclining her head at the path that wound around the bungalow. By the time he gotten there, she was pushing the back door open with her shoulder, and walking out with two open beer. "There you go," she said, passing him an ice cold bottle. "I figure we can sit out here and enjoy the weather." She laid back on an Adirondack chair that faced out toward the river, and he took the seat next to hers. "Cheers," she said, holding out her bottle, and he clinked his against it.

"Cheers."

He took a long, cold sip of beer, closing his eyes as it slipped down his throat. "I needed that."

"Me, too." She smiled at him. "It's been one of those days."

"You can say that again."

Her left eyebrow lifted up. "How're the repairs going?"

"Slow. Hard. And made worse by the constant worry that I'll flood the whole place, and my dad will never let me hear the end of it."

"You really care what your dad thinks?" she asked.

"I care if I flood him and he ends up in the hospital again," Gray said, lifting the bottle back to his lips. "Or if I leave Aunt Gina without water for days."

"You have enough money to fix any of that. Just whisk them away to Hawaii for a few days and get a professional in. I'm pretty sure they'll forgive you real quick."

"I'm starting to learn that money can't buy everything."

She laughed. "It can buy a damn lot." He watched as her lips closed over the rim of her bottle and she tipped her head back to swallow another mouthful. He tried to ignore the desire shooting through him.

This was Maddie. Little Maddie Clark. His fucking libido needed to take a hike. He crossed his legs in case it didn't.

"So why is it one of those days for you?" he asked her, trying to distract himself.

She sighed and pulled at the label around her bottle, tearing off the paper. "Every day feels like one of those days sometimes, you know? Like you're swimming against the tide when everybody else is on a motorboat, and right when you think you're making progress, they circle around you and make sure their wake sends you under the surface."

"Was it Murphy's eggs?" Gray asked, his face serious.

She laughed, and it gave him way too much pleasure. "It's *always* Murphy's eggs." She turned to look at him, her warm eyes catching his again. "They're enough to ruin anybody's day."

"How does someone run a diner for that long and still not know how to make eggs?"

She shrugged. "It takes a lot of skill."

It was Gray's turn to laugh. For the first time all day he felt his muscles relax. A mixture of the beer, the cool air, and the woman sitting next to him. It reminded him of something, but he couldn't quite put his finger on it.

"Look at that," Maddie said, lifting her hand toward the trees. "Fireflies. There are so many this year."

He followed the direction of her finger, taking in the glowing insects as they rested in the old oak tree at the end of her yard. From here they looked like a thousand tiny lights, glowing in the night air.

"Pretty."

"Yeah. I always love the fireflies. There are some years they don't seem to be around at all. But then others they're here every night, lighting up the way."

"There was a year when they were everywhere," Gray said, his eyes drawn back to her. "I must have been sixteen, and I remember thinking if only they could stay until Christmas, it'd be like having our own living, breathing decorations. But they never did."

Maddie smiled at him. "I didn't know sixteen-year-old boys thought like that. I thought it was all girls, sports, and well..." she pulled her lip between her teeth.

"Sex?" he asked, biting down a grin.

"I was thinking more about solo fun."

"You were thinking about masturbation?" His voice was low. "Don't let a teenage boy hear you say that."

"You have a dirty mind."

"Not as dirty as a teenage boy."

"You sure about that?" She tipped her head to the side, her brows rising up.

"You're the one who brought up sex," he pointed out.

"Oh my god," she said, shaking her head. "You're twisting my words."

Yeah, maybe. But now he couldn't get the image out of his mind. Maddie Clark touching herself.

He took another mouthful of beer.

"Why don't we change the subject?" Maddie asked him.

"Sure. What should we talk about?" he replied, his voice low. He couldn't remember the last time he felt so relaxed, and yet so aware of a woman, too. His body responded every time their eyes met.

"Tell me about your next album," Maddie suggested, leaning her head back as she spoke. And as Gray told her about the concept he had planned, he watched her expression. He liked the way her eyes lit up as he spoke about the music, the way her questions were so pointed and intelligent as he talked her through the latest song he was writing. But more than anything, he liked the way she looked at him. Like he was as big and bright as that plate moon hanging low in the sky.

And if a part of him wanted to kiss his teenage sweetheart's little sister? Well, he was a grown man. He could ignore it.

CHAPTER ELEVEN

"*M*addie? I just saw Rachel Garston pull up outside."

"I'll be right there."

Rachel Garston's son was a regular pupil, one Maddie had been teaching since he was five years old. He didn't have any particular flair for the piano, nor did he want to. But he liked to please his momma by playing for her friends at Christmas and on birthdays, and Rachel never missed a payment for his tuition.

And he was a sweet little kid, so there was that.

Maddie glanced at the message she'd been reading on her phone as she walked out of the kitchen. She hadn't heard from Sarah Mayhew for months, not since they exchanged Christmas cards the previous December. Seeing her name flash on the screen had made Maddie's stomach do a weird flip-flop. Sarah was the only person from The Ansell School of Performing Arts she kept in contact with, and seeing her name always reminded Maddie of those days.

Of what could have been and what wasn't.

Walking down the hallway, Maddie thought about her

message.

Can you believe it's been five years since the Class of Fifteen graduated? We've decided to have a long-overdue reunion. Right now, we're in the organizational stage – we've set up a Facebook page and are asking for suggestions of dates and locations. You should join us. I know you didn't graduate, but you were still part of the class. Everybody would love to see you!

Maddie pulled the front door open and lifted her hand to wave at Rachel. Little Charlie ran up the pathway, clutching his music book. She grinned as he reached the steps.

"Come on in," she said. "My mom's made some lemonade. I figure we can have a glass before we start."

"Yes!" He did a fist bump that made Maddie want to laugh.

She slid her phone in her pocket, and pushed away thoughts of Ansell and all those who'd graduated from it.

It was a lifetime ago. It didn't matter any more.

"Come on," she said, putting her hand on Charlie's shoulders. "Let's go fix you a glass."

When Friday night came around, Maddie found herself wishing for rain, even though she hated getting wet and being stuck indoors. Right now it felt preferable to wheeling her mom to *Chairs* and subjecting herself to the good townsfolk of Hartson's Creek.

But like a dutiful daughter, she did it anyway, loading up a cooler with drinks and helping her mom get ready. The only silver lining she could see when she carried the cooler of drinks and cupcakes to the large table in the center of the field was that Gray's Aunt Gina and sister, Becca, were there, unloading their own baskets of baked goods.

"Hey." Becca greeted her. "Long time no see." She was

pouring lemonade from an oversized glass jug into cups. "Want one?"

"That'd be great." Maddie took the proffered glass. "Thank you. Is this your Aunt Gina's recipe?"

"Yup. And we're lucky to have it. Until an hour ago we had no water in the house." Becca sighed. "I have to be up by six every morning if I want a shower. Right now I'm counting down the weeks until I get to sleep in."

"How's the plumbing going?" Maddie asked. "Has Gray drenched anybody yet?"

"You know about that?" Becca asked.

"Gray told me…" Maddie trailed off, noticing Becca's curious expression. "Nothing's secret around here for long," she added quickly.

"I heard about you rescuing him," Becca told her. "But that was before he agreed to replace all the pipes. Have you seen him since?"

Maddie's thoughts drifted back to the other night, and their long talk in her backyard as they watched the fireflies. She'd loved listening to him talk about music, about his homecoming album, and the songs he wanted to write.

Becca was staring at her, waiting for a reply.

"He came in the diner the other day," Maddie told her. It wasn't a lie.

"Oh. I didn't know."

"So apart from the early mornings, how is the job going?" Maddie asked her, hoping Becca didn't notice the abrupt change in subject. After they talked about Becca's work at a local distillery, Maddie made her mom a plate of sweet treats and poured a cool drink, telling Becca she'd catch up with her later before heading back over to her mom.

"Thank you, honey," her mom said when she'd laid a napkin and plate on her lap. "This looks delicious."

"The tea is Aunt Gina's finest," Maddie told her.

87

Her mom took a sip. "Like drinking a little piece of liquid sun."

An hour later, her mom was in deep conversation with Jessica's mom. Although Maddie ached to go home, she didn't have the heart to interrupt her. Taking a cookie from the still-laden buffet table, she wandered across the grass toward the field where a group of teenagers had set up a flag football game. Her lip curled up as she watched them run and bicker, reminding her so strongly of a decade earlier, when she'd been one of them.

"Maddie, come sit with us."

She turned to see Jessica looking at her expectantly. When Maddie hesitated, she tapped the empty chair to her right and smiled.

Maddie opened her mouth to refuse when she saw that Laura and Becca were among the group seated there. It couldn't be all that bad, could it?

"I hear you've been hurdling over fences," Jessica said before Maddie's behind hit the seat. "I didn't believe it when Della Thorsen told me. What woman our age goes climbing fences?" She gave a fake laugh. "I guess it helps that you've never given birth."

"What?" Maddie asked. "Why would that matter?"

"Oh, you'll understand when it happens to you." The woman next to Jessica grimaced. "Let's just say that trampolining, acrobatics, and even coughing can cause a problem after childbirth."

"That's why I always do my pelvic floor exercises," Jessica proclaimed, flipping her hair behind her back. "Use it or lose it, ladies. Plus Matt appreciates the... ah... difference." She winked.

"Can we talk about something else?" Laura asked, wrinkling her nose. "I really don't need to know your sexual secrets."

Jessica huffed. "I'm just saying Maddie is lucky. She doesn't have to worry about that stuff." She turned back to Maddie. "I don't think it's right, though. Gray leading you astray like that. What did Ashleigh say?"

Maddie stole a glance at Becca. Her expression revealed nothing. "He didn't lead me astray. I'm the one who made him jump. He was only trying to escape from all the attention."

"I bet he actually likes it," Jessica said. "What guy wouldn't love girls running after him? He's pretty much begging for it with all those album covers. I swear I've seen his naked body more than I've seen Matt's."

"That's not fair," Maddie said, trying to push down her annoyance. "It's like saying a girl with a short skirt is begging for guys to hit on her. He's allowed to express himself."

Becca smiled warmly at her, appreciation all over her face.

"Girls with short skirts *are* asking for it." Jessica shrugged. "We all know that."

Laura shook her head. "The nineteen fifties called. They want their bigoted opinions back."

Maddie bit down a laugh. "I like Gray's album covers. They're beautiful and artistic."

"All those tattoos." Jessica gave a mock shudder. "I like my men to look like men, not canvases."

"I think tattoos are hot." The words escaped from Maddie's lips before she could stop them. Jessica turned to her with a raised eyebrow.

"You think Gray Hartson is hot?"

Maddie swallowed. "I didn't say that."

"Yeah, you really did."

She was sick of defending herself against the Jessicas of this town. Their small minds and judgments felt like burdens weighing Maddie down. She looked over at Becca who was watching with interest. When their eyes caught, Maddie winked.

"Well, if you're asking for my opinion, then Gray's definitely the hottest guy in Hartson's Creek right now. But he doesn't have a lot of competition, does he? Tanner's pretty good looking, I guess, but who else is there?"

Jessica blinked. "I think Matt's very good looking."

"Of course you do," Maddie said. "Bless your heart."

Laura coughed out a laugh.

It didn't feel as good as Maddie thought it would. Maybe it was too easy. Jessica got up to get herself another drink, calling her friends – minus Maddie, Laura, and Becca – to join her.

"That was sweet," Becca said to Maddie when they'd gone. "And hopefully one day I'll get over you describing my brother as hot."

"She was just telling the truth," Laura said, shrugging. "Your family breeds good looking children, you included."

Becca blew her a kiss. "Thank you kindly. And for that you should both come to Tanner's birthday party tomorrow night. He's rented out part of the Moonlight Bar."

"Rich is already going," Laura said, letting out a sigh. "Which means I'm on babysitting duties. But thanks for the invite."

"How about you?" Becca asked, smiling at Maddie. "Tanner's promised Karaoke. I always win when I sing with you."

"Yeah, but will you two beat Gray?" Laura asked them. "He's the famous singer, after all."

"Ugh. I didn't think of that." Becca pressed her lips together. "In that case, you have to come tomorrow night. We can't let my brother take our crown." She wiggled her eyebrows at Maddie. "Be there by nine. That's when the fun begins."

CHAPTER TWELVE

*G*ray walked into the Moonlight Bar and looked around, taking in the dark wooden floors, the peeling walls that might once have been painted a dark red, and the neon lit signs that were hanging at an angle.

He'd only ever been in here once, and he'd been quickly ejected before he could even produce his fake ID. Why he'd thought he could get away with underage drinking in the only bar in Hartson's Creek he had no idea. Maybe because he'd been eighteen and cocky as hell.

He did a double take at one of the lighted signs on the far wall.

"Live nudes?" he asked Tanner, frowning. "Seriously?"

"In Sam's dreams," Tanner said, inclining his head toward the bar owner. Sam was pulling a pint, his grey hair falling over his eyes. "Somebody bought it for him last Christmas as a joke."

"He'd never get away with it," Becca said, joining them at the bar. "Imagine Reverend Maitland's sermon on Sunday if he did." She looked down at her phone. "I got a message from

Cam. He and Logan are about twenty minutes away. Their flight was two hours late."

"Nothing changes." Tanner rolled his eyes. "Those two are always late."

Gray shook his head, smiling at his brother and sister. Tanner had been right. It was good being able to come here with them and share a drink as adults. He'd missed out on all their birthdays after he was twenty. Never got to celebrate their graduations, their first drinks, and much more, so this was making up for lost time. And he was glad to have the opportunity.

"Two Sierra Nevadas and a dirty martini," Sam said, sliding their drinks over. "You want me to add them to the tab?"

"Yep." Gray slid his black Amex over the counter. "Put all the drinks on this tonight."

"All of them?" Sam raised an eyebrow. "As in everybody who comes in and orders?"

Gray nodded.

"You can't do that. I invited a lot of people. It will cost hundreds," Tanner protested.

"Maybe thousands," Sam added helpfully.

"It's all good. Consider it payback for all the drinks I should have bought you over the last six years," Gray reassured Tanner. "I'm your big brother, let me do this."

"Will you throw me a birthday party, too?" Becca asked him, grinning as she took her cocktail glass.

"Of course."

"In that case, say yes," she told Tanner. "Never look a gift horse in the mouth."

"Are you sure, man?" Tanner asked again. "At least let me pay half."

"No way. I figure this way you'll let me skip the karaoke."

"Oh no," Becca said. "No way. You can't back out of that. I've got bets riding on it."

"You bet on Gray winning?" Tanner asked, grinning. "What idiot would bet against you?"

"Nope. I've bet *on* me. Well, me and Maddie. We've won every time there's been a Karaoke competition. I figure we'll do it again tonight. And since Gray's here, the odds are amazing."

"Maddie's coming tonight?" Gray asked. He took a sip of beer and tried to ignore the way his pulse quickened.

"Yeah. She's my partner in crime here. And I hate to say it, but her voice is as good as yours." Becca shrugged. "It's game on, bro."

Gray opened his mouth to respond but the door opened and more of Tanner's friends walked in, followed by two familiar faces that everybody turned to look at. He grinned as he recognized them.

"Oh my god!" Becca shouted out, running to her other two brothers and hugging them. "You're here. God, I've missed you idiots."

"Of course we are," Logan, the eldest of the two, ruffled her hair. "I told you we wouldn't be long." He glanced at Tanner. "Happy birthday, bro. Sorry we couldn't be here longer. Staffing crisis at the restaurant."

As the owner of three restaurants in Boston, Logan was constantly busy. He could only get away once in a blue moon.

Cam was an NFL player, a cornerback for the Patriots. His schedule was as rammed as his twin's. It was rare they got to spend time together.

Gray stepped forward and hugged his brothers, grinning widely. He was just over a year older than them, and when they were small he'd been like the third twin. It was only as they grew that he became the protector, making sure they were okay, along with Tanner and Becca.

"All the Heartbreak Brothers in one place," Becca said, laughing when they groaned at their old nickname. "Who would have thought?"

"How's work?" Gray asked Cam. Of all his brothers, Cam was the one who knew how hard fame could be to deal with. When he was in Boston, it was almost impossible for him to go anywhere without being recognized.

"I'm keeping busy." Cameron ran his hand over his cropped hair. "About to begin offseason training. And how about you? I hear you've been working on the old homestead?"

"Who'd have thought Gray Hartson would be into plumbing," Logan said, slapping Gray on the back. "I hope you're recording it all for posterity."

Tanner brought their drinks over, and they all raised their glasses in a toast. A warmth washed through Gray, the kind of warm that only family gives you. It was like the other side of the coin to his relationship with his father. Strange that without the old man none of them would exist.

"Twenty minutes until Karaoke," Sam called out from behind the bar. More of Tanner's friends spilled in, along with some younger women he didn't recognize, who headed straight for Becca.

He scanned every face that came in, but none of them were Maddie.

"You guys are going to sing, right?" one of Becca's friends asked Logan and Cameron.

"Of course." Logan grinned. "We can't let Gray steal all the limelight."

"I'm not singing," Gray told them.

"Ah, yeah you are."

"How about you, Tanner?" Cam asked.

"Yep. I've already put my song request in." He grinned. "And since it's my party, I get to go first."

Becca glanced at her watch. "Maybe I should call Maddie. It's not like her to be late."

The air inside the bar was getting warm, the noise levels rising as Tanner's friends and family laughed and talked with each other. Gray glanced at the door as it opened, and Maddie walked in. She stood in the doorway for a moment, looking around until she spotted Becca and smiled.

God, she looked good in her tight jeans and white strappy top, her dark hair cascading down her back. He took another mouthful of beer and pulled his eyes away, not wanting anybody to notice him looking.

"Who's that?" Logan asked Becca, his eyes wide.

"Maddie Clark."

"No way." His brother looked at Gray. "You hear that? That's Maddie Clark. Jesus, she's changed."

"Ashleigh's sister?" Cam asked, turning to watch her walk across the bar. "They sure know how to make gorgeous girls in that family."

"Hey, you seen Ashleigh since you've been back?" Logan asked him.

"No."

"Probably for the best." Cameron laughed. "She hated your guts after you left."

Gray swallowed hard, and looked over at Maddie again. Couldn't help himself. Her eyes met his and it felt like a punch in the gut. A pleasurable, yet painful punch. Then Logan stepped between them and cut off the connection. Gray took a deep, calming breath.

What was it with her? Every time they were together he felt a visceral connection. It was crazy and stupid, and so damn good.

He took another mouthful of beer and glanced at his watch. It was almost nine o'clock.

"Okay, Tanner," Sam called out, walking from behind the bar. "It's Karaoke time and you're first up." He led Gray's younger brother to the makeshift stage in the corner, handing him the microphone and pointing at the screen. "Ladies and gentlemen," he called out. "Welcome to the Moonlight Bar Karaoke Competition. First contestant is our very own Tanner Hartson. And tonight he'll be singing *Along the River*, a song made famous by his brother, Gray Hartson."

~

MADDIE BIT down a grin at the way Gray's mouth dropped when Sam called out Tanner's choice of song. His brows pulled together and she had the biggest urge to reach out and trace the furrows that formed at the top of his strong, straight nose.

"You chose *my* song?" Gray asked, perplexed.

Tanner grinned and leaned into the microphone. "Think of it as a homage, bro."

"That's Tanner-speak for massacre," Becca mock-whispered while Logan and Cameron laughed. But then the familiar notes of *Along the River* began, and Maddie's heart clenched like it always did. It was such a slow, heartbreaking melody. Every local radio station seemed to play it constantly when it first came out. It reminded her of school dances and Homecoming and evenings at *Chairs*.

Her eyes slid to Gray's again, and her breath caught in her throat when she realized he was looking at her.

"Hi." She smiled at him.

"Hey." He walked over to her, stopping a few feet away. "I'm glad you came."

Yeah, so was she. *Now*. She had an almost-panic attack

about an hour ago when she realized she'd be singing in front of Gray Hartson. Which was stupid because she never cared about singing in front of people. Not here in Hartson's Creek, anyway. Karaoke in the Moonlight Bar was only a bit of fun, unless you were Becca who took it very seriously.

The instrumental intro ended and Tanner sang the first words.

"Remember when we were kids? And everything we did? The days we spent at school right by the river."

"Ouch." Logan covered his ears. "Could he hit any more bum notes?"

"The day that love died. And everybody cried. We held each other tight by the river."

Tanner was looking right at his brother, serenading him. Gray shook his head and Maddie grinned because it was so damn sweet watching them.

"Come on, bro," Tanner called out. "Come and sing with me."

Gray lifted his hands up and shook his head. "No," he mouthed.

"Go on," Logan urged.

"It's his party," Becca said, grabbing Gray's arm. "Go and join him."

Tanner launched into the chorus and pointed at Gray. He turned his hand over and beckoned him with a curled finger. Maddie laughed again and Gray looked at her with raised eyebrows.

"What?" she asked.

Gray grinned sheepishly at her and walked to the stage, and damn if watching his long-legged easy stride didn't make her heart beat a little faster. He walked onto the platform and Tanner hugged him, his grin so wide it was infectious. Tanner held the microphone up to Gray's mouth as the chorus repeated, and the crowd in the bar cheered loudly as he began to sing.

"The day I walked along the river was the day we said goodbye." Gray's voice was low and achingly soulful. A shiver wracked its way down Maddie's spine.

"The day we walked along the river was the day I made you cry." His eyes scanned the crowd as he leaned in, landing on her. Maddie's breath caught in her throat.

"Now I sit here all alone and all I think about is then."

Everybody was clustered around the stage, their arms up, their voices loud as they joined in the song.

"Why can't we walk along the river again?"

"Shit," Becca whisper-shouted in Maddie's ear. "Do you think we can top that?"

"Sure," Maddie lied. "Piece of cake."

Becca muttered something about their A-game before she wandered over to where Sam was standing by the stage, and whispered something in his ear. Maddie stayed exactly where she was. She couldn't have moved if she'd wanted to. It was as though she was glued to the spot, her pulse thumping in time to the music.

"You're so fucking hot," one of Becca's friends shouted at Gray over the music. Almost everybody laughed.

Maddie wanted to join in, she really did. But there were too many emotions rushing through her, and not a single one of them was amusement. There was confusion and desire and a wistfulness that she could taste on the tip of her tongue.

But not humor. Not at all.

As the song came to a close, and Gray sang the final note, another roar went up, along with whistles and claps. Gray ruffled Tanner's hair and Tanner slapped his back, then they both climbed down from the stage.

For a moment they disappeared into the crowd, and all

she could see were the tips of their heads as Tanner's friends congratulated and hugged them. Then Gray emerged, walking toward her, and Maddie had to curl her fingers into fists and dig her nails into her palms in an attempt not to throw herself at him.

The need to touch him was overwhelming. His t-shirt was clinging to him, his skin glowing, his eyes sparkling. She swallowed hard and tried to remind herself who he was. Her sister's ex.

But her heart didn't want to listen. It was too busy pounding at her ribcage.

"How was I?" he asked her, his eyes heavy-lidded as he looked down at her.

"You were okay." She somehow managed to keep her voice steady. "Not as good as the original, but who is?"

He grinned, and it about broke her. "Damned with faint praise."

"Okay, next up is Becca and Maddie," Sam shouted into the microphone. The feedback crackled through the speakers, making her wince.

"Good luck," Gray said, still smiling at her.

"And as a treat, Maddie will be playing the piano while they sing."

"You will?" Gray asked her.

It was news to her. So *that* was what Becca had been whispering to Sam about. She looked over at the old piano at the end of the stage. She knew from experience it was out of tune, and covered with about two inches of dust.

"Come on, Maddie," Becca called out over Sam's shoulder, almost bouncing with excitement.

Gray slipped his warm palm under her elbow and led her over to the piano, stepping back so she could slide onto the stool. She traced her finger along the lid, and sure enough it came back grey. Sighing, she lifted it up and turned to Becca. "What am I playing?"

"Lady Antebellum. *I Need You Now.*" Becca spoke into the microphone. The people in front of the stage whooped.

Maddie shook her head and looked at the keys. It would have been better with a guitar, but she could make it work with the piano. As she put her fingers on the ivory, Becca walked over, carrying the microphone, and sat down next to her.

"You do Hillary's vocals and I'll do Charles'," Becca whispered, as Maddie pressed her fingers on the first four notes, then repeated the melody, silently counting herself in.

As Becca held the microphone in front of her, Maddie opened her lips to sing, and forgot everything around her.

Everything except the gorgeous man leaning on the top of the piano, watching her intently.

CHAPTER THIRTEEN

The entire room was silent as Maddie sang the first line. Her voice was pure, perfectly in tune, and it cut right to his core. Beneath the keyboard he could see her knee moving up and down to the beat, her fingers speeding up as the verse segued into the chorus.

Becca leaned in and the two of them sang about being drunk and needy, and he believed every word. Maddie's expression was animated, her lips soft as she lived the words she was singing.

She was a natural performer. That much was clear. It wasn't just that she could play piano – he'd met a lot of people who could do that, some of them better than her. It wasn't the sound of her voice, either, though it sent shivers down his spine every time she opened her mouth. No, it was in the way she moved, her head turning to capture the audience who stood swaying in front of the stage, their expressions rapt. She didn't need to strut her stuff or belt out the tune, because she'd already made them hers.

It was intoxicating.

Becca took over the next verse, stumbling over a note,

and Maddie caught her eye and grinned. Then the chorus began again and the crowd joined in, their bodies swaying, their arms raised up.

Gray found himself mouthing the words along with them. Maddie glanced up at him, her lips curling as she caught his eye. God, he wanted her. Wanted to kiss those words right out of her mouth. Wanted to show her how damn sexy her talent was. His fingers ached with the need to touch her soft lips, to push his way inside and watch her reaction.

"Maddie's good, huh?" Tanner asked, passing Gray a fresh bottle of beer. He leaned on the piano next to him and made a face at Becca, who stuck her tongue out at him.

"She's more than good. She's better than half the professional singers I know."

"That's why nobody likes singing Karaoke after them. She and Becca always win the competitions." Tanner grinned at him. "Until we came along."

The song was coming to an end. Becca and Maddie were leaning in close, singing about how much they needed their baby, their voices breathy and low. As Maddie played the final note, the crowd cheered loudly, stamping their feet and calling for more. Becca grabbed her hand and pulled her up, the two of them bowing to their audience. Somebody whistled appreciatively, and Gray frowned. That was his sister and his...

Friend?

Why did that word make him feel so disappointed? He looked back at Maddie. Watched the way her chest rose and fell rapidly as she took shallow breaths. Then someone put a glass in her hand, and another person pulled her away, and all Gray could do was watch her.

His friend.

"Next up we have some fresh Karaoke meat. Twins Logan

and Cameron. Give a big Moonlight welcome to them both," Sam shouted into the microphone. "And don't forget, at the end you'll have the chance to vote for your favorite. Whoever gets the loudest applause wins the coveted Moonlight Karaoke Trophy."

"He doesn't have one," Tanner told Gray. "Someone stole it last year. But he's hoping by the end of the night everybody will be too drunk to notice."

Gray chuckled as he scanned the room, looking for her. "I'm just gonna..." he inclined his head at the bar.

"Good plan. Logan and Cam sing about as well as I do."

Gray walked across the room, smiling and shaking hands as people told him how great it was that he came here tonight. But his attention was elsewhere, looking for *her*.

She wasn't at the bar, nor in the crowd of people staring at the stage as Logan and Cam ruined a perfectly good song. He looked at the bathroom for a while, but gave up when he started to worry what people might think.

Becca was talking to a couple of girls by the bar. Gray walked over to her and hugged her, congratulating her on her performance.

"Have you seen Maddie?" he asked her.

"No." Becca looked around. "But she must be here somewhere."

"No worries. I'll catch her later."

She'd gone home. He was sure of it, though he had no idea why. He put his beer down on the counter and grabbed his jacket, heading out through the peeling green door. The night air surrounded him, cooler than he'd expected.

That's when he saw her. Sitting on a bench in the square – the same bench she'd sat on that first day they'd met. Her feet were propped up on the seat and her arms were wrapped around her knees, hugging them tight. For somebody who'd just had everybody in the Moonlight Bar –

including him – wrapped around her little finger, she didn't look happy.

It only took a minute to cross the square to join her. She looked up as he reached the bench, but she didn't move.

"Hey." He sat down next to her. "You okay?"

"Yeah." She sighed. "I just needed some fresh air. It's hot in there."

"It's cool out here."

"You're telling me. I've got goosebumps on top of goosebumps." She looked down at her bare arms.

He shrugged his jacket off and laid it across her shoulders, not bothering to ask for permission. He knew enough about her already to know she would have insisted he keep it, and he wasn't in the mood for bullshit.

She was cold. He could make her warm. Simple.

"You were good in there," he told her. "*Really* good."

A ghost of a smile passed her lips. "Thanks. Though it's an old favorite. I can't tell you how many times we've performed that one. It always gets people going."

"I guess it resonates with everybody. Who hasn't been up at one in the morning thinking about somebody?"

She nodded, pulling his jacket sleeves across her chest.

"You have an amazing voice. Better than half the ones I hear in the business. Have you ever thought of becoming professional?" he asked.

She looked up at him, the moonlight making her skin glow softly. God he wanted to touch her. "I like things the way they are."

There was no conviction in her voice. No truth. It sounded like a line she'd rehearsed too many times. "You like living in a dead end town serving shitty eggs for a living?" he asked her. "And spending every Friday night gossiping with old women who are more interested in who's dating who than what's happening in the real world?" He curled his fingers into his palms, wondering where his anger had come from.

"I teach piano, too," she replied, raising an eyebrow.

He laughed. A short, humorless laugh that made him wince. "That's bullshit. You don't get to have a talent like you do and hide it away. You have it for a reason. You should be out there, recording songs, putting them in front of the industry." He turned, his eyes staring straight at hers. "I could help you."

"I don't want your help," she told him, pulling her lip between her teeth. "I don't need it. I'm fine here. I have a good life, people who need me. I can't walk away from my responsibilities."

"I got away."

"You were lucky enough to have a big family who could take care of each other when you were gone."

Maybe she was right. He never had to worry about who was going take his dad for doctor appointments or make sure he ate something every day. Gray got to travel the world and leave it to Gina and Becca and his brothers.

Maddie didn't have that luxury.

"Your mom has Ash, too," he pointed out, to himself more than her.

Maddie winced. "Ash has her own family. She shouldn't have to look after us."

"So how come she's the one who left?" Gray asked her. It all felt wrong. As though she was throwing excuses out to cover something else up. "Didn't you go to Ansell? Why did you come back?"

Maddie paled. "You know about that?" Her bottom lip wobbled, and he wanted to make it stop. God, he wanted so many things but had no idea how to make them reality.

"I heard you went there for a while then came back. You didn't graduate?"

She swallowed. "No."

"Why not?"

Maddie looked down at the sleeve of his jacket, her fingers twisting the cotton. "It doesn't matter," she said. He had to lean forward to hear her. "I'm here and this is where I'm going to stay."

"So that's it? You stagnate because your mom needs you? You'll regret it if you do."

Her head lifted and he could see the moon reflecting in her watery eyes. "Maybe I'd regret it more if I left. Not everybody succeeds, Gray. Not everybody gets the life they've always dreamed of. You might have gotten the fairytale, but there are nightmares out there, too. Sometimes it's better to stick with what you know." She stood and pulled his jacket off, holding it out to him.

"Keep it."

"I'm heading home. Can you tell Tanner for me? And make my excuses to Becca?"

"Don't you want to know if you won the contest?"

He took a step toward her, reaching out to cup her jaw. Her skin was as soft as he'd imagined. Warm, too, in spite of her shivers.

"You're better than this," he whispered, his thumb brushing her bottom lip.

"I'm not." Her voice cracked. "I'm Maddie Clark. Ashleigh's sister. I'm the girl nobody sees because there are so many better things to look at. I'm not you, Gray. I'm not star material. And I've come to terms with that."

A single tear rolled down her cheek, her jaw, and it felt like somebody was twisting every muscle inside him. He wiped the dampness from her skin, his gaze dropping to her lips. God, they were perfect. Pink and full and slightly open.

"Maddie." His throat was tight as he leaned closer. "Maddie Clark."

Her lips were trembling. Her eyes were wide, full of questions he didn't have the answers to. He swallowed hard, feeling the need to kiss her hot in his blood. He wanted to consume her until he knew all the answers. Kiss her until she understood every one. Pull her body against his until she knew how much he desired her.

He slid his hand around her neck, angling her head until her gaze met his. And for a moment he drowned in them. In her. Unsure if he'd be able to breathe again.

"I should go." She pulled away, leaving his hand dangling in mid-air. "I'm sorry."

Gray watched as she hurried across the square, his brows scrunched together as she ran through the gate and onto the sidewalk. Within moments she was gone, disappearing into the shadows, and he was all alone.

What the hell just happened? He wasn't certain, but one thing was for sure. He didn't like it one bit.

MADDIE HURRIED ALONG THE SIDEWALK, clutching Gray's jacket tightly across her chest. The smell of him clung to the cotton. Warm and masculine, it made her stomach flip with the memory of his expression. He'd been about to kiss her, of that she was certain.

But she had no idea why.

Was it sympathy? Or some crazy flashback to Ashleigh? Her cheeks burned at the thought. She'd been so close to closing the gap between their lips. All it would have taken was a roll of her feet and their mouths would have touched. She swallowed hard as she turned the corner onto her road, mortification wrapping around her as she spotted her house at the end of the block.

She was such an idiot. Had she really cried in front of

him? She ran her fingers along her cheek. Any dampness was gone, but her skin was still heated. And maybe that wasn't a surprise.

Because Gray Hartson had almost kissed her. Even worse, she'd *wanted* him to. Felt the need for him drumming through her veins until she could barely concentrate on anything else. And for a moment – just one perfect slice in time – it had felt so right. As though a woman like her could be with a guy like him.

Until reality hit her like a Mack truck.

Maddie knew she was okay looking. But she was no Ashleigh. Growing up in her beautiful sister's shadow had taught her that looks were currency. They bought you attention and admiration, and guys like Gray Hartson.

She knew from an early age that she'd never be *that* kind of girl. So she made people laugh or was kind to them. Did things that built other kinds of connections. When all else failed she'd hide away in her music. Her happy place.

And they might not have bought her a life like Ashleigh's – living with a rich husband in an expensive house with two beautiful children – but she'd never wanted that kind of life. Here in Hartson's Creek, she knew who she was. Where she stood. She had friends, people she took care of. It was a good life.

So why did her heart feel like it was cracking in two? She let out a sigh as she turned into the pathway to her home. The porch light was on, the way she'd left it, but the rest of the cottage was dark.

Once inside, she checked on her mom, who was sleeping soundly, then walked to her own bedroom with that jacket still warmly wrapped around her. She'd give it back tomorrow – or maybe give it to Becca to pass back to Gray. She wasn't sure she could have another conversation with him without revealing herself to him.

Or fearing he wouldn't like what he saw.

Kicking her shoes off, she laid down on her bed, breathing in the warm scent that clung to his coat. She shook her head and stood up again, laying it on her desk chair before sitting back on the mattress.

She wasn't a teenager anymore. She didn't get to make the kind of decisions she had when she was naïve. She'd done that once before and look where it got her? Alone and afraid in New York, calling her sister at midnight and begging her to come and save her.

She wouldn't put herself in that position again. Better to be alone and safe than with somebody and vulnerable.

Even if it was becoming almost impossible to fight her feelings.

CHAPTER FOURTEEN

"Aunt Gina says stop working and come outside," Logan said, craning his head to where Gray was working in the attic. "There's a beer out there with your name on it."

Gray wiped the sweat from his brow and looked down at his brother. "How was church?"

"Boring without you," Logan said, grinning. "I was promised crowds of screaming girls outside. And Tanner just sat in the corner looking green. I told him that last whiskey wasn't gonna do him any good."

"I think it was the five before it that hurt him," Gray said, climbing through the attic door. "And the six beers." It was hard not to laugh at Tanner's hangover.

"He's drinking a bottle in the garden right now. Said something about kill or cure."

Gray followed his brother down the stairs and through the kitchen. Aunt Gina was cooking up a storm, muttering to Becca who caught Gray's eye. She rolled her own at him.

"Do you need any help here?" he asked as his aunt opened the stove and squealed at the smoke coming out.

"No. Go outside with your brothers and get out of my hair."

"You coming?" he asked Becca.

"In a minute." She nodded. "I figure I'll let you get all the boy talk over with first."

Logan passed him a beer as they walked outside. Tanner was laying on two chairs, his face inclined to the sky, eyes closed as he listened to Cam. The younger twin was regaling him with stories of his last game.

"You carried on playing with a head injury?" Tanner asked, his eyes still closed. "Are you crazy?"

"I wanted to win." Cam shrugged. "The rush was incredible." He grinned as he spotted his older brothers walking out. "Gray must know what I mean. I've seen your face when you walk out on stage."

"Kinda like his face when Tanner made him sing Karaoke of his own song," Logan said, grinning. "Man, that made me laugh."

Tanner shook his head. "I can't believe we lost to Becca and Maddie. I could have sworn we were a sure thing."

"They won fair and square," Logan said, glancing at his phone and wincing. "They got the biggest cheer."

"Don't remind me," Tanner complained. "Becca was shoving it in my face all night."

"I gotta make a phone call," Logan told them, his jaw set hard. "I'll be right back."

"Restaurant problems?" Gray asked Cam as the older twin walked around the front of the house.

"He's lost five staff since Friday to a rival place. Any more and he'll have to close temporarily. He was bitching about it the whole way here." He shrugged and took another mouthful of beer. "Talking of bitching, how are you finding the old man?"

"He's being his usual asshole self," Tanner muttered. "Everything Gray does with the plumbing is wrong."

"Is it bad that I was relieved he stayed in bed today?" Cam asked. "I can take about ten minutes with him, but a whole afternoon? No way I want to listen to him dissecting every play I made last season. I'd have to win the Superbowl single handed to make him happy."

Gray pressed his lips together. Yeah, it was bad, but he felt exactly the same way. Though his father's health was improving, he was still nowhere near well. And having all of his children in the house at once was proving too much for him.

"Hey, how's that girl you were seeing?" Tanner asked Cam, opening his eyes a chink. He immediately shaded them with the palm of his hand. "Alice was it?"

"Andrea. And we ended things. She nagged too much."

"Big surprise," Tanner muttered.

"How about you, Tanner?" Cam asked, raising an eyebrow. "Are the girls pushing down your door in New York?"

"I saw you looking at Maddie Clark," Tanner said to Cam, ignoring his question. "She's grown up and looking better than her sister."

Gray lifted the bottle to his lips. He'd barely slept last night. Too much thinking about Maddie and their conversation in the square.

He'd been a hair's breath away from kissing her. Could still smell the sweet fragrance of her perfume if he tried hard enough. It was messing with his head, this attraction he had for her.

No matter what he did, he couldn't get her out of his mind.

"She's a beautiful girl." Cam shrugged. "But I've sworn off women. At least until I retire from the NFL."

Was it weird that Gray's shoulders felt lighter at that?

"What about you, Gray?" Tanner said. "Any stories about actresses or singers you can tell us?"

"Nope."

"Oh come on. At least one of the Hartson brothers has to be getting some." Tanner sat up, but his face remained ashen. "You have to fight them off. I see all the comments on your Instagram pictures."

"I haven't. My publicist deals with that."

"Some of them put their phone numbers and describe everything they want to do to you. You should call them."

Gray lifted an eyebrow. "I'm not interested in a hook up."

Cam tipped his head to the side, his eyes scrutinizing his brother. "What are you interested in? Settling down?"

"No." Gray frowned. "I'm not looking for anything permanent. I'm not looking for anything at all. But if I ever do, I want a connection. Some emotion. I'm sick and tired of sex just for the sake of it."

"Whoa. I never thought I'd see the day when one of my brothers would say that," Becca said, grinning as she walked out to join them. "And if you don't mind, can we change the subject? Because the thought of any one of you having sex is going to ruin my Karaoke winning high."

"Shut up," Tanner told her. "It was fixed. You only got all those cheers because you paid for them."

Gray finished his beer and put the bottle on the ground. When he looked up, Cam was looking at him, a speculative expression on his face. As though he could see right through Gray's brain to the thoughts inside.

He hoped to god it was just an illusion. Because if he could read Gray's thoughts, he'd probably think he was crazy. Because they were full of the girl who happened to be his ex-girlfriend's sister.

If that wasn't a mess, Gray had no idea what was.

~

"Your father's feeling well enough to join us for breakfast," Aunt Gina said a few days later as she poured out four glasses of orange juice. "Isn't that wonderful?"

"Great." Gray took a sip of his juice and tried really hard to smile.

"That *is* wonderful," Becca said, jumping up from the table. "I'll go help him."

When she'd left the room, her bare feet slapping against the floorboards in the hallway, Aunt Gina glanced at him. "It's a shame he couldn't get up while your brothers were here. Maybe they can come visit again soon."

Logan and Cameron had left early the Monday morning after Tanner's party, making hurried excuses as they raced to catch their flight. Tanner had left a few hours later.

Gray already missed them like crazy, which was stupid considering how little he'd seen them in the past few years. They'd made promises of coming to see him in L.A. when he was back there, but he knew it would take a lot of organizing to get them all in the same place at the same time again.

"Here he is," Becca said as she walked with her father into the kitchen. He held tightly onto her arm as he shuffled along. Gray stood and pulled a chair back and Becca helped him sit down.

"Orange juice?" Aunt Gina asked him.

"Just a dash."

Gray could feel the atmosphere in the kitchen change. It was like somebody had dimmed the lights and turned the volume down.

"What's happening at work today?" Aunt Gina asked Becca as she buttered a slice of toast.

"We're having a new still fitted and the bosses are bitching like crazy about the loss in production, so I'm going to put in my headphones and pretend I can't hear them." Becca shrugged. "Oh, and I'm still lording it over Gray that I beat him at Karaoke." She winked at him, and he raised an eyebrow back at her. "Did I tell you about that?"

Aunt Gina laughed. "About a hundred times."

Becca shrugged. "It's not often I get to beat a Grammy winner. I'm thinking of putting it on my resumé."

"I was thinking of putting it on my next album cover," Gray told her. "The second best singer in Hartson's Creek."

"Third, really, if you count Maddie," Becca pointed out with a grin.

Maddie. The mention of her name was enough for his grip to tighten on his glass.

"You planning on doing any work this morning?" His dad's voice cut through Gray's thoughts.

"Yeah. Once breakfast is over, I'll get changed and cut the water off."

"Better hurry, then," his dad said, pointing at the uneaten toast in front of him. "I'll help you with it today."

"You're sick," Gray pointed out. "You should be resting."

"I'm feeling a little better. And I'll just sit and watch. Make sure you're doing it correctly."

"I am doing it correctly." Gray tried not to show his irritation.

"Oh let him help. It'll be good for the two of you to spend some time together. This afternoon your father can rest." Aunt Gina smiled at him.

"I don't need rest," his dad grumbled.

Yeah, well Gray didn't need his supervision, but it looked like none of them were getting what they wanted today.

"You want another?" Sam asked as Gray leaned on the

counter of the Moonlight Bar eight hours later. Gray nodded and Sam filled his glass with another shot of whiskey. His third, which felt restrained considering the day Gray'd had.

Nothing was good enough for his father. He should have known that by now. But being told he needed to rip out everything he'd done so far and start again was bad, even for him. It had led to a full-blown fight, followed by a huge coughing fit before a teary Aunt Gina had shot him a look and made his father go back to bed.

So much for family bonding.

"You still sore about losing the Karaoke competition?" Sam asked with a grin. The bar was practically empty, but Gray still kept his cap pulled down low and sat in the shadows at the far end. More because he was pissed than because he was worried about being spotted.

He swallowed a mouthful of whiskey, the warm liquid searing the back of his throat in such a pleasurable way. He wasn't drunk – unlike Tanner, it took more than a few drinks to get him that way – but he was more relaxed than he'd felt in days.

"I'm not sore about losing," Gray said as he put down his empty glass. He shook his head when Sam lifted the bottle again. "I just needed a quiet place to sit."

Sam cocked an eyebrow. "It's funny, because that's where your old man used to sit back in the day. I was just a kid then. But I remember pouring him out whiskies while he lurked right there."

Gray frowned. "My dad used to come here?"

"Yup. Regular as clockwork. I felt kind of sorry for him. His wife gone, and five kids to feed and clothe. It's tough on any man to have to handle that." Sam poured himself a glass and leaned on the counter. "Everybody thought he'd get remarried real quick. There was even talk of him marrying your Aunt Gina, but that went nowhere."

Gray could remember wishing they would get married, even though there was never anything more than friendship between his dad and his mom's sister. He'd been afraid of losing her the way they'd lost their mom. Scared that she'd get sick of taking care of them and leave them alone with their dad.

But she always stayed, and he was grateful for that.

"Maybe he *should've* gotten remarried," Gray muttered into his empty glass.

"Sometimes you only get one chance at love," Sam said, shrugging. "Maybe your mom was his soul mate. What's the point in trying to replace the irreplaceable?"

"You really believe that?" Gray asked him. "That there's only one soul mate out there for each of us?"

"I don't know." Sam leaned his chin into the vee of his thumb and forefinger. "But maybe your dad did. I've never seen a man so lost. To be honest, it scared me to death. Maybe that's why I stayed single." He chuckled. "You see a lot of heartbreak in this job."

Gray tried to picture his father sitting here as a younger man. He could barely remember a time before his mom died, and couldn't remember what his father had been like then. His memories were full of the anger, the arguments, and the fire that rose up in his stomach every time he and his father clashed.

"One thing that your dad didn't do when your mom died was leave. For a while I wondered if he might. I see that a lot, too. Guys who abandon their families and walk away." Sam pressed his lips together. "I hate that."

"I know a bit about walking away," Gray said, holding his glass up for one last whiskey. It had done its job. Soothed away the pain and doused the fire. He didn't need it to do any more than that. He'd drink this last glass and head home.

And maybe be a little thankful that he wasn't a widowed man with five children depending on him.

A man who'd had love and lost it.

Gray wondered what it was like to have a love to lose.

YOU'VE BEEN INVITED to the Ansell Class of 2015 Reunion Group.

Maddie clicked on the little notification, her stomach lurching as it took her to the group Sarah had messaged her about. At the top was the option to join, along with a little note stating she was in preview mode, able to read any posts in the group, but unable to comment on them unless she joined.

She felt her throat get tight as she scrolled down. There were over fifty members already. And a whole list of posts from them, thanking Sarah for creating the group, updating everybody on their lives.

Some of them were playing in Symphony orchestras, traveling the US. Others were working for music publishers, or teaching music at a college level to new students. She recognized a couple of them who were now working in Hollywood in the movie industry, composing scores.

Not one of them seemed to be working in a diner, or teaching music to the local youth.

She tried to ignore the little voice in her head telling her she was a disappointment. That if only she'd stayed at Ansell she'd be one of them. All those hopes and dreams she'd had when she'd opened her acceptance letter came flooding back.

Once upon a time she'd really believed she could be someone.

With a swipe of her hand, she closed down Facebook. It was just a stupid reunion. She wouldn't be going. Her life was here, in Hartson's Creek, and for the most part it was a happy one.

She wasn't going to dwell on what could have been. That would be madness.

～

TAP, tap.

Maddie blinked at the noise, looking around the room. It was late, almost eleven, and she was thinking about turning off her light. It had been a long day of teaching.

Then there was a knock. Louder, surer. Maddie frowned and stared at the closed curtains across her window. Sometimes birds would walk along the ledge and tap their beaks on the glass, but not at this time of night. She swallowed hard and walked over to the window, her pulse racing, as she curled her fingers around the thick cotton curtain.

Oh so slowly she lifted it, just enough to be able to peek through. On the other side, a hand lifted again, knuckles connecting with the glass, making her jump.

"Gray?"

She yanked the curtain and unlatched the window, pushing it open. It really was him. Gray Hartson in the flesh, staring in at her with the strangest expression on his face.

"I hoped this was still your room," Gray said, a half–smile curling his lips. "I didn't want to knock on the front door in case your mom was asleep."

"Is everything okay?" she asked him.

His eyes were soft. Was that whiskey she could smell on his breath? It was warm and spicy and made her want to step closer.

"Yeah. I just wanted to see you. Tell you I'm sorry."

"You're sorry?"

Gray pulled his cap off, using his other hand to rake his

fingers through his hair. It fell in a perfect messy style over his brow. "For being an asshole the other night. I shouldn't have said what I did."

"You could have told me that while it was light," she teased.

He lifted an eyebrow. "Yeah, I coulda. I probably should have. But I'm here now."

"Have you been drinking?" she asked him.

"Just a little." He shrugged. "I had a bad day and needed to take the edge off."

"I know the feeling." She thought about the two bottles of beer she'd drunk that evening.

He nodded. "So that was it, really. I just wanted to say I'm sorry." He grinned at her again. "And I am. Good night, Maddie."

Was he leaving? She tried to swallow down the disappointment. It wasn't as though she wanted him to try to kiss her again. It was good that he hadn't. Even if he was soft and warm and a little drunk.

"Good night," she whispered. She stood at the window and watched as he started to walk back up the path. Then he turned on his heel to face her again, his body wobbling.

"Oh and Maddie?"

"Yeah?"

"What you said that night about nobody seeing you? You were wrong. *I see you.* I've always fucking seen you." The corner of his mouth lifted up, as he took the few steps back toward her. "You're impossible to miss."

Her chest tightened at his words. "You see me?" she asked softly.

"Yep. Every single glorious inch of you. I hear you, too. Even when I've got my eyes closed and I'm trying to sleep. You're everywhere and I've no idea what to do with that."

She was finding it hard to breathe. She wanted to, she

really did. But every time she tried the air caught in her throat.

"It's crazy, right?" he asked, that smile still on his lips. "You're Maddie Clark. Ashleigh's sister. I keep trying to remind myself of that. But the heart wants what the heart fucking wants, Maddie. I should know that. I've sung about it enough times. I never really believed it though." He shook his head and laughed. "I'm sorry, you must think I'm fucking crazy."

"I think you're swearing a lot," she said, smiling.

"Blame the whiskey."

"So it's the drink talking for you?" she asked him, a twinkle in her eye. "Okay then, good night." She went to close the window.

Before she could, he pushed it open further and leaned in, staring right at her. "Don't go."

"I wasn't the one going," she told him. "This is my bedroom. I'm planning on staying right here."

He smiled goofily.

"Maybe you need to go to bed, too," she suggested. "You're drunk. You should probably sleep it off."

"You know what?" he said, completely ignoring her suggestion. "We should kiss. Just once. See if there's something there." He shook his head. "Who am I kidding. Of course there's something there."

"Is there?" she asked softly.

"Isn't there?"

Yeah, there was. And the thought that he felt it too made her whole body feel on fire. Like one of those little lightning bugs they watched together, she could feel herself start to glow.

"You want to kiss me?" she asked, just to be sure she was hearing him right.

"Yeah. I really think we should. Get it over with."

God, he was cute when he was drunk. "Here? Through the window?"

He looked at her with dark eyes. "Nah. This isn't Romeo and Juliet."

"He had to climb up to her balcony. I live in a bungalow."

"It's a damn good thing I don't have to climb. I'd probably break my neck."

She grinned at him. "So where do you want to kiss me?"

"On the lips." He winked.

Talking to Gray was like foreplay. It made her body ache.

"I'm kidding," he said, leaning in through the window. "Come out here and let me take you somewhere. First kisses shouldn't be through windows. Not if you're over the age of fifteen."

"Where do you want to go?"

He was close enough to reach out and touch her. He threaded his fingers through her long thick hair. His touch made her shiver. Her body was pressed against the sill, a thin barrier of bricks between them. She wanted to pull them down one by one to get closer to him.

"If we were in L.A., I'd drive you down to a little beach just past Malibu. We'd park and take our shoes off and paddle in the waves. Then I'd turn you just right until the moon caught your face. And I'd look at you until I couldn't take it any more. Maybe you'd laugh a little because I'd have this stupid damn expression on my face because I wouldn't want to mess up this kiss."

She tried not to swoon at his description. "Then what would you do?"

"I'd twist my fingers through your hair like this," he murmured, sliding his hand to the back of her head. The window sill dug into her hips. "I'd need to tip your head up because you're so damn short and I'm so damn tall."

"That's rude."

He winked again. "And then I'd tell you how goddamn beautiful you are. How I can't get you out of my mind. How every night I think of the way your hips swing when you walk, and how one of your eyes closes a little whenever you smile. And how your voice is so damn sweet it makes me want to drag you to bed until I make you sing out with pleasure."

"And all this before we've even kissed?" she asked, a little breathless.

"I like to do things properly."

She tilted her head. "Well, it's a six hour flight from here to L.A.. Another couple for boarding and landing. Add in the drive to Malibu and we're looking at ten hours. One way." She glanced at her watch. "And my shift starts at six in the morning. I don't think we're going to make it."

"Come out here, Maddie Clark." He reached for her hand, sliding her finger through his. "I know you can climb. I've seen you."

"And then what?"

"Then I'll work out where I'm going to kiss you."

She shook her head. "You're crazy. You know that?"

"Yep."

"And drunk."

"Just a couple drinks." He held up four fingers.

"And you broke my sister's heart," she reminded him.

"What's her name again?"

"Gray!" She couldn't help but laugh, because it really was crazy. But maybe she needed a little crazy in her life. God knows, her body thought so.

"Come on. Get out here." He tugged at her hand.

"I need to get some shoes." She turned to look at her closet.

He pulled her back. "I'll carry you."

"Gray…"

"Seriously. If I let you go grab some shoes you might change your mind. Then we'll have to have this discussion all over again. And I want my kiss, Maddie. I really, really want it."

Damn it, she really wanted it, too.

Taking a deep breath, she pulled her hand away and grabbed the window frame, then climbed through it with her socked feet. He helped lift her through, his warm, strong hands circling her waist. Her breath hitched at the contact.

"Put your feet on mine," he whispered, pulling her close. "That way your socks won't get dirty."

"That might be the most romantic thing I've ever heard."

"Stick with me, babe. I'll keep your soles clean and make your soul dirty." He frowned. "That would read so much better than it sounds."

"If it makes you feel any better I got it."

"Yeah," he said, brushing a lock of hair from her eyes. "It really does."

The way he was looking at her made Maddie's legs shake. It was exactly how he'd described. Like she was entrancing him with her eyes and her voice and the way she swung her hips. It made her ache inside.

"Maddie."

"Mmm?"

"If you close your eyes will you pretend you're on a beach in the moonlight?"

"I thought you were going to take me somewhere special," she said, biting down a smile.

"I am, baby. I am."

She looked up at him, still standing on the top of his sneakers. It made her a few inches taller than normal, but she still had to tip her head back to meet his gaze.

He shuffled his feet, moving her with him, until the moonlight fell across her face. "There," he said. "Perfect."

"What do you see?" she asked him, putting her palms on his chest to steady herself. And also to check out those pecs. Yep, as firm as she thought they would be.

"I see," he said, kissing the skin on her temple, "a beautiful woman." He slid his mouth down to her jaw. "One who makes me laugh and want to scream at the same time," he whispered, kissing his way to the corner of her mouth. "A woman I'm going to kiss, or die trying."

"By the beach," she whispered. "After splashing in the waves."

"Hush. I changed my mind."

The way his lips lingered at the corner of hers was tantalizing. She held her breath, waiting for the kiss. Needing it. He slid his hand down her back, pulling her even closer against him, and her body arched in response. Just a few sweet words and the briefest of touches and she was on fire. He exhaled and the feeling of his breath against her skin sent a shiver down her spine.

He slid his hand over the swell of her behind and she pressed against him, feeling his desire. Hard and big, and everything her aching body wanted.

"Gray," she whispered. "You're driving me crazy."

His lips curled up against her skin. "The feeling's mutual." He pulled his head back and she saw herself reflected in his dark eyes. "Keep looking at me like that and I'll do more than kiss you."

"You wouldn't dare."

"Yeah. Yeah I would." He turned around, spinning her with him, and pushed her against the brick frontage, his head dipping to kiss her neck. He slid his hands under her behind and without thinking she circled her legs around his hips, and dear god, pleasure shot through her. Her head tipped back as he kissed his way up her throat, the sensation forcing a moan from her lips.

"Christ. I'm harder than a teenager."

She let out a laugh as his mouth reached hers once again. "This is the longest wait for a kiss I've ever had," she told him. It was entirely possible her body would succumb before her lips did. He was pressing himself against her in an enticing way. Her toes curled up with delight.

"I like the anticipation," he told her.

"This isn't anticipation. It's sex with clothes on."

"If you think this is anywhere close to sex, you have a lot to learn." He raised an eyebrow.

"And you're the one to teach me?"

He pushed himself against her again and she swallowed her cry. She was embarrassingly responsive, and he knew it.

"Is your mouth always this smart?" he asked her.

"Pretty much." She batted her eyelashes at him. "But I think you know what to do about it." Her thighs tightened around him and he groaned. Such a sweet sound.

He was staring at her again, the humor had melted from his expression, replaced by dark desire. Her breath hitched as he leaned closer and slowly, pressed his lips to hers.

If she thought she was needy before, it was nothing compared to now. He deepened the kiss, his mouth parting hers. The tip of his tongue slid against the tender skin inside her bottom lip. She kissed him back hard, her lips moving without conscious thought.

God, he felt good. So good. He knew how to kiss – not too hard and not too soft. A goldilocks kiss that sent her soaring. His mouth ignited a fuse that kept on burning, her body on fire as he held her against the wall and swallowed her sighs. And when they finally parted, both of them breathless, it felt as though she'd lost a little piece of herself.

"Damn." Gray shook his head. "There's definitely something there."

"Yeah," she agreed with a smile. "I guess there is."

CHAPTER FIFTEEN

"*Y*ou wanna take a walk?" he asked her when he finally let her slide back down the wall.

"Now?"

"Why not?"

"Um, because it's getting late and we both have to work tomorrow. And the town is full of busybodies who'll take one look at us and light up the grapevine." She raised an eyebrow and put a finger across her lips as though she was thinking. "Oh yeah, and I don't have any shoes on. There's that, too."

It was crazy how much her sarcasm turned him on.

"Go get your shoes." He nodded at the window. "And we'll keep to the shadows. Everybody's probably asleep, anyway."

"And if they're not?"

He shrugged. "Let them talk."

"Says the guy who doesn't live in a small town anymore."

"America's my small town. If I make a wrong move it gets plastered all across the Internet, not just at *Chairs*," he pointed out.

"Another good reason not to make waves." She looked

pale. He wasn't sure if it was a trick of the moon or the blood draining from her beautiful face.

"I just want to walk with you," he told her. "I promise nobody will see us." He wrapped his hands around her waist and lifted her onto her window sill. "If you don't want to come, that's okay. I understand." And he'd really try not to be pissed. But he didn't want to go home. He wanted to be with her.

"I do want to," she said quickly. "I'm just careful, that's all."

"Careful is good," he told her as she climbed inside. He stepped forward, leaning on the sill to take a look at her room. It was small and neat. Her plaid sheets were tightly tucked, though there was a dent in the middle where she'd been sitting. The walls were painted a pale color that he couldn't discern in this light. There were a few framed photographs on her dresser. He leaned in further to try and make them out. One of her, maybe, standing next to a piano in a long black dress. Another of a wedding – *was that Ashleigh?* And then another of two children, their blonde hair neatly combed, both cream-and-pink faces lit up with delight.

"Are those Ash's kids?" he asked Maddie as she pulled on her sneakers. Her back immediately stiffened and he realized he'd messed up. He bit on his bottom lip, trying to figure out how to make it better.

"Yes. Grace and Carter," she said, tying her laces. "They're five and three." She looked up. "Is it strange, knowing they could have been yours?"

"No. They couldn't have been mine." He shook his head. "Not at all." He was still trying to find the right words. "Ashleigh and I were kids ourselves when we dated. There was no future in it. Not for either of us. We wanted such different things."

Her expression was still guarded as she climbed back out

of the window. He found himself missing smart-mouthed-Maddie. The one who could walk verbal rings around him.

"Come on," he said. "Let's get out of here."

He turned right and she followed him, heading toward the edges of town. "Where are we going?"

"I don't know." He shrugged. "Just somewhere." He reached for her hand, sliding his fingers through hers. "You okay?"

She looked up at him, her chin jutting out. "Yeah, I'm good."

He took a left then a right, his hand still enveloping hers. His body was buzzing, like he'd put his finger in a live socket. When was the last time he'd felt like this? Even singing an encore in front of fifty thousand fans who sang his lyrics right back didn't feel this good.

The houses were thinning out, replaced by thicker rows of oaks that clustered together along the roadway. Taking a left, he pulled her down the dirt path.

Maddie stumbled on the rocky ground, and he slid his arm around her waist to steady her, activating the light on his phone to guide their way.

"Here," he said as they reached the edges of the brook. "There's a fallen log here. We used to climb on it when we were kids."

"You were allowed down here on your own?" she asked him.

"Yeah. The bonus of having a widowed dad, I guess. He didn't give a shit as long as we came back home at night and kept our grades up."

Her eyes softened. "I'm sorry."

"Don't feel sorry for me. A million people out there have it worse."

She reached for his face, cupping his jaw with her soft hand. He leaned into it, closing his eyes for a moment. It was a crazy idea, knocking on her window, yet this felt so damn good. Like he was taking in oxygen after a lifetime of holding his breath.

He heard her shuffle, then felt the warmth of her lips on his jaw. His body immediately responded. She only had to touch him and it turned him on.

Opening his eyes, he wrapped his arms around her and lifted her, straddling her body across his. She leaned her face close, enough that he could see the specks of pigment in her blue irises. She hooked her arms around his neck, her fingers massaging his scalp and he groaned at how good it felt.

"What is it about you, Maddie Clark?"

Her eyes sparkled. "You tell me."

"Let me show you instead." This time there was no hesitation, just pure electric need. He kissed her hard and deep until they were both breathless, their bodies pressed against each other like there was no other choice. She fit into him like her body was made for his; soft where he was hard, yielding where he put pressure. He stroked her hair, feeling the strands caress his palm, and kissed her again. She intoxicated him, stronger than any alcohol, more potent than any drug.

He was high on Maddie Clark and it felt so good.

"Two pancakes, one eggs benedict, and a side of bacon." Maddie smiled and laid the plates on the table in front of Reverend Maitland and his wife. "Enjoy your breakfast."

Theirs was the last order of the breakfast rush, and boy did that make her happy. It felt like all of Hartson's Creek had decided they wanted to eat at Murphy's this morning. Every now and then, Maddie would walk toward the kitchen then turn back abruptly to make sure nobody was talking about her. And they weren't.

Didn't make her any less paranoid, though.

That was the problem with only getting three hours sleep. Her brain was jumpy, and slow at the same time. She didn't like it.

"I'm heading to the bathroom," she told Murphy as she carried another pile of dirty dishes back to the kitchen. "I just refilled the coffee pot and everybody has full mugs. I'll only be a minute."

"Sure." Murphy didn't look up as she walked past him, too busy staring at the funnies. He still read the paper religiously every day. She'd given up trying to convince him he could read on his phone instead.

The staff bathroom was out back, across the alleyway in a small brick building. Word had it that Murphy built it back when he was married and his wife ran the kitchen. It was his one escape from her sharp tongue. His wife had long since left – probably before Maddie was even walking – but the bathroom remained.

She washed her hands and stared at herself in the rust-specked mirror. There were dark shadows under her eyes that no amount of concealer could fight. Her lips were red and swollen, and her chin and cheeks felt raw with beard burn. She was too old to spend all night kissing and grinding in the middle of the woods, but it was impossible not to sigh at the memory.

By the time Gray had walked her home, the first light of dawn was dancing its way across the sky. He'd kissed her again outside her home until her body sang, then watched until she made it inside safely before he left.

She splashed her face with cold water then dried it on a fresh towel, grabbing her cosmetic bag and repairing her mascara and lipstick. Her phone lit up with a message and she grabbed it eagerly, frowning when she saw it was from Ashleigh.

Ash and Gray hadn't been an item for more than ten years, yet she immediately felt guilty.

I just had coffee with Jessica. What's this about karaoke? Call me. A.

Maddie stared at it for a minute. The last person in the world she wanted to talk to right now was Ashleigh. Not just because of the guilt, but because Ash could read her like a book. A few strategically placed questions and the truth could come tumbling out.

I'm working. Will call later. M.

She paused for a moment and added a couple of kisses. Then she deleted them because Ash hadn't added any. Shaking her head at her reflection, she slid her phone into her jeans pocket and headed out of the door.

"Hey."

"What the hell?" She jumped about a mile.

"Sorry. Murphy told me you were out the back." Gray's eyes crinkled as he grinned at her.

"Did he tell you I was in the bathroom, too?" She couldn't help but smile back.

"Kinda. He started on a graphic description so I got the hell out of there."

"I don't want to know." She closed her eyes and shook her head. When she opened them again, he was still grinning at her.

"Let's start again," he suggested, stepping closer. "Hi."

"Hi." She lifted her head to look at him. "I thought you'd be elbow deep in plumbing by now."

"I am, I just came to pick up a few things from the hardware store." He shrugged. "Thought I'd stop by and see you while I was here."

"You did? Why?" The smile was still clinging to her lips.

"I have a question for you." He lifted his cap and smoothed out his hair.

"Sounds interesting."

"I've got a hazy recollection of talking to you last night. I remember leaving the bar, but can't really remember what happened next. I didn't do anything stupid, did I?"

She swallowed hard. He didn't remember? All those sweet words, those sweeter kisses. Not a bit of it?

"Um..." Her mind was blank. Of all the things she'd expected him to say, that wasn't it.

And then he started laughing, tipping his head back and exposing his stubbled jaw. She watched him, open mouth, as tears came to his eyes. "Your face," he said between chuckles. "You should see it."

"You're an asshole." She swatted his arm. "You had me believing you'd forgotten it all."

"You think I could forget something like that?" He was still laughing. "Think I could forget kissing you for almost an hour straight? I only had a couple drinks."

"Four." She held her fingers up.

"A couple of couples."

"Whatever." She shrugged. "I hope your memory isn't too hazy, because it's not happening again." She was kidding, but the dismay that flashed across his face was gratifying.

"It's not?" His voice dipped.

"Nope." She tipped her head to the side, biting down a smile.

He traced a finger along her jaw, his eyes flickering when she let out a sigh. "That's a shame," he said gruffly. "Because I liked kissing you a lot."

"I know."

He laughed again, his finger trailing across her bottom lip. "I remember how sweet you tasted. How good you felt on my lap. How you kiss like a wild woman when you let go."

"A wild woman?" She tried to ignore the heat working up her chest and neck. "Really?"

"Yeah. I was going to ask if you wanted to do it again tonight, but I guess you don't." His eyes crinkled with amusement.

"I'd rather pull out my fingernails," she said grinning.

"You're right." He nodded. "There's some paint I need to watch dry."

"What time are you gonna pick me up?"

"Eight," he told her. "And wear shoes."

She laughed. "You planning on taking me somewhere fancy?"

"Yeah, I thought we'd fly to Malibu." He winked.

Maddie paused for a second. "You're not serious, are you?"

"Not really. But now that I've said it I might look into it. I promised you a kiss on the beach."

"I'm not going with you to Malibu."

"Okay. Then how about a restaurant in Stanhope?"

"And end up trending on Instagram? No thanks."

"You don't like people knowing your business, do you?" he asked, tipping his head and scrutinizing her. "Why is that?"

"Because I don't like being talked about." She looked up at him. "Do you?"

He shrugged. "Okay. No Malibu and no restaurant. I'll think of another plan." He cupped her face with his palm and leaned down to brush his lips against hers. "But still wear those shoes. Just in case."

CHAPTER SIXTEEN

*M*addie saw the silver Mercedes as soon as she turned the corner into her street. It was parked in the driveway, its shine looking completely out of place next to her rusty Honda Accord.

She looked inside the back seat when she walked past and smiled when she saw the car seats firmly fixed in. Ashleigh only ever put their car seats in when the kids were with her. She didn't like the way they dented her soft leather seats.

"Are there any monsters in here?" Maddie called out when she opened the front door. She barely had time to take a breath before Carter came barreling down the hallway, yelling loudly with his three-year-old sister toddling behind him, screeching out with delight.

He flung himself into Maddie's arms and she lifted him into a bear hug. Grace clung to her legs, jumping up and down with delight.

"Can we play the piano?" Carter asked her.

"Yeah. Wanna play the peeno." Grace nodded, her blonde locks catching the hall light. Her face was so serious Maddie had to bite down a smile.

"Give your aunt some space," Ashleigh said, walking out of the kitchen. "She's just come home from work. And you were both in the middle of drawing, remember? Come back and finish what you were doing."

"I don't want to!" Carter stuck his bottom lip out.

"Excuse me?" Ashleigh said tartly, pressing her lips together. Maddie immediately sensed the change in her nephew. His head drooped and he nodded, grabbing his sister's hand and pulling her back into the kitchen.

"Mom, can you watch the kids for a minute?" Ashleigh called out. "I want to talk to Maddie."

"Sure." Their mom's voice was warm. "Come on, Carter. Show me your picture."

"Is everything okay?" Maddie asked as Ashleigh walked into the living room.

"Of course." Ashleigh smiled, though it didn't quite reach her perfectly made-up eyes. "We were just passing and I thought I'd come say hi."

"Passing from where?" Maddie leaned against the wall, folding her arms across her chest.

"It doesn't matter," Ashleigh said quickly, closing the door behind them. She turned to the fireplace, and picked up an old photograph of her and Maddie, turning it to examine it further. "So what's this I've been hearing about karaoke at the Moonlight Bar?"

So that's why she was here. Ashleigh never could stand being out of the loop. Growing up, she was always the one people were talking to – and about. Though she'd always proclaimed she hated the way Hartson's Creek ran on gossip, maybe her old habits died hard.

"It was nothing." Maddie slumped in a rose patterned high back chair in the corner. "Just something Becca dragged me into."

"Becca Hartson?" Ashleigh replaced the photograph,

dragging her finger across the glass then turning it to check for dust. "How was she involved?"

"Why does this feel like you're the mom and I'm the kid?" Maddie asked her. "Have I done something wrong? It was a bit of singing and some fun. I've no idea why you'd be interested in that."

"I'm always interested in you," Ashleigh said softly. "You know that."

That was true. Ashleigh had always taken her big sister role seriously, from the time they were as young as Carter and Grace. "Well, you don't need to worry about this one. I sang a song with Becca, we won the competition, and I came home and got up the next morning for work. That's all there is to the story." The lie tasted strange on her tongue. Almost dirty.

Ashleigh picked up another photograph. This time one of her in her prom dress. Maddie could still remember that night so well. How beautiful her sister had looked. Their mom took photograph after photograph, Ash's blonde hair pinned up in curls, her neck slender, her shoulders bare, leading to the silver dress she'd saved up for months to buy. Maddie could remember staring at her, wondering how it must feel to be that beautiful. Knowing she could never ever look that way.

Maybe that's why she'd skipped her own prom. The thought of having her photograph next to Ashleigh's was too much to bear.

"I hear Gray was there." Ashleigh turned to her. "Jessica told me she saw the two of you talking in the square. Said you looked mighty close."

"Jessica has too much time on her hands."

The ghost of a smile passed Ashleigh's lips. "She does like to gossip."

"Yeah, even when there's nothing to gossip about."

Ashleigh sat down in the chair next to Maddie's, making sure to straighten out her skirt to avoid any wrinkles. "I worry about you. After everything that happened in New York..." she trailed off, reaching for Maddie's hand. "There's nothing going on with you and Gray, is there?" she asked. "I'm just fretting over nothing, right?"

New York. Those two words were like a bucket of ice water over Maddie's head. Ashleigh was one of the few around town who knew what had happened, and in the years since she'd arrived to bring Maddie home, she hadn't breathed a word to anybody. She might drive Maddie crazy sometimes, but Ashleigh had been there for her when she needed her the most. For that reason alone she loved her sister like crazy.

"There's nothing going on that you need to worry about." It was only a half-lie. And a lie told to protect somebody wasn't really a lie at all, was it? "It's a small town and I work in the diner. I'm bound to bump into him sometimes. But he's only here for a few more weeks and then he'll be gone again. Probably for another ten years."

And wasn't that thought like a kick to her gut? Or a reminder to guard her heart.

"You see him in the diner?" Ashleigh asked, her eyebrows raised. "I would've thought he could afford to eat somewhere nicer. There are some lovely restaurants in Stanhope."

Maddie thought about pointing out that the diner was nice, but she'd already told enough lies. "He's working on his dad's house. He doesn't have much time to drive somewhere nicer."

"What?" Ashleigh laughed. "That's not true. Why would he be working on his dad's house? He must have enough money to buy it ten times over."

Maddie shrugged. "It's a family thing, I guess."

Ashleigh pulled her bottom lip between her teeth, then

released it, looking down at her skirt. "Has he asked about me?"

"I don't know," Maddie said. "Probably. I must have mentioned you and the children."

"Does he know I live in Stanhope?" Ashleigh asked. "Did you tell him I married Michael? And that his parents own the First State Bank?"

"Um." Maddie was trying not to grin, but it was a challenge. "I don't know, but I'll make sure I do if I see him again."

"Oh no, don't do that. He'll find out from somebody." Ashleigh shrugged. "I just want him to know that I'm doing well." She straightened her back. "That he's not the only one who managed to leave town and make something of themselves."

Maddie wasn't sure what to say. If it had been anybody else she would have rolled her eyes, but this was her sister. And she could hear a note of hurt in her voice. A reminder of how devastated she'd been when Gray left for L.A. and didn't look back.

If Ashleigh ever found out about Maddie kissing her ex, she'd be apoplectic. The thought of it twisted Maddie's stomach into knots. Another reminder of what a bad idea it was to flirt with Gray Hartson, as if she didn't know that already.

You didn't flirt with him, you kissed him, the little voice in her head reminded her.

Maddie sighed. Yes, it was a terrible idea to kiss Gray Hartson. But the thought of *not* kissing him felt even worse. And if it meant she had to lie to her sister, to her mom, to the whole damn town to feel his lips on hers again? Then, god forgive her, that's what she'd do.

"Mom, I finished my picture," Carter said excitedly as he pushed the door open. "Wanna see?"

"Sure." Ashleigh flashed Maddie a wary smile.

"Here you go." Carter shoved the piece of paper in his mom's hands before he turned to Maddie with a hopeful expression. "Can we play the piano now or are you two still arguing?"

Maddie burst into laughter and took Carter's proffered hand. "Sure, we can go play for a while."

"Ten minutes," Ashleigh told him. "And we weren't arguing, we were talking."

AT EXACTLY EIGHT O'CLOCK, Maddie pulled on her shoes and called out to her mom. "I'm heading out. I'll be back before midnight. Call me if you need anything."

"Who are you going out with again?" her mom asked from her bedroom.

"Just a few friends," Maddie said hurriedly. "Good night."

Before her mom could ask her anymore questions, she grabbed her sweater and purse and walked out onto the stoop, planning to sit on the porch swing until Gray arrived. But then she saw him walking up the path, wearing a pair of jeans, a dark grey hoodie, and a baseball cap, and she stopped at the top of the steps.

"Hey." He looked up at her, pulling his hat off. "I was just about to knock."

"I decided to wait out here. I didn't want to disturb my mom."

A slow smile curled his lips. "You look pretty," he said, taking in her blue-and-white summer dress, fitted at the bodice before flaring at her hips. She was wearing her hair down, her dark waves cascading down her back. When she'd taken a look in the mirror, she'd breathed a sigh of relief that she'd managed to tame it.

He reached the bottom of the stairs and held his hand out to her. She slid hers inside his palm, feeling the warmth of it, the calluses from playing the guitar. And the strength in his fingers as they curled around hers.

"Where are we going?" she asked, as he led her to a truck parked across the driveway. It was shiny and new from the looks of it. Expensive, too. Not the kind of truck you usually saw around Hartson's Creek.

"I thought we could go for a drive." He opened the door and helped her inside. "I packed some food and drinks. Wasn't sure if you'd eaten."

"I can eat again." She shrugged. "Especially if it's Aunt Gina's cooking."

"How did you guess?" He grinned.

She winked. "Women's intuition. But what I'm more interested in is what you told her you needed the food for."

He climbed into the cab and pulled his seatbelt on, pressing the ignition so the engine roared to life. "She didn't ask and I didn't tell. But if she had, I would've told her I'm trying to woo a beautiful woman, and I need all the help I can get."

"Woo?" Maddie laughed because it reminded her of her conversation with Carter the prior week. "That's the second time I've heard that word in the past few weeks."

Gray lifted an eyebrow. "Is somebody else wooing you?"

"Not unless you count my nephew." She grinned. "I'm hoping you might do it a little better."

"Maybe." He pressed his foot on the gas. "Is it working?"

Was it? She turned to look at him, taking in his profile. Strong nose, soft lips, jaw shadowed with evening beard growth. He'd thrown his cap into the back seat and his hair was mussed, but that made him look even more good looking, if possible.

Even before he'd headed to LA and become famous, he'd

been out of her league. Now he was a million miles up in the stratosphere. Yet here he was, talking about wooing her, and it made her feel funny inside.

"Can I ask you something?" she said as he took a left onto the main road out of town.

"Yeah. Shoot."

"Why am I here?"

The corner of his lips quirked up. "I already told you. I'm wooing you."

"But why me? Of all the people you could be sitting next to right now, why me?"

He pressed his foot to the brake, bringing the car to a stop in the deserted lane. "What people do you think I want to be sitting next to?" he asked, turning to face her. His brows were knitted together.

She had to fight the urge not to smooth out the lines in his frown. "It doesn't matter," she told him. "I'm just being stupid."

"It clearly matters to you. So it matters to me, too. So let me tell you something right now. There's nobody in the world I'd rather have sitting in that seat than you. When you agreed to let me pick you up I felt like I'd won a goddamned prize. Because I get the impression you don't agree to this kind of thing very often."

"No, I don't," she said softly.

He reached out to take her chin between his fingers, his grasp soft but sure. Slowly, he angled her head until she was staring right into his eyes. "So why did you agree to it today?"

Her breath caught at the intensity of his stare. It made her whole body heat up, like the sun was beating down on her. If he kept this going for too long she was going to get burned.

Any smart remarks she might have thought of melted on her tongue.

"Because I couldn't *not* agree," she said quietly. "I haven't stopped thinking about you since you arrived back in Hartson's Creek. And the way you kissed me last night..." she trailed off, shaking her head. "I can't get that out of my mind, either."

He swallowed, his Adam's apple bobbing beneath the taut skin of his throat. "Yeah," he said, his voice scratchy. "I'm finding it hard not to think about it, too." He released his hold on her jaw. "Let's get out of here before you change your mind." The engine sprang back to life as he put his foot on the gas.

"Where are we going?" she asked again, a smile curling at her lips.

"Wait and see."

CHAPTER SEVENTEEN

*S*he was thinking about kissing him again? Well that made two of them. As he took a left onto the road that wound up to the hills, he couldn't bite down his smile anymore. Couldn't stop glancing at her from the corner of his eyes, either. Damn, she looked good. Like one of those cute, take-no-shit girls next door he always sung about but rarely met. When she'd asked him what she was doing sitting next to him in his cab he'd wanted to laugh; because he'd been asking himself exactly the same question about her.

The entrance to their destination was right where he remembered. A broken gate hung at a strange angle from a paint-peeled post, and he maneuvered his truck through the gap with just enough space not to scratch it. Pulling up on the left, he shut off the engine and looked out of the windshield to the view below. The dotted lights of Hartson's Creek laid out before them.

"You brought us to Jackson's Ridge?" Maddie asked, her voice lifting with surprise.

"Yeah. Figured we could eat up here without being disturbed." He climbed out of the cab and walked around to open her door, offering his hand to help her down. When she jumped to the ground, he grabbed the blanket and cooler he'd stowed in the flatbed, still holding her hand as he led her over to the grassy ridge.

"I've never been up here before," she told him. "I didn't know it had such a beautiful view."

"I used to come up here with my guitar after arguing with my dad. Once I camped out all night. I caught hell for it from Aunt Gina." Gray reluctantly let go of Maddie and laid the blanket on the soft grass, placing the cooler on top. "Got grounded for a month I think."

Maddie grinned. "You were always a rebel."

Gray couldn't help but laugh. "Is that what you thought? I actually was a pretty good kid. Didn't cause too many problems."

"Oh come on. Everybody used to talk about you and your brothers. How you all ran wild and crazy." She pulled her lip between her teeth, her face illuminated by the moon. "Remember the time you put whiskey in the communion wine?"

"That wasn't me. It was Tanner." Gray raised an eyebrow and opened the cooler, pulling out a bottle. "And talking of drinks, would you like one?"

"Champagne?" Maddie knelt down next to him. "What are we celebrating?"

Gray shrugged. "I finished the plumbing today. Only the roof left to finish and I'll be done. I figure it's worth raising a glass to." He winked. "And it'll only be one glass for me. I'm driving." He popped the cork and poured two glasses, handing one to Maddie and raising the other one up.

"To home improvements," she said with a grin, clinking her glass against his.

"And not flooding my dad's house." He took a sip, his gaze catching hers. Everything about her felt fresh and new.

Like a wind blowing through the house, clearing out the cobwebs.

"When was the last time you did this?" Maddie asked, running her finger around the rim of her glass.

"Came to Jackson's Ridge?" he asked. "I don't know. Ten years ago, maybe longer."

She looked up at him. "I meant drank champagne. With a woman."

There was something in her voice. A tone somebody else might have missed. The merest hint of uncertainty that made his chest fill up. "I don't know. I don't drink a lot. Not anymore. I did, for a while but…" He took a deep breath. "But it messed with my mind and my music." It was his turn to feel awkward. He looked up at her, his eyes hooded. He didn't talk about this. At least not to anybody who wasn't paid to listen. And yet the need to spill his guts to her pulled at him.

She ran the tip of her tongue over her bottom lip. "You were drunk the other night."

"Yeah. I was a little."

"I kind of liked it," she admitted, staring at him with hooded eyes.

He put his glass down and leaned forward. "You did?"

"Yeah."

"What did you like?"

"The things you said to me. That you see me. And you always have."

"I do," he whispered, reaching out to trace her cheekbone. Her eyelids fluttered at his touch. "I see every single bit of you. And I like it more than I can say."

Her breath hitched and it made him want to touch her more.

"I wish you could see yourself the way I do," he whispered, leaning closer. "You're beautiful, Maddie Clark. And you're kind. Funny as hell, too. Every time I think of you trying to climb that wall I laugh."

"Asshole." She smiled, her cheeks plumping against his fingertips.

"And I have no idea what you're still doing in Hartson's Creek, but because I'm a selfish bastard I'm so glad you're here. I would have gone crazy without you to talk to."

Her eyes were glassy. She blinked and he could see the clouds forming inside them.

"I can see you're overthinking this," he told her as her gaze darkened. "Stop it."

"I can't help it. You're right about one thing, I'm still a small town girl, and you're not a small town boy."

"I'm still me, Maddie. You of all people should know that. Just Gray Hartson who spikes the church wine."

"I thought you said Tanner did it."

He winked. "So I did." He took the glass from her hand and set it down beside him, pulling her close until her face was a breath away from his. "Let me show you something," he said softly, laying her down on the blanket, positioning himself beside her.

"What?" she breathed.

He brushed his thumb against her lips. "Can you feel that?" he asked.

"Yeah."

"What does it feel like?"

Her brows drew together. "What do you mean?"

"Close your eyes. Describe the sensation." He caressed her lips again.

"It feels soft and warm. But strong. Skin against skin with nothing in between."

"It's me," he whispered. "Just me. I'm the same as any other guy. I eat, I sleep, I go to the bathroom." He laughed.

"And I think you're the most beautiful creature I've ever seen."

She sighed, and he felt the warm air on his hand. God, he wanted to kiss her. Wanted to pull her body on top of his and feel every inch of her pressed against him.

He swallowed, trying to push down his insatiable desire. "Touch me," he said hoarsely, moving her hand to his face. She feathered her fingertips against his cheek, her thumb brushing his jaw, slowly moving down to his neck.

It was getting hot. Too hot. He pulled his hoodie over his head and threw it on the blanket, his skin immediately cooling as the evening air caressed it.

Maddie ran her finger around the sleeve of his t-shirt, then traced down his bicep, outlining the tattoo etched there.

"When did you get this one?" she asked him.

"That was my first tattoo. I got it on the anniversary of my mom's death before I drank myself to oblivion." He looked at her with a wry smile. "I'd only been in LA for a year then."

"It's pretty. A dove, right?"

"Yeah. My mom's favorite bird."

A smile played at her lips. "How many do you have?"

"Tattoos? I don't know. A lot, I guess."

"Can I see them?"

He tipped his head to the side. "Are you asking me to take my t-shirt off, Miss Clark?"

"I'm asking you to show me your tattoos, smart-ass." She shook her head. "The rest is just gravy."

He pulled his black t-shirt over his head, watching her expression change as she took him in. Her eyes roved over him, and he liked it too much. Couldn't get enough of the darkness in her eyes. "Can I touch you?" she asked him.

He grinned wickedly. "God, yes."

"Turn onto your back," she whispered, and he did as

directed. She leaned over him, her face close to his chest. He held his breath for a second until her fingers began to trace the tattoo on his left pectoral, long thick black lines depicting a growling wolf. "When did you get this?" she asked, her fingers perilously close to his nipple. He was already hard as iron.

"Sydney. About eight years ago."

She slid her hand across his chest, and he held his breath as she leaned closer, her mouth inches from his skin. He was hanging on by a string. "And this one?" she asked, her fingers tracing down the ridges of his abdomen.

"The eagle? I got it in London when I'd been in Europe for a few months. I was missing home."

"Will you get any more?" she looked up at him.

"Yeah." His voice was gruff with restraint. "Probably."

"Where will you put them?" she asked, tracing circles on his hard abdomen. "It's getting pretty crowded around here."

"I've still got a lot of bare skin," he said, his voice low. "My legs, my forearms, my ass."

Her lips twitched. "Your ass?"

He raised an eyebrow. "I hear it hurts less there." Reaching for her hands, he pulled her back up until her face was next to his. "What about you? Any tattoos?"

"Nope. I'm as unmarked as the day I was born."

"Can I check?"

This time she laughed. "You want me to take my clothes off?"

"You started it," he joked, never in a million years expecting her to show him.

But the next moment, she was sitting up and pulling her dress over her head, revealing a white lace bra and matching panties, and her creamy, unmarked skin.

Damn. If he'd thought he was hot before, now he was burning up. Not just because she was beautiful, but because

149

she was so damn unpredictable. He loved the way he could never guess what she was going to do next.

MADDIE HELD her breath as Gray stared at her. His eyes were hooded and dark, as his gaze dipped from her face to her shoulders, and then to her chest. He swallowed hard and then turned toward her, reaching out a hand to roll her onto her back.

"It's my turn," he whispered. "Okay?"

"Yes." It was more than okay. She craved his touch the way she craved him. The panic she'd felt when she'd taken her dress off was long gone, melted by his heated response. Her head tipped back, her eyes closed, and she held her breath as she waited for his touch.

When it came her body arched off the blanket. Soft, warm lips pressed against her ribcage, his hands curling around her waist to hold her in place.

"Is this all right?" he murmured into her skin.

"Yeah." She nodded. "Don't stop."

She cracked open her eyes to see a wicked grin curl his lips.

"Wasn't planning on it," he told her.

He kissed his way across her ribcage, his breath warm, her skin warmer. Then he moved lower, reaching the softer skin of her stomach. She tightened her muscles and he chuckled, before continuing his way down, his lips grazing the top of her panties.

She held her breath again, feeling the ache between her thighs, waiting to see what he'd do next.

"No," he murmured, so quiet it seemed he was talking more to himself than her. "Not yet."

He pulled himself over her, his denim-clad thighs sliding

between her bare ones, and cupped her face with his hands. "Can you feel what you're doing to me?" he asked, pressing himself against her.

Yeah, she could feel it. Her thighs tightened around him in response.

"You're beautiful," he whispered, brushing his lips across hers. She slid her arms around his neck, needing the connection.

"So are you," she told him, meaning every word. *So damn handsome it shouldn't be allowed.*

"Nobody's said that to me before. Sexy, yeah. Beautiful, never."

"Then they're crazy," she said smiling.

He laughed again, then kissed her, sliding his hands around her back to unclasp her bra. Her breasts were aching, needy, and as soon as he released the fabric encasing them, her skin puckered at the cool night air. He lowered his head to capture a nipple between his lips, sucking soft, then hard, until she couldn't help but moan.

He was setting her on fire, inch by inch. A kiss, a caress, a curl of his tongue, they were music on her body. He pulled back to take his jeans off, then moved his hands up her legs, warm and firm on her thighs. His fingers traced the elastic of her underwear.

"These need to come off."

"Yeah, they do." Her breath caught.

He nodded as he hooked his fingers around the white lace, dragging them down her heated thighs and throwing them behind him.

And then she was naked. On Jackson's Ridge with Gray Hartson, and for some crazy reason it felt like the most natural thing in the world. He was still wearing underwear – black shorts that did nothing to hide his impressive excitement – but her eyes were drawn to the beauty of his body.

He was a work of art. Even the parts of him that weren't painted with ink and history. Wide shoulders, sculpted chest, abdominal muscles that rose and fell like a symphony. And his face. Dark, needy eyes, lips parted, his breath coming in short pants the same way hers was.

Then he slid his fingers between her thighs and all thoughts of faces and chests were gone, replaced by a need building inside her. She was achy in a way she could barely remember feeling. How long was it since anybody had touched her like this?

Forever... never.

Nobody had ever touched her the way Gray was.

"Christ, you feel good," he whispered, his voice catching. Then he put his fingers between his lips and sucked, making her eyes widen with shock. "You taste good, too." He smiled at her response, touching her there again, and making her cry out his name.

"Do you know what you're doing to me?" he asked her.

"The same thing you're doing to me." And she wanted it. *All of it.* Every part of him. Wanted him to play her the same way he played his songs. Soft, then hard, until the sound filled every cell in her body.

"Gray..." She slid her arms down his back, tugging at the waistband of his shorts. "I need..."

"What do you need?" he whispered in her ear, his voice hot and harsh.

"You. I need *you.*"

He slid his fingers inside her once more, then pulled them out. "Yeah, you do." A smile pulled at his lips. He grabbed his wallet and pulled out a condom. Her throat was dry as she watched him slide it on. "But not as much as I need you."

He hovered over her, his eyes trained on hers, and she could see herself reflected in their depths. They stared at each other for a long moment before she could feel his hardness against her.

Dipping his head, he captured her lips with his, swallowing her cries as he pushed inside. He groaned. His hips moving fast, his lips taking everything she could give, his body making hers sing until they reached the crescendo.

And when he took her there, watching with dark eyes as the pleasure overtook her, she could feel him following close behind. He was moaning, his elbows digging into the blanket beside her, his hips thrusting against hers as he reached his peak.

And when it was over, pleasure still washing over her, he pulled her close and wrapped his arms around her, whispering sweet words in her ears.

It felt like heaven and hell had collided and made a whole new world just for them.

A world she never wanted to leave.

CHAPTER EIGHTEEN

*I*t was a beautiful day. The hazy sun had beaten its way through the wispy clouds, leaving behind a cerulean blue sky that stretched for miles above him. Gray was kneeling on the roof of his father's house to assess the damage, taking photographs of the holes that he'd send to the Johnson brothers for their advice when he heard a car pull into the driveway.

He didn't turn around at first. Mostly because he was used to people coming and going. Aunt Gina's friends, Becca's old schoolmates, and the occasional visitor for his father. And he'd noticed that Tanner still had everything delivered here – even his online shopping. Funny how home always had that pull on him.

"Hey," a female voice called out a minute later. This time he turned, pressing his foot down to keep his balance on the camber of the roof. The sun was so bright it still hit his eyes in spite of the shade his hard hat provided. He blinked and lifted his hand.

The car in the driveway was a sparkling silver Mercedes. And standing next to it was the last person he expected to see.

"Ash?"

She smiled at his instant recognition. "I heard you were back in town. I thought I'd come say hi."

For a moment he thought about telling her he was busy – which he clearly was – and send her away. But he knew without a doubt that Aunt Gina had already seen her, and would give him hell if he didn't show any hospitality.

"Give me a minute," he called out. "If you go around the back, Aunt Gina's in the kitchen. I'll meet you there in a few."

Her smile faltered a little. "Oh, okay."

As she walked around the side of the house, Gray let out a sigh. He'd been riding a high all morning on memories of last night. His father had bitched him out about the pipes creaking throughout the night and he hadn't given a damn. It was like listening to a bird chirping to him. He was too busy thinking about the way Maddie's body had felt so goddamn soft and enticing to care what his father had to say.

But now her sister was here and it was like she was holding a needle, ready to puncture a balloon. He'd have happily gone a hundred years without seeing her.

When he walked into the kitchen, pulling his hard hat off and ruffling his hair, he saw her sitting with Aunt Gina, the two of them sipping sweet tea. They were leaning over Ashleigh's phone, flipping through pictures. Their heads lifted to look at him as his feet stomped against the floor.

"There you are," Gina said as he kicked his boots off and left them on the mat. "Ashleigh was showing me photos of Grace and Carter. I can't believe how much they've grown. Have you seen them?"

"I saw a picture at Maddie's house."

Ashleigh blinked. "You've been to my house?"

Damn. He had absolutely no idea what Maddie had said to

her sister about him – if anything at all. Were they supposed to be friends? Acquaintances? Enemies?

"She helped me out at church a couple of weeks ago. I went to thank her." He leaned casually against the door, taking Ashleigh in. She'd always taken care of her appearance, but there was an expensive sheen to her she hadn't had before. Like somebody had airbrushed her in real life, taking away the interesting features and blemishes that made her human.

That made him think about the cluster of freckles on the back of Maddie's neck that looked like the big dipper. He'd kissed his way down them last night, making her shiver against him. Her ass had been pressed against his groin and it had sent a jolt of pleasure right through him.

"I heard about that. Typical Maddie, making you jump over fences." Ashleigh unleashed a smile. "She gave Della Thorsen such a fright. You'd think my sister was still a teenager, not twenty-five-years old."

"I'm thirty-one," Gray pointed out, his voice deep. "If anybody was leading anybody astray it was me."

Ashleigh's smile faltered for a second. "Well thank you for protecting her. She's still so young in many ways. I guess that's what comes of never really leaving home. Not like the two of us. She's never been wise in the ways of the world."

Was she talking about Maddie Clark? Smart-mouthed, sharp as a knife, and never knowingly taken advantage of?

"I don't think she needs my protection."

"No, she doesn't." Ashleigh took a sip of the sweet tea. "Actually, while I'm here there's something I'd like to talk to you about." She slid her eyes to Aunt Gina. "Alone, if that's okay. Maybe we can take a walk in the yard."

Gray took a deep breath. He'd rather be up on the roof listening to his father bitch than talking to his long-ago ex, but from the way Aunt Gina smiled, he knew that wasn't an option. "Yeah, sure."

"Great." Ashleigh stood and walked over to where he was standing. He could smell the deep notes of her perfume. "Thank you for the sweet tea," she said, smiling at his aunt.

"You're very welcome. It was lovely to see you again."

He slid his boots back on and opened the door, gesturing for Ash to walk through. She took her time, lifting her head to smile up at him before sliding her body past his. She was wearing a navy dress that skimmed her slim body, her hair tied up to expose her long, slender neck. There were no freckles there, just pale creamy skin.

As soon as they were outside, she turned to him. "Actually, a walk in the yard is a bad idea. It'll ruin my shoes. Perhaps we should sit somewhere."

He gestured at the old bench by the gate and she shook her head. "Not in this dress."

"Maybe standing will be better," he said, trying to bite down his annoyance. This was Ash. the girl he'd once cared about. He owed her politeness at the very least. "What can I help you with?" he asked her.

"How's your music career going?"

He stared at her for a moment, trying to decipher what the hell it was she wanted. "Yeah, pretty good."

"And you'll be leaving soon?"

"I will?"

She shook her head. "That was a question. I'm asking you when you'll be going back to wherever it is you live."

"I live in L.A."

"Okay, so when will you be going home?"

His lip curled up. "You seem pretty set on getting rid of me. Should I take that personally?"

She let out a sigh. "You can take it as you want. And I'm not set on anything, I was simply making small talk."

He glanced at his watch. It was almost lunch time. "Okay." He shrugged. "I'll be heading back home in a few weeks. And how are you? I hear you're living in Stanhope. Is that going well?"

"It is." Her voice was icy cool. "I'm very happy there. And I want to make sure I stay that way."

"You think I might be a threat to your happiness?" His brows knitted together. "Why would that be?"

"Because everywhere I go, all I hear about is you and Maddie, and I've no idea what's going on. I have people calling to tell me you've been spotted together in all kinds of places, and I don't like it." She lifted her head defiantly. "Whatever happened between us should stay between *us*, Gray."

This time he couldn't stop the laughter from exploding. "You think I'm chasing your sister to hurt you?"

"Aren't you?"

"No." His expression was incredulous. "Why would you think that?"

"Because we parted on bad terms."

"I left and you were angry at me. I got over it." Gray rubbed his chin with the heel of his hand, still trying to figure out what she was thinking. "It's old news, Ash. More than ten years old. I'm not here to hurt anybody."

"So there's nothing going on with you and Maddie?"

He licked his dry lips, staring at her through narrowed eyes. "Have you asked her that?"

"Yes."

Of course she had. "And what did she say?"

"That there was nothing between you two at all."

He ignored the jabbing pain of her response. "Then that's your answer."

"But I know she has a crush on you, she always did. Even after you left she was always talking about you. I couldn't go anywhere without hearing that damn song you wrote. And she played it constantly."

Well that made him feel better.

"A lot of women have crushes on me."

Ashleigh rolled her eyes. "I see stardom hasn't deflated your ego."

He shrugged. "It's part of the job. And not the part I enjoy, frankly. It gets old pretty quick."

"That's another reason you should stay away from Maddie. Your job. I don't want you hurting her."

"Why would my job hurt her?" he asked, perplexed.

Ashleigh pressed her lips together and looked him in the eye. "You're a rockstar, Gray. A musician. People like you aren't made for people like her. Maddie's a simple, small-town girl. She tried leaving once, and it almost killed her."

"What?" He frowned. "How?"

"It doesn't matter. Just stay away from her. That's the only way you won't hurt her. Promise me that."

She had to be talking about New York, and how Maddie left Ansell without graduating. "How did it almost kill her?" he asked again.

"That's not my story to tell. But I've seen her at her lowest and I never want to see her like that again. Don't hurt her, Gray. She's not resilient like we are. Just leave her alone." Her phone buzzed, and she sighed, pulling open her navy leather purse to check it. "I need to go, I have an appointment in half an hour." She looked up at him, the sun glinting against her eyes. "Goodbye, Gray. I hope you found whatever it was you were looking for when you left town all those years ago."

He blinked even though he was shaded from the sun. "Goodbye," he said. Her words were ringing in his ears as he watched her walk around the corner of the house. A minute later, her engine fired up, and he could hear the whine of her wheels against the driveway as she reversed out.

Did he find what he was looking for when he left Hartson's Creek right after his twentieth birthday? Or was it here all along after all?

～

"GIVE ME CAKE. Lots of cake. And coffee." Laura slid into a chair at the counter and leaned heavily on it, shaking her head. "Cream, five sugars, and keep the caffeine coming."

Maddie grinned at the expression on her friend's face. "Bad day at the shop?"

"The worst." Laura shook her head. "If I have to spend another hour with Marie Dean I swear I'm going to get arrested for murder. How can one woman hate so many clothes? I ordered twenty different dresses at her request and she's not happy with a single one of them. I tried to suggest she try online shopping, but then she told me that she hates paying to send things back. I tried to point out that I'm going to be paying to send all those dresses back, but it went right over her head." Laura took in a mouthful of air. "Sorry, I'm ranting."

"Rant away. We all have those days." Maddie poured her a mug of coffee, adding plenty of cream. "Here, you add the sugar," she said, pushing the bowl toward her. "I don't want to be held responsible by your dentist."

"Ah, he loves it when I get cavities. I always make sure I wear a low cut top so he can look at my chest." Laura almost smiled. "We should set up a union or something. Start refusing to work when we get awkward customers."

"You own your shop," Maddie pointed out with a smile. "You'd only be hurting yourself."

"Ugh." Laura slumped down in her stool and grabbed her coffee as Maddie slid a slice of carrot cake onto a plate. "I hate myself sometimes."

"No you don't."

Laura spooned more sugar in. "Okay then. I hate my life."

"No you don't." Maddie grinned.

"Hey. I'm looking for some support here. You're supposed to be cheering me up." Laura lifted the cup to her lips for a sip.

Maddie leaned on the counter. It had been a quiet day, which meant nothing had soured her good mood. Not a customer sending her plate back three times thanks to Murphy's eggs, nor Murphy's X-rated response as he threw the plate of food on the floor in a fit of pique.

Nothing could push away the glow she was feeling. It was too warm, too deep, too good.

"Hey, you're still smiling. What's up with you?" Laura asked.

"What do you mean?" Maddie tried to force her cheek muscles to relax, but they weren't playing ball.

"I mean you're all glowy and grinning and stuff. It's not like you. What happened?"

"Maybe I'm just smiling because it's a beautiful day." Maddie shrugged and gestured out of the windows. The sun was beating down on the verdant town square, bouncing off the bandstand and the white painted benches. "Is that a crime?"

"Hmm." Laura pressed her fork into the cake and scooped up a piece. "I don't know. What've you been doing?"

Maddie laughed. "Nothing. Just working the way I always do. I'm allowed to smile, aren't I?"

For the first time since she'd stormed through the door, Laura smiled. "Yeah, you are. And you're pretty when you do it."

"All that sugar's gone to your brain," Maddie teased. "And your tongue, you sweet talker." Behind Laura's shoulder, she could see her sister's Mercedes pull up in the space outside.

161

She watched as Ashleigh climbed out and smoothed her dress with her palms, clicking the car shut as she walked toward the diner. Suddenly, Maddie's good mood disappeared. Replaced by a strong sense of guilt as she remembered last night.

Her body tensed. Why should she feel guilty? Gray wasn't Ashleigh's boyfriend anymore. Hadn't been for years. They were two grown adults doing what adults did. It wasn't anybody else's business.

Even if everybody seemed to think it was.

"You okay?" Laura asked, turning to glance over her shoulder. "Oh," she said, turning back with wide eyes. "Big sister is here."

"Yup."

Ashleigh pushed the door open, causing the bell to tinkle, and she looked up as though it was a personal affront. Her chest rose as she took in a deep breath of air and walked over to the counter.

"Hey," Maddie said, trying to keep her voice light. "To what do we owe this pleasure?"

"I was just passing." Ashleigh smiled. "I decided to visit Gray and say hi. It seemed stupid him being back in town and me ignoring it. So I decided to be the bigger person."

"You did?" Maddie felt any of her remaining happiness ooze away. "Was he there?"

"He was on the roof when I arrived. He pretty much scrambled down to say hi. It was kind of sweet. Reminded me of when we were at school. He could never do enough for me then."

"Oh." Maddie desperately searched for words, but her mind was blank.

"Does Michael know you're visiting old boyfriends?" Laura asked.

Ashleigh turned around, her eyebrows rising up at the

intrusion. "Oh, it's you. I didn't see you there. And since you're asking, I didn't tell Michael because it was a spur of the moment decision. But I know he'd support my choice. I never give him any reason to doubt me." She turned back to Maddie. "We talked about you a little."

Maddie's breath caught in her throat. "You did?"

"Yeah. He said you were sweet, and he told me you were like his kid sister." Ashleigh glanced at the gold watch wrapped around her delicate wrist. "Can I order a coffee to go? I need to pick up Carter in twenty minutes."

"Sure." Welcoming the opportunity to turn her back on her sister, Maddie walked over to the coffee machine and took a deep breath. No drip coffee for Ashleigh Lowe. She always ordered a skinny cinnamon latte. But even the mechanical action of filling the filter and steaming the milk wasn't enough to push away the hurt of Ashleigh's words. Had Gray really said that about her? Even if he was trying to throw Ashleigh off the scent, describing her as a kid hurt.

It reminded her of how it was growing up. Always in her sister's shadow. Even now, when she finally had something good happen in her life, Ashleigh was here to remind her that he'd been hers first.

She put a lid on the cup, then slid a sleeve over it and passed it to Ashleigh, who was standing silently next to Laura. "There you go."

"How much?"

"It's on me."

"Don't be silly. I know how tight money is. Here you go." Ashleigh pulled a five-dollar bill from her purse and left it on the counter. "Keep the change. And I'll call you later, okay?"

"Okay." Maddie swallowed, though there was still a lump in her throat.

Ashleigh left as swiftly as she came, the door slamming

closed behind her. Maddie stood there for a moment, already missing her good humor from this morning.

"Well, your sister's a bitch," Laura said, forking the last piece of cake into her mouth. "But we already knew that."

"She's not so bad. She has her good qualities."

"Yeah, well we can discuss those later. Right now I've got a few questions for you. What the heck is going on between you and Gray Hartson?"

CHAPTER NINETEEN

"*I* don't see much progress on the roof," his dad said. He coughed loudly, covering his lips with a white starched handkerchief the way he always did. He was well enough to walk outside for a few minutes – and he'd obviously decided to use that time to rile Gray up.

Good luck, old man. Even Ashleigh hadn't been able to kill Gray's good mood completely.

"I'm waiting for the materials to be delivered," Gray said, keeping his voice light. "After that it's a few days work." That's what the Johnson brothers had told him, anyway. "It'll be done before you know it."

His dad looked up at the roof with narrowed eyes. "I want it done properly," he wheezed. "No half baked measures."

Gray bit down the urge to tell his dad where to go. "I didn't take half measures with the plumbing and I won't do it with this."

"Maybe if you weren't so busy flirting with married women, you'd get the job done quicker."

"What?" Gray leaned on the side of the house, surprise pulling his brows together.

"I saw you with Ashleigh Lowe. The two of you looked thick as thieves. You know she has a husband and children?"

"Yeah, I know. And I wasn't flirting. She came over to say hi and I was polite in return." He had no idea why he was explaining himself. He didn't owe his old man anything. Still, the heat started to rise up inside him, the way it always did when his dad was near.

"Best thing she ever did, marrying that man. She's a clever woman. She knew you weren't reliable."

"Is that right?" he asked through gritted teeth.

"You're not the type who sticks around, are you, Gray? Too busy chasing after the next big thing to think about the people you left behind." His dad's eyes narrowed. "Too important to visit your home or think about the people who love you."

Gray swallowed hard, but the bile kept rising. "Why do you think I'm here? Why do you think I'm spending my free time repairing this goddamned house when I could have paid to get it done a hundred times over? For the goodness of my heart?"

"Guilt." His dad pressed his lips together. "You think it makes up for all those years you never came home. All those times you broke your aunt and sister's hearts. But a few pipes and shingles prove nothing. You'll leave again, and we won't see you for another ten years."

"You think they're nothing?" Gray's voice rose up, it was all he could do not to shout. "All these hours I've spent making the house watertight and useable? You want me to stop now? Just leave you with a roof full of holes because you're too cheap to pay for professional help?"

His dad coughed loudly. "If you want to leave, then go. We'll deal with it the same way we always have. Without you."

Gray curled his fists together and closed his eyes for a moment, trying to push down the urge to punch something. *Anything.* His dad knew how to push his buttons. What the hell was he doing here anyway? He could be home in L.A., playing music and relaxing. Instead, he was here, in the small, cloying town he grew up in, getting criticized by his dad for trying to do a good thing.

There was no winning with him. There never was. Why the hell did he keep trying?

"You're a miserable old man, do you know that?" Gray told him through gritted teeth. "You made my childhood hell after mom died. You pushed every one of us out. We couldn't wait to leave. Me, Tanner, Logan, and Cam, we were counting down the hours."

"And yet here you are, right back where you started."

"Yeah, but not to see you. To make sure Aunt Gina and Becca are okay."

"They're fine. They always will be. I make sure of that." Another cough. "They don't need your concern or your money. None of us do."

"You're going to die a lonely, miserable, old man."

His dad laughed. It was short and angry and had no humor in it at all. "Not as lonely as you. At least I have my family and my memories, and a town full of friends. What have you got, Gray? A body ruined by tattoos. People who are only your friends because they want what you have to offer. How many of them are real friends? How many of them have called you since you've been here? You haven't had any visitors. So don't talk to me about being lonely when you're the one who's alone." His dad shook his head and turned away, shuffling off around the corner of the house.

As soon as he disappeared from sight, Gray slammed his hand against the wall. "Fuck!" he shouted. He hated this. He hated him. Why did he still let the old man rile him up like this?

"He doesn't mean it, you know."

Gray looked up to see Aunt Gina standing at the back door. From the look on her face, Gray knew she'd heard every word.

"Yeah he does."

She shook her head. "He loves you, Gray. But he has no idea how to show it. It scares him."

Gray wanted to laugh. "Nothing scares him."

"Some things do. Losing your mom scared him so bad he never let himself open up again. He pushes you away because he's scared you're going to leave anyway. This way he can tell himself it's what he wants."

"That's fu… I mean, that's crazy."

Aunt Gina ignored his almost-swearing. "It's who he is. He never got over your mom's death." She sighed.

"Yeah, well maybe he should have. That way he wouldn't make everybody else's life hell."

"If you think yours is hell, imagine losing the one person who was everything to you. Your soul mate. Then imagine having to stay in the same house and seeing her face in the expressions of your five children. Imagine having to watch them cry and hold in your own tears because those little children need stability." She reached out to stroke the side of his face. "I know he's no angel. And that he's impossible when he talks to you. But he did his best for you. We both did. But sometimes it isn't good enough."

He hated seeing the sadness in her eyes. Gray pulled her close and hugged her tight. "You were more than good enough," he said gruffly.

"Maybe one day you'll be able to talk to your dad without butting heads and tell him the same," she suggested when he released her.

"Maybe," he told her. "But I wouldn't bank on it."

The smallest of smiles curled her lips. "Maybe is good enough for me."

"WHY IS everything so much easier when I'm with you?" Gray murmured, pressing his lips against Maddie's hair. It was almost eleven, and they were sitting in her backyard in one of the old Adirondack chairs. When he sat down, she'd gone to sit in the other one, but he'd pulled her into his lap instead, telling her he needed to feel her. And yeah, maybe she'd needed a little of that, too.

"Because the rest of the world is full of assholes."

He chuckled. "Truth. Wherever I go, I can't seem to escape them."

"Me either. I hear my sister paid you a visit earlier." Though her voice was light, those words laid heavy on her chest.

"Yeah, she did. But I have no idea why. She said a few strange things then left as quickly as she arrived."

Maddie turned in his arms until she was facing him. She'd never get sick of looking at his beautiful face. Deep blue eyes, high cheekbones, strong, square jaw. The face that melted a million women's hearts. "What kind of strange things?"

He brushed his lips against hers, making her spine tingle. "She said that New York almost killed you."

Maddie's mouth went dry. "She did?"

"Yeah." He frowned. "What did she mean? Why did going to Ansell nearly kill you?"

She squeezed her eyes shut for a moment, not wanting to look at him. "It's old news," she said softly. "I had a bad experience and wanted to come home."

"A bad experience? With who? Was it one of your teachers?"

Her ribcage felt like a tightly closed door. He was prodding, trying to pry it open, and part of her wanted to let him. The other part? It knew that once he opened it she was going to have to deal with him knowing the truth. She wasn't sure she was ready for that. Not yet. Maybe not ever.

"I had a boyfriend," she said, her voice thin. "And something happened between us that really hurt me. And everybody knew about it. People were whispering about me in the hallways. In the end, all I wanted to do was come home."

Gray slid his hands around her waist, as though he was protecting her. "What did he do?"

She buried her face against his shoulder. "It doesn't matter. It's old history." She took a deep breath, trying to center herself. She didn't want to think about those memories now. Not while she was in his arms.

"It isn't old history if it stopped you playing music."

"I still play. I teach piano. I write some songs. It's enough for me." She licked her lips. "How about you, has anybody hurt you?"

"As in girlfriends?" he asked, his voice low.

"Yeah."

The corner of his mouth quirked up. "Are we having *that* talk?"

"What talk?" She looked up again. There was so much warmth in his eyes. She loved the way he knew to stop asking her questions about New York. He never pushed further than she could handle.

One day she's have to tell him, though. She knew that.

"The one where we tell each other all our guilty secrets about our past relationships. I ask you if you've ever been in love, and you ask me if I've ever cheated. Then we assess whether the other person is good enough for us."

"Have you ever cheated?" she asked him, suddenly interested.

"Nope. But I've done some things I've regretted."

"Like what?"

It was his turn to look cornered. "Stupid things. Had one night stands with women who were looking for more. Drunk too much and woken up to women whose names I didn't know."

"Women?" she asked him. "As in more than one."

He laughed. "Yeah, there's been more than one."

"I meant at the same time." Her chest tightened at the thought.

"Are you asking me if I've ever had a threesome?"

Her breath caught in her throat as she nodded. The difference in experience between them was all too evident. She'd only woken up once to find something she wasn't expecting. And that had ruined everything.

But it sounded like for Gray it was a way of life.

He pulled her tighter, his eyes meeting hers. And inside them she could see the honesty she was looking for. He was an open book, and she was desperate to turn the pages.

"I told you before that when I first found success I took advantage of it. Too much drinking, too many drugs, and yeah, there were too many women as well. I used them the way I used everything else. To make me feel better. Less alone. I wanted to feel like a star because deep down inside I didn't feel like I deserved any of it."

There was a rawness to his words that touched her. "But you *did* deserve it. You're so talented."

His mouth twitched. "It's okay. Years of therapy mean I don't need that kind of validation any more."

"No?"

"Nah uh."

She traced her finger down the bridge of his nose. "So have you had any longer relationships since then?"

"A couple," he said, his lips parting as her finger brushed against them. She could feel the heat of his breath against her skin. "Nothing too serious. Both of them were women in the industry."

"Do I know them?"

He shrugged. "Probably. But they're history now. How about you? Any suitors I should know about in Hartson's Creek? Should I be getting ready to fight for you?"

She grinned. "No. The only guy I spend time with is Murphy. And I can guarantee that he'd give me up without a fight."

"I can make better eggs than him."

"I have no doubt of that."

He traced her spine, his fingers slow and lingering. "So there's nothing standing between us."

She shivered at his touch. "There's a small matter of two thousand miles between your home and mine. And the fact that Ashleigh would throw a fit."

"Why didn't you tell her about us?" he asked her.

Maddie swallowed. He was so close she could feel every part of him against her. "Because I don't want to deal with the fall out."

He blinked. "You don't think this is worth it?"

"Of course it's worth it," she told him quickly. "That's not what I meant. But you're only here for a few more weeks and then you'll be back in L.A. I'd rather keep it between us while it lasts."

He dipped his head until his eyes were in line with hers. "You think this ends when I leave?"

"Won't it?" she asked, a little breathless. "Because I can't see how a long distance relationship will work."

"You'll come see me, I'll come see you. In between we'll have hot cyber sex to keep us going." He smiled. "The usual."

"You make it sound so easy."

"It is."

"And when people find out about us, and they start to wonder why a star like you wants to be with somebody like me?"

He frowned. "What does that mean?"

"Look at us. You're you and I'm... not."

"You're doing it again. Not seeing yourself the way I do."

"I'm being honest. You must have a PR company representing you. And probably image consultants. They'd advise you against this. Tell you to find somebody more your level. One of those other singers you've had a relationship with."

His fingers feathered her neck. "I don't want one of those other singers. I want *you*." His voice was thick. "I want to take you out in public, show people how goddamned lucky I am. I want us to be together, Maddie. And I don't give a damn what anybody else thinks."

"You're lucky. I care too much."

"Why?" He looked genuinely confused.

"Because I know what it's like to be talked about. To have gossip whispered behind my back while people laugh at me. It hurts, Gray. Cuts like a knife. I don't want to give anybody that kind of ammunition again."

"So that's it? We end this when I leave?"

Her heart clenched. The thought of not seeing him again made everything ache. "No," she whispered. "I don't want that."

He blew out a mouthful of air. "Thank god. Because I couldn't let you do that." He tipped her chin up with his fingers, and pressed his lips against hers. "So where do we go from here?"

She thread her fingers through his thick hair and pressed

herself against him, feeling the hardness of his excitement against her stomach. "I've got a few ideas," she whispered throatily. "But we may need to keep it quiet."

He slid his hands down her back and grabbed her ass. Then he kissed her hot and hard. "I can do quiet," he whispered. "If you really insist."

CHAPTER TWENTY

*G*ray was enjoying repairing the roof about as much
as he'd liked replacing the pipes in the house. It
wasn't the time it took, nor the physical effort he
had to expend each day to remove the old shingles and nail
new ones in their place. It was just so damn tedious. His
hands ached with the repetitive nature of the task, pushing a
crowbar under each broken shingle and maneuvering at it
until it finally came free, then replacing it with a fresh row,
making sure it lined up perfectly so no rain could seep
through.

His mind was elsewhere today. Too caught up thinking
about the song he'd started writing last night. *Second Chances.*
He was stuck on the bridge that linked the verse to the
chorus, and he kept humming combinations that could work.

So the pain, when it came, shot straight up his arm,
squeezing the breath from his lungs in a deep groan. He
looked down to see the sharp end of the crowbar digging
into the thick skin between his left thumb and forefinger.
Blood was pouring down his wrist and the metallic glint of
the bar. He pulled his hand back, and the pain made his toes

curl. He didn't realize he'd shouted out until he saw Aunt Gina run out of the kitchen door.

There was a jagged cut about two inches long, exposing the soft tissues in his flesh. Blood was gushing everywhere, and he had to grit his teeth against the dizziness threatening to overtake him. He sat down hard on the roof to try to catch his breath.

"Gray!" Aunt Gina called out. "What's happened?"

"I cut myself," he said, his voice thinner than he'd expected. He really needed to get down from the roof before he lost too much blood.

"Is it bad?"

"Pretty bad." There was too much blood to tell if he'd caught any tendons. "I need to get down." He let go of the crowbar and it clattered down the roof. Clenching his teeth against the pain, he scooted to the edge. He grasped the roof ladder with his good hand, keeping the other lifted up in an attempt to stem the flow of blood.

"My god, Gray," Aunt Gina whispered by the time he made it down. "Let me get a cloth to clean you up."

"I think I might need a doctor," he said, his teeth still clenched together.

"You need the hospital. Sit right there," she told him firmly, pointing at the bench. "I'm going to call an ambulance, then we need to stop the blood. Keep your hand up and try to breathe."

"Yeah." He nodded, trying not to look at the way the sleeve of his grey Henley was stained dark.

But before he could even sit, the world turned black. The last thing he remembered was the sound of blood rushing through his ears.

~

Maddie ran into the emergency room, her heart galloping like it was trying to win the Kentucky Derby. She stopped at the desk, still breathless from her mad dash, and told the clerk she was looking for Gray.

"Are you family?"

"No," she panted. "A close friend." She looked across the waiting room and spotted the familiar sight of Aunt Gina's gunmetal grey hair. "It's okay, I see his aunt. I'll go sit with her."

Had it really only been half an hour ago that Laura had ran into the diner to tell her Gray had been rushed here? The town's grapevine had been working overtime. Eleanor Charlton had been having a dress fitting in Laura's shop when her best friend, Lula Robinson, had called. Lula's son worked for the fire department who'd been called out to the Hartson home, and he'd wasted no time in telling his mom that they'd transported a superstar to the Sandson Memorial Hospital.

Aunt Gina showed no signs of surprise when Maddie appeared in front of her. Instead, she stood and smiled at her, offering her cheek the way she always did.

"Is Gray okay?" Maddie asked her after she'd kissed her cheek. "I heard he cut his hand. Is it bad?"

"I'm still waiting to find out. There was a lot of blood and he lost consciousness for a minute. He's with the doctors now." She patted the chair next to hers. "Why don't you sit with me for a minute?"

Maddie wasn't sure her body would slow down enough to sit. She wanted to pace the hallways until she found him. Still, she tried, taking a deep breath as her legs bent and her behind hit the seat.

"It's nice of you to come check on him," Gina said, her voice light.

Maddie's feet started to tap the floor. "Do you think he hit

177

any tendons?" she asked. That would be so bad for his career, and she felt sick at the thought of it.

"I don't know. It was hard to tell through all the blood."

Maddie winced.

"He's a strong boy," Gina said, patting her hand. "Don't worry so much."

But she did. She was worrying like crazy. She couldn't imagine what it would be like if she couldn't play the piano. It felt as important to her as breathing. And for Gray, his hands were everything.

"You're fond of him, aren't you, dear?"

Maddie turned to look at her. There was understanding in Gina's eyes.

"Yeah, I guess I am."

"I had a beau once," Gina said, her gaze soft. "He was everything to me. But I was seventeen and he was twenty-three and my parents were strict. We'd pass notes after church and if I could get one of my girlfriends to cover for me, we'd take Sunday afternoon walks by the river." Her smile was full of memories. "Then one day, right before my eighteenth birthday, his number came up on the draft lottery. Turns out he was one of the last, but we didn't know that at the time."

"He went to Vietnam?" Maddie asked her.

"Yes he did. He was placed into the Marines after basic training. And while he was away he sent me the sweetest letters. He'd talk about what we'd do when I turned eighteen. Told me about his dream of a pretty white house full of children." Gina pressed her lips together. "And then one day the letters stopped. And I couldn't talk to my parents about it, because then they'd never let me see him again. So I'd come home from school and check the mailbox every day."

"Did they start again?"

As if she hadn't heard her question, Gina continued, "So I

started to hang around his parents' house. Just to see if the mailman delivered any letters there. His mom must have noticed me lingering, because one day she asked me to come in for a glass of lemonade." Gina took a deep breath. "That's when she told me about the visit she'd had that morning from a Marine Corps colonel. According to her, the poor man looked so white she was afraid he was going to faint. Then he told her about David. How he'd fought bravely but had died of gunshot wounds in battle." She looked at Maddie. "He'd only been there for two months."

Maddie's chest ached. "Did you go to his funeral."

Gina shook her head. "They buried him in a military cemetery miles away from town. I'd have had to ask my father, and explain why. I wasn't brave enough to do that."

"That's so sad." Maddie blinked away her tears. "What a waste of a life."

"It really was. And for a while it felt like my life was over, too. No pretty white house, no picket fence. But do you know what the worst thing was?"

"What?" Maddie asked softly, her head tipped to one side.

"Not being able to tell anybody how sad I was. Not being able to talk about what I'd lost. Looking back, I wish I'd been braver. Told my parents about David and how I felt about him. Maybe then I wouldn't have bottled it all up and felt like I was dying inside."

"It sounds like you were very brave to me," Maddie told her. "I'm so sorry for your loss."

"It's okay. These things often turn out for the best. Being single and alone meant I could take care of my sister's children when she died too young. Maybe that was God's plan for me all along."

For a moment Maddie wondered if that was God's plan for her, too. Whether she was supposed to be there for

Carter and Grace the way Gina had been there for Gray and his siblings.

"But you're not like me," Gina told her. "And we live in different times. There's no need to hide the way you feel about somebody any more." She looked right at Maddie, her brows rising up.

She knew.

Maddie had no idea how much, or how she'd found out, but she knew.

And for some reason, right now that felt reassuring.

"I just hope he's okay," she whispered.

"I do, too. But I want him to be more than okay. I want him to be *happy*. And I have a feeling he hasn't been happy for a long time."

"But—" Maddie started to protest.

Gina held up her hand. "Oh, I know he's successful with all those hit songs and Grammys and goodness only knows what else. But those things aren't what make us happy. They're just little bits of sparkle on the cake. But it's the cake that matters. That's what sustains us, keeps us going. Anything else will rot your teeth."

"I want him to be happy, too," Maddie admitted.

Gina smiled. "Well that's half the battle. The other half is allowing yourself to be happy. Do you think you're up for that?"

"IF YOU HAVE ANY PAIN, you can take ibuprofen or aceta-minophen. No aspirin, though. We don't want to thin your blood. The dressing will need to be changed in twenty-four hours. Your family doctor will be able to do that for you, but if you have any problems, give us a call." The nurse smiled at him. "If you notice any increase in pain or oozing from the wound, come in right away. The stitches should dissolve in a couple of weeks, and we'd advise you to rest your hand until then."

Gray looked at his bandaged hand. There were eight stitches holding the wound closed. They'd injected it with a local anesthetic before closing it up, and thankfully right now he felt no pain at all.

"And no more messing around on roofs," the nurse told him. "Leave that to the professionals."

"I plan to." Gray managed a smile. "Can I go now?"

"Of course. I'll walk you to the waiting room."

She led him to the double doors and said her goodbyes, leaving him to walk to where he knew Aunt Gina was waiting. A few people looked up with interest as he passed, then leaned across to their companions to whisper frantically.

And then he saw *her*, and it felt like somebody had lit a fire inside him.

"Hey," Maddie said, standing up as he approached. "How are you doing?"

He held up his bandaged hand. "All good." It was impossible to stop himself from smiling. "You came."

"Yeah," she said softly. "I was worried about you. Did they say if you damaged any tendons?"

He shook his head, still grinning. "It's just a flesh wound. A few stitches and a bandage and I'm good to go."

She sighed with relief, and it heated him more. It was the sweetest damn thing somebody had done for him in a long time. All he wanted to do was take her in his arms and kiss the hell out of her. Then somebody cleared their throat and he realized Aunt Gina was right next to them, and he leaned forward to hug her.

"Thanks for picking me up off the ground," he whispered in her ear.

She shook her head. "Don't make me do it again. Now I'm

going home to make some sweet tea, I figure Maddie can give you a ride home."

Maddie didn't look surprised at her request. "Yeah, sure."

"And I'll call around for some roofers," Aunt Gina continued. "Don't worry about your father. If he protests, he'll get a piece of my mind."

Gray bit down a grin. Over the years, he had enough pieces of his aunt's mind to know what a threat that was.

She shuffled toward the main entrance, leaving Gray with Maddie. He still couldn't get over her being here.

"Shall we go?" he asked her. She smiled and nodded.

He slipped his good hand into hers, his grin widening when she didn't protest. She felt warm and soft and everything he wanted right now. Maybe that's why he spun her around and pulled her against his side. His body relaxed as he pressed her against him. "You're a sight for sore eyes, and hands," he whispered, dropping his head to brush his lips against hers. She let out a sigh, and the warmth of her breath fueled his desire. If they'd been anywhere else – somewhere private, he'd have shown her just how much. But they weren't. They were in a hospital lobby, and he had to be satisfied with deepening the kiss, letting his tongue caress hers as he slid his hand down to that perfect dip at the base of her spine.

When he pulled away, her eyes were heated, and he loved the way he affected her the same way she affected him. "Gray…" she whispered. "We shouldn't."

"I know." His grin was lopsided. "But I can't help it. Every time I see you all I can think about is those lips." And that body, those legs, the way her voice got all rough when she sighed.

The way he felt real when she was in his arms.

He waited for her to chide him again, but instead her face paled. Her throat undulated as she swallowed, and he turned to glance over his shoulder, trying to determine what had caused such a change in her mood.

That's when he saw the woman staring at them. He frowned, because she looked familiar, though he couldn't quite place her.

"Who's that?" he asked Maddie.

She squirmed out of his hold. "It's Jessica Martin. She used to be Jessica Chilton."

Jess Chilton. Ashleigh's best friend at school. She was still staring at them, her red-painted lips pressed together.

"I should talk to her," Maddie said, her words coming out in a rush. "Tell her it isn't what it looks like. She can't tell Ashleigh..."

"Why not?"

She looked up at him, her eyes still wide. "Because she'll go crazy."

He shrugged. "So let her. What happens between us has nothing to do with her or anybody else." He reached out and ran his finger down her face, aware of Jessica's continued scrutiny. "I don't give a shit what anybody else thinks."

"I wish I didn't." Maddie inhaled deeply. "I really do."

"Then just try it," he urged. "It's not as bad as you think. Trust me."

"How do I do that?" She blinked.

"You realize people can't hurt you unless you let them." His mind turned to his dad. "That the words they say and the way they look at you can't kill you. And what doesn't kill you..."

"Makes you stronger," she whispered.

He nodded. "That's right."

He could see the struggle on her face, as she thought about his words. And he realized how much he wanted her to ignore what everybody else said. To shuck off the expectations of this town and the people who lived in it. To shout from the rooftops that she wanted to be his girl.

Until now, he hadn't realized how much he craved it. For her to tell everybody about them. For their relationship to be open knowledge, instead of a dirty little secret they both had to deny.

Because it wasn't dirty. It was good and it was right, and it was the best damn thing that had happened to him in years.

"Maddie?" he whispered, his chest tight as he waited for her to say something.

She nodded, her eyes catching his. And he saw it. The strength and determination that had characterized her from the first time they'd met. It pushed down the vulnerability, cloaking it in a suit of iron.

"You're right," she whispered, reaching her hand out to cup his jaw, her palm soft against his rough skin. "I don't give a damn what Jessica thinks. Or anybody else for that matter." She rolled onto the balls of her feet, her head tipping up until her lips were a breath from his. "Gray Hartson, you're making me break all my rules."

His brow lifted up. "I've already thrown mine out." He closed his eyes as her mouth brushed his, warmth flooding his body. He slid his good arm around her waist. "Christ, you feel good."

When he pulled away, she was smiling, and it about broke him. This pretty, funny, strong woman had chosen him. And she wasn't afraid to show it.

"Come on, I'll let you take me home," he said, tucking her against his side.

As they walked out of the hospital, he saw Jessica furiously tapping against her phone.

CHAPTER TWENTY-ONE

"Your record company is pissed," Marco said down the telephone line. Gray was sitting in the summerhouse, his denim-clad legs stretched out in front of him, his feet rested on a box. "I promised them you'd be ready to record in September. They're not happy about postponing for two months."

"It was an accident," Gray reminded him. He was used to Marco's high strung responses. Liked them, even. He paid his manager to panic, so Gray didn't have to. "Just tell them I'll be ready in November."

"I already did. And they're still worried, Gray. You left the tour on a high. They don't want you disappearing for months. They were planning on releasing your next single in December."

"We still can. It'll just be tight, that's all." He stretched his injured hand in front of him, wincing at the momentary pain his movement caused. There was no way he could even hold a guitar right now, let alone play. The record company would have to wait.

"I spoke to the PR department and they're making a plan

in the meantime," Marco continued. Gray could picture his manager sitting in his office, wearing his usual designer suit and thin, knotted tie, his wire glasses pitched low on the bridge of his nose. He was younger than Gray, but he acted about ten years older. "They want to get you back in the limelight. Let people see what you're doing back in your home town. *Rock Magazine* has agreed to do a feature on you. They're sending a journalist down next week."

"What?" Gray sat forward. "I didn't agree to that."

Marco paused. "Okay, let me rephrase. Gray, is it okay if a journalist comes to interview you next week? It'll be good for your career."

"No."

A big sigh reverberated through the telephone line. "You gotta throw them a bone. They've paid a huge advance for your next album, and now you've injured yourself doing something stupid. Something *I* told you not to do, by the way."

A smile lifted the corner of Gray's lips. "You gonna tell me you told me so?" He knew Marco never would. He was too diplomatic for that.

"I'm going to tell you to listen to me for a change. Let me earn the money you pay me. Just do this interview and it'll keep the folks at Vista Records very happy."

The thought of a journalist coming to interview him here, in Hartson's Creek, made Gray want to groan. It was like two worlds colliding, and he had no idea where the fallout would be. In L.A., he was Gray Hartson. Rock singer, Grammy winner, owner of a beautiful house in the hills above Malibu. Over there he was in control of who he was.

But here? He felt bare. And yeah, some of that was due to Maddie and the way she made him want to be. But there were other things, too. His relationship with his father for one. He never wanted the world to know about that.

"Okay, I'll do the interview, but I'll fly to L.A. to do it," Gray said, leaning back in his chair. "Tell me the time and date and I'll be there."

Marco hesitated for a moment. "That won't work," he said quietly. "They've done a whole load of interviews with you in L.A. before. They want an exclusive. And the record company wants to start building the hype for your album. The journalist wants to see you in your home town. Wants the insider scoop regarding the inspiration behind your next album."

"And it has to be next week?"

"Yeah. Rick Charles is flying down. Bringing a photographer with him. I'll arrange for a hair and makeup artist to be there. And of course I'll be there."

"Of course." Sarcasm dripped from his tongue.

Next week. The thought of it brought a heavy discomfort over him. He'd have to speak to Aunt Gina and Becca, not to mention his father. And explain it to Maddie, too, even though he had no idea what she'd make of it.

"So I'll tell them to go ahead?" Marco prompted. "We'll fly in Sunday night for a Monday morning start. They shouldn't be there for more than a couple of days."

"Yeah, tell them it's on." Even if it made him feel a little dizzy, like the world was tipping. More than most he knew that interviews and publicity were the price you had to pay to get the kind of success he had. He'd scratch their back, they'd scratch his, and hopefully everybody could move on to the next thing.

It didn't stop him feeling weird about it, though.

GRAY WALKED into the diner right as Maddie's phone lit up. She glanced over at him, her heart skipping a beat as she took in his long, strong body and the tight black t-shirt he was wearing. The tattoos she'd traced more than once with her lips were visible in colorful glory on his thick biceps.

"Hey." She smiled as he walked over to the counter. It was the lull between lunch and dinner – only two tables were occupied, and neither customer seemed particularly interested in the rockstar who'd just walked in.

"Hey." He leaned on the counter. "I just got back from getting my bandage changed. Thought I'd soothe the pain with some pie."

Her grin widened. "You want me to kiss it better?"

He leaned closer, catching her eye. "I can think of a better place for those pretty lips."

"That's because you're dirty." She lifted an eyebrow. "I'll have you know this is a reputable establishment, Mr. Hartson."

He tipped his head to the side, his lip curling up. "So what are you doing working here?"

"I'll ignore that question and get you some pie." She reached for a plate. "How's the hand? Does it hurt a lot?"

"Not too bad. The wound is clean which is good, and I took some painkillers before I went. I'd still like that kiss though." He winked.

"Later."

"I'll hold you to that."

Her phone lit up again, her sister's name flashing across it. Maddie sighed and slid it into her jeans pocket. "It's Ashleigh," she said. "I'm guessing the word is out." She pressed her lips together in an attempt to smile. "It's time to face the music."

"You not going to answer her?"

"I'll ask her to meet me after work," Maddie said, her stomach dropping. "There are some things that should only be done face to face."

"You're going to tell her about us?" He tipped his head to the side, his eyes scanning her face. God, he was good looking. Every time their gazes met she felt a jolt of electricity shoot through her. All she wanted to do was curl up with him and pretend the rest of the world didn't exist.

But it felt like everybody else had other ideas.

"Yeah," she said softly. "I am." And it scared her to death. Not because of Ashleigh's response, but because she'd finally be admitting to having feelings for Gray. Strong ones. Ones that could hurt her if this went wrong.

Oh god, she didn't want to think about that.

"Then I'll be there with you."

Her eyes widened. "You're kidding?"

"Nope. If you're telling Ashleigh about us, then I want to be there to support you." He shrugged, as though he was talking about coming over for dinner, rather than the kind of family-ageddon Maddie imagined it was going to be.

"That's really sweet," she told him. "But she'll take it so much worse if you're there. I should tell her alone."

He looked at her, and she saw questions behind his deep blue eyes. She waited for him to protest again, but instead he slowly nodded. "Okay. But if she goes too crazy, feel free to tell her it's all my fault for seducing you."

"You think you seduced me?" Maddie asked, the smile returning to her face. He grinned back at her, and the intensity of it took her breath away.

"Yeah," he said, closer still. It was a good thing there was a counter between them or she'd probably be rubbing herself on him like a cat in heat. "I seduced you. And the memories keep me company at night."

"Good job you're right handed," she whispered, and he laughed out loud. "And for the record, I let you seduce me."

"I know." He reached out to tuck a stray hair behind her ear. She shivered at the warmth of his touch. "I'm under no

189

illusions who's in charge here, Maddie." He looked at her with heated eyes. "You've got me wrapped around your finger."

"I do?" she breathed.

"Yeah. And I like it too goddamned much."

The door opened again, and this time two chattering women walked in and headed for a booth.

"I should go take some orders," Maddie said. "Before Murphy gives me the boot."

Gray pushed himself off the counter. "Call me later. Once you've talked to Ashleigh."

"Okay."

"And if you want to let me seduce you again, I'm up for that, too."

She laughed. "I'll bear that in mind. You want that pie now?"

"Yeah, but I'd better take it to go. I've got some things to do this afternoon. A reporter's flying in next week to write up a profile on me."

"You're doing an interview here?" Maddie asked him.

"Yeah. *Rock Magazine* wants to talk about the next album, and the publicity will make my record company happy. Because currently they are pretty angry about this." He waved his injured hand.

"When are they coming?" A wave of alarm washed over her.

"On Monday. And don't look so worried. They're just here to talk about the music and my upbringing."

"Okay," she said softly, but the anxious feeling didn't disappear. If anything it increased.

"I wasn't planning on talking about us," he told her. "If that's what's worrying you."

She exhaled, the warm air rushing from her mouth. "Thank you," she said. "I'm not sure I'm ready for that."

A fleeting expression crossed his face. One she couldn't quite put her finger on. Then he smiled again and it disappeared.

"I'll get you that pie," she said, putting the plate back under the counter and grabbing a cardboard box. She lifted the glass lid up and cut a wedge. "You want whipped cream?"

"Nah. Got to watch what I'm eating before a photo shoot." He tapped his flat-as-heck stomach and winked.

And all those fears and worries disappeared, replaced by a neediness that made her thighs ache and her heart race like a stallion.

He slid a five dollar bill into her hand. "I'll see you later, Maddie," he told her, his eyes soft as he squeezed his fingers against hers. Then he pulled his hand away, grabbed his to go box, and walked out of the diner with long, sure strides.

Yeah, she'd see him later, if Ashleigh didn't kill her first.

"You lied to me," Ashleigh said, her eyes flashing with anger. "I *specifically* asked you if there was something going on between you two and you told me there wasn't. Do you know how it felt when Jess called to tell me what she saw at the hospital? The whole town is laughing at me. At the fact that you're messing around with the guy who broke my heart."

Maddie swallowed hard. Her sister had every right to be angry at her.

"You're my sister," Ashleigh continued. "And sisters support each other. They don't go sneaking around and lie to each other, and do God knows what else. After everything I've done for you, you turned around and stab me in the heart."

"I know there's history between you and Gray," Maddie

said, her voice tentative. "But it all happened a long time ago. Can't you let bygones be bygones?"

"It's not about me and Gray. It's about me and you. What's going to happen when Gray goes back to L.A.? Are you going with him?"

"I don't know. We haven't talked about that."

"So you'd leave?" Ashleigh asked, her voice rising an octave. "You'd walk away from mom and me? And from Carter and Grace? You'd break their hearts."

"I'd never want to hurt anybody. And I'm not planning on going anywhere right now."

"So you're going to have a long distance relationship?" Ashleigh's laugh was short and humorless. "You really think a virile man like Gray would settle for that? You're crazy, Maddie. He'll end up hurting you the way he hurt me. The way you were hurt when you went to New York."

Maddie's chest tightened at her sister's words. "He won't hurt me," she whispered.

"That's what I thought, too. All those times he held me in his arms and told me we were forever." Ashleigh's eyes sparkled with tears. "He made me promises, and then he broke them. You saw what he did to me. You saw how much I hurt. And you're hurting me again by being with him."

"I don't want to hurt you," Maddie told her. She reached out, tried to take Ashleigh's hand, but her sister pulled away. "You have Michael. And Grace and Carter. If things hadn't ended with you and Gray the way they did, you wouldn't be their mom."

"It doesn't matter," Ashleigh insisted. "You're my sister. You're supposed to be on my side. Always."

"I am. I am on your side."

"Then end it with Gray. Let him go back to L.A. and we'll go back to the way things were. We were happy, Maddie. We all were. I have my family. You have mom and your music and the diner. It works for us. Don't let Gray ruin it."

Maddie blinked. "It worked for you. I'm not sure it did for me. It feels like I've been living in the dark for so long. Then Gray came along and let the light in. I don't want to go back to who I was. I like my life better this way."

"Oh for god's sake. The next thing you'll be telling me is that you love him."

Maddie swallowed hard.

"You don't love him, do you?" Ashleigh asked, her narrowed eyes boring into Maddie's. "Tell me you're not in love with Gray Hartson."

Maddie's thoughts were full of him. Of the softness of his eyes whenever he spoke to her. The heat in his hands whenever he touched her bare skin. And those kisses. Those teasing, heartbreaking kisses. They filled her soul in a way she'd never experienced before.

"I have feelings for him," she admitted.

Ashleigh shook her head. "Does he know what happened at Ansell?"

"I haven't told him yet."

"Then those feelings you have mean nothing. If you don't feel safe enough to tell him everything about you then it's just pretend, isn't it?" Ashleigh leaned forward, her voice urgent. "If you can't rely on him to be there for you, what's the point? And you *can't* rely on him, Maddie. The way I couldn't rely on him. He'll use you up and toss you aside, and I don't know if you'll recover from that a second time." She folded her arms across her chest. "And if you think I'll be there to help you when he leaves you, you're wrong. I saved you once, but I won't do it again."

There was hurt in Ashleigh's eyes, and it killed Maddie to see it. "I'm so grateful for everything you've done for me," she said, her heart aching. "And I've done everything I can to pay you back. I've been there for you, too. Supported you when you had Carter and Grace. Taken care of mom so you didn't have to worry." Maddie took a deep breath in. "But I can't do this for you. I can't give up my one chance at happiness."

Ashleigh's expression was tight. "If you want to throw your family away for some guy we all know is bad for you, go ahead. But I won't be here to watch it. Nor will Carter and Grace." She unfolded her arms and turned on her heel, her blonde hair swinging behind her as she stomped across the room. Her stiletto heels banged against the wooden floor. Wrenching the door open, she turned back to Maddie, her eyes tight and dark. "I hope you're happy," she told her. "Because you've just broken my heart."

CHAPTER TWENTY-TWO

"*Y*our sister's a bitch. That's all there is to it." Laura crossed her legs, her bare toes skimming the water rising and falling against the harbor wall. She and Maddie were sitting on the old flagstones, their jeans rolled up, their shoes and socks placed carefully beside them. It had been warm today, enough for this Friday's *Chairs* to be full to bursting with townsfolk. Behind them, they could hear the rumble of gossip from the adults clustered in circles, and the shouts of the children as they played makeshift football games.

"She's right, though. Family should come first." Maddie traced a circle in the water with her toes, watching as it disappeared. "I upset her."

"Over a guy she used to date when she was a teenager?" Laura said, shaking her auburn curls. "That was a decade ago. They were kids. Jeez, if I wasn't allowed to date any guy one of my family or friends used to crush on, I would've been a spinster for the rest of my life." She raised an eyebrow.

"Oh shut up." Maddie nudged her with her shoulder.

"Guys used to cluster around you like flies before you got married."

"Yeah. Like flies cluster around manure." Laura shook her head, though Maddie could tell she was biting down a smile. "Anyway, we're not talking about me. Your sister has no right to tell you who you can or can't date. It's none of her business."

"She thinks she knows best."

"Because of what happened when you were in Ansell?" Laura lowered her voice, her eyes glancing around.

"Ashleigh saved me that day," Maddie said softly. "When I called her she dropped everything. Drove all the way to New York by herself and raised hell with the administration. And when I begged her to take me home, she packed everything up while I cried my heart out, before driving for hours through the night. I owe her."

"You owe her nothing. You're always there for her. How often do you babysit your niece and nephew?" Laura asked her. "And then there's your mom. Ashleigh never does anything apart from visit every so often. You're the one who takes her to the doctor, who makes sure she's in bed safely every night. Hell, you bring her here every Friday and I know how much you hate it."

"I get to see you." Maddie smiled.

"Yeah, that's the only saving grace of *Chairs*." Laura grinned back. "I get to talk to you without Murphy shouting at us." Her face turned serious. "You're not going to do what she asks, are you?"

"My mom wants me to," Maddie admitted.

"Your mom?" Laura frowned. "What's she got to do with it?"

"She heard us arguing. She was so upset when Ashleigh slammed her way out of the house without saying goodbye. I got a lecture about how we're sisters and we should always take care of each other." Maddie sighed. "Maybe she's right."

"You'd really stop seeing Gray Hartson because your sister's throwing a fit over it?"

The thought made Maddie's chest contract. The attraction between them was crazy. Even now, sitting here surrounded by people, all she really wanted to do was talk about him, be with him.

But that was crazy, too. Because then everybody would start talking about her, and she'd hate that.

"I don't think I can," she said softly.

"Good. Because I'd have had to push you in the water if you did. I know you, Maddie. Not as well as Ashleigh, maybe, but well enough. If you like this guy, then you should go for it. You'd regret it if you didn't."

"And if he hurts me?" Maddie asked, the tightness in her chest not feeling any better. "What then?"

"Then you'll deal with it the way you deal with everything. You're not a naïve kid anymore. You've grown since returning from New York." Laura tipped her head, the dying sun catching the red in her curls. "You're a strong, intelligent, kick ass woman who doesn't let people walk all over her. And if Gray hurts you the way you've been hurt before, I'm pretty sure you'll rip his balls off."

"You're pretty fierce," Maddie said, grinning at Laura's flashing eyes.

"Well, thank you. If you need any help with the ripping part, I'm your girl." She pulled her legs out of the water and shook her feet, tiny droplets flying through the air. "I'm going to grab some lemonade. You want some?"

"Yeah," Maddie agreed, a smile curling her lips. "I can't think of anything better right now."

～

THE LITTLE FACEBOOK icon on Maddie's phone screen had been racking up all day. She rarely got notifications on Facebook – hardly any of her friends even used it anymore. And yet every time she checked her phone the little red number next to the icon was increasing. It was now up to twenty, and it was making her twitchy.

It wasn't until she got home from work that she finally brought herself to check it. And when she saw that every notification came from that damn Ansell Reunion Group she'd been invited to, Maddie sighed. She'd thought by not accepting it she wouldn't be part of it anymore, but it seemed like Facebook had other ideas.

There was a post in the group that was going crazy with replies. Maddie blinked as she read it, her mouth feeling as dry as the desert.

Has anybody invited Brad Rickson? Or are we not going there? Somebody had posted. With a masochistic finger, Maddie clicked on the comments that followed.

HMM. Not sure whether we should invite him or not. Y'all remember what he did, right?

DID you hear he has a record deal? Somebody told me he signed with Vista Records.

YEP. According to a friend in the business, his debut album comes out next year.

WHY DO good things happen to bad people?

. . .

TALKING OF BRAD, has anybody heard from Maddie Clark?

POOR, Maddie. He was such an asshole. Has anybody heard from her?

SHE'S in the member list, doofus. So be careful what you say.

GUYS, nobody is inviting Brad. And yes, I've invited Maddie. I'm closing the comments. Let's concentrate on the reunion, okay?

MADDIE IGNORED the way her hands were shaking as she pressed the 'decline invitation' button, before closing down Facebook. For good measure, she uninstalled the app and threw her phone down on her bed.

There was no way she was going to the reunion, Brad Rickson or no Brad Rickson.

So why did it feel like somebody was stabbing her in the gut?

THE CIRCUS ARRIVED at ten o'clock on Monday morning. Okay, so there weren't animals or clowns spilling out of the black sedans at the end of the driveway, but as Gray watched his manager, the journalist, a photographer, a makeup artist, and a hairdresser walk up the graveled path, it felt like his sleepy home town was being invaded.

"Wow," Becca breathed, as she stood next to him and stared out of the living room window. "They've come mob-handed." She looked at him and grinned. "You will tell them about me beating you at Karaoke, right?"

Gray raised an eyebrow. "I'm pretty sure they'll ask you some questions. You can spill the beans if you want."

She grinned. "I can?" Her eyes widened as she took in the huge cases the makeup artist and hairdresser were wheeling. "Do you think they'll want to take a photo of me, too?"

"I can ask them." He smiled at her. "Not for the magazine, though. Just for you to keep." The thought of exposing Becca to the world like that made him want to squirm.

"Yay!" Becca clapped her hands. "Yes, please."

Ten minutes later and they were all clustered in Aunt Gina's kitchen, drinking freshly-made iced tea. Even though the kitchen was large, it felt claustrophobic with so many strangers sitting around the table. Even still, Aunt Gina was doing her best to make them feel welcome.

"Can I offer you some cake?" she asked them. All six shook their heads in horror, like she was trying to give them some kind of poison.

"What about lunch?" she asked. "Will everybody want something to eat?"

Marco shook his head. "We'll probably take Gray around the town to shoot some photos. We can pick something up there. Do you have a juice bar?"

"A juice bar?" Aunt Gina repeated, her brows pulled together.

"We don't have a juice bar," Becca said, biting down a grin. "But we have a diner."

"We can head over to Stanhope for lunch," Gray added hastily. "There are a few locations that way that should give us some good shots."

"What's wrong with the diner?" Aunt Gina asked.

"Yeah, you seem to spend a lot of time there," Becca added, a wicked gleam in her eye.

"You do?" Rick Charles, the lead writer for *Rock Magazine* scribbled something on the pad in front of him. "I'd like to check it out. A few photographs in there could work."

"I don't spend a lot of time in there," Gray told him. "I'm mostly in the summer house at the end of the backyard. That's where I write my songs. You could take photographs there."

"Can I take a look?" Andie, the photographer asked. "I want to see which way the light is facing."

"Sure. It's out there," Gray pointed at the door.

"I'll come, too," the make-up artist said. "I can work out what kind of products we'll need."

"I can show you the way if you like," Becca suggested, finishing the last of her tea. She glanced at Gray for his approval, and he nodded. "It was like Gray's second home growing up. He wanted to move his bedroom out there, but dad said no."

"Where is your father?" Rick asked, looking around the room. "He still lives here, right?"

"He's working in his room," Aunt Gina said, refilling their glasses with iced tea. "He doesn't really like fuss, so we thought it was for the best."

"I was hoping to meet him," Rick told them, looking straight at Gray. "If I'm writing about your beginnings, he's kind of where it all started."

Marco leaned forward. "I'm sure we can make that happen. Can't we, Gray?"

"He's been sick," Gray told them, his voice low. "I don't want him disturbed."

"I've been around for all of Gray's life," Aunt Gina interjected, her voice unusually light. "I can answer the questions you have."

"Okay." Rick's tone made Gray feel uneasy. "We can start with that." He grabbed his recorder from his bag and set it up on the table, before he turned his note pad over to a fresh page. "But if your dad feels any better later, be sure to introduce me to him."

~

MADDIE WIPED the counter down and tidied up the menus, then glanced at her phone one more time to see if she had any messages.

She hadn't heard from Gray since his manager and journalist arrived in town yesterday. It was weird how strange it felt not to connect with him for more than twenty-four hours. She didn't like it. Even worse, she didn't like that she didn't like it. Her happiness shouldn't be dependent on a message or phone call.

News of a journalist being in town had spread like wildfire, the way gossip always did in Hartson's Creek. According to Laura, who heard it from Sonya Chilton – Jessica's mother – the journalist had been asking questions about Gray all over town. He'd been into the church and grilled Reverend Maitland, had walked into the high school and spoken to Gray's old music teacher. He'd even sat down on the bench in the town square for an hour, standing to talk to anybody who walked by.

But he hadn't been in the diner. Not yet.

"According to Mrs. Chilton, he looks like a 'Beatnik'," Laura had told Maddie with a grin. "I asked her what that meant, and it turns out he wears jeans that hang below his underwear, which is some kind of a crime around here."

"I heard he has a t-shirt with *Black Sabbath* written on it," Doris, one of their regulars, joined in, her voice rising up an octave. "And he wore it into church."

Her friend gasped. "I'm surprised Reverend Maitland didn't throw him right out."

"Oh come on now. You know that Reverend Maitland is too kind to do that. But if I see him wearing that t-shirt I'd be happy to give him a piece of my mind."

"*Black Sabbath* is a rock band," Laura said, her amused gaze meeting Maddie's. "I don't think he's going around advertising he's the devil's disciple or anything."

"Ozzy Osborne was the lead singer," Maddie added, though neither of the women next to Laura seemed to know what she was talking about.

"Is he the one that bit the head off of a bat?" Laura asked, her voice light. There was a wicked glint in her eye.

It was hard not to laugh at the older ladies' expressions of distaste.

"Yeah." Maddie nodded. "And apparently he once gave hash cake to a priest."

"Hash cake?" Doris asked. "What's that?"

"It's cake laced with marijuana," Laura told her. "He drugged the priest."

"I hope that boy doesn't drug Reverend Maitland," Doris said, alarmed.

Maddie grinned at the memory of the old ladies' shock. It had been a moment of lightness in a hard day. Hard because her mom was still upset about Maddie and Ashleigh's argument, and because Gray had been ominously silent while the journalist was in town.

The bell above the door rang, and Maddie stopped clearing the counter and automatically reached for the menus. When she looked up, a man was walking toward the counter.

As Laura had described, his jeans were baggy and hanging from his thin frame. His dark t-shirt didn't have *Black Sabbath* emblazoned on it today, but instead there was a religious image of a dead man lying on an altar, with *Joy Division* printed across the top. She could tell from the faded gray of the fabric and the way it looked thin and crinkled that it was old, probably an original.

She couldn't help but think his clothing had been carefully chosen to cause a stir in the small town.

"You can take a seat," Maddie said to him, nodding at the booths. "I'll bring a menu over. Would you like coffee?"

"I'm okay at the counter." He walked over and pulled out the stool closest to Maddie, sitting on it and leaning his arms on the countertop. "You're Maddie Clark, right?"

Her back straightened. "Yes," she said carefully. "That's right."

"I'm Rick Charles from *Rock Magazine*." He offered her his hand and Maddie took it. "You might have heard that I'm in town doing an article on Gray Hartson."

"I might have."

"Yeah." He smiled. "I figured word gets around fast here. Who needs the internet, right?"

"People sure like to talk. Can I get you a coffee?"

"That would be good."

She turned to the pot, taking a deep breath as she lifted it up and filled his mug. He was only interested in Gray. That's why he was here. It was okay, it really was.

"Cream and sugar?" she asked him, turning back, her face impassive.

"No thanks. Black is good." He took a deep sip then smiled at her again. "So I guess you know Gray as well as anybody around here, right?"

"Not really." She shook her head. "We've never been close."

"But you helped him escape from the church a few weeks ago, didn't you? I heard you caused quite a scene jumping over fences and running through yards."

"I'd have done it for anybody. Nobody should be chased by teenage girls after church."

Maddie noticed Rick had pulled a notepad out from his pocket, before he lifted his hand to pull the pen from behind his ear. She felt like she was sitting on the stand of a courtroom, waiting to be questioned.

"You've known him for a while, right?" He flipped his note pad, scanning through the scrawled words written there. "He dated your sister during high school. Ashleigh, is it?"

"Yeah." She managed a smile. "But it was a long time ago. She's married with children now."

It felt strange, watching him write her own words down.

"Do you know why they split up?"

"Shouldn't you ask Gray that?" she said lightly.

"I have. But sisters are close and I'm guessing they confide in each other. I just wondered if she has the same reasons as Gray."

"I don't think my sister would like me talking for her."

"Do you have a number that I can call her at directly?"

She shook her head. "I don't think she'd like me giving that out either."

"That's okay," he said nonchalantly. "I'm sure I can track her down."

Maddie's spine tingled at the thought of him talking to Ashleigh. Would her sister tell him the truth about her and Gray? Maddie didn't think she would, but she hadn't seen Ashleigh this angry in a while. She tried to ignore the rising panic in her stomach.

"Can I get you something to eat while you're here?" she asked. "We have an impressive menu."

"The coffee is fine. But I'd love a top up," he said, smiling. "I did have one other question for you while I'm here."

"Ask away," she said, turning to grab the coffee pot. It spluttered as she lifted it from the warming plate.

"Somebody I talked to said you've been spending a lot of

time with Gray over the past few weeks. They mentioned you being there when he was at the hospital for his hand."

She turned to see Rick staring straight at her.

He tipped his head to the side. "They also said they saw you kissing, which is kind of strange for a girl who doesn't know him that well."

CHAPTER TWENTY-THREE

"You should have warned me," Marco said, leaning his elbows on the old kitchen table. "If I'd have known about you and this girl I would've played this differently. Or argued more for you coming to L.A. for the interview."

"I did suggest that," Gray pointed out. He was pissed. More than pissed. After a frantic call from Maddie, and Rick's suggestion that he wanted to talk to Ashleigh and his dad, he was completely over this whole damn interview. And his hand was throbbing like a bitch.

"But you didn't tell me why." Marco sighed. "I've spoken to Rick. He's agreed to keep it to a minimum about the two of you. But you have to admit, Gray, it's a great angle for him. *Big Rockstar Falls for Small Town Diner Waitress.* I can see the headline now."

"She's not just a small town diner waitress," Gray grumbled. "She's a musician, too."

Marco raised an eyebrow. "That's convenient."

"What do you mean?" Gray frowned.

"I mean, if I was some hick looking for a big break, I'd

probably be falling all over you, too."

"Yeah, well fuck you," he said, his voice graveled.

"You're tetchy as hell today."

"I'm injured, I'm tired, and now I'm dealing with all this crap. I knew this whole thing was a bad idea."

"It'll be fine. And your publicist will love it." Marco looked up. "Have you written any songs about this girl for the album?"

"*Maddie*," Gray said pointedly. "Her name's Maddie."

Marco's lip twitched. "Okay, have you written any songs about Maddie?" he asked. "Because that would give us a great angle."

"I'm not using my relationship with Maddie for an angle." He shook his head. "I don't like it and she wouldn't either. So that's a no-go."

"Gray, does she understand what she's getting into?" Marco's brows dipped with concern. "The gossip sites are going to be all over this. It's big news. You haven't dated anybody seriously since Ella Rackham a few years ago. And you remember what the response was to that, right?"

Yeah, he remembered. They couldn't go anywhere without the paparazzi being all over them. That had been part of the reason their relationship had ended.

"I don't want that for Maddie."

"You might not get a choice," Marco told him.

Gray leaned back in his chair and ran his good hand through his hair. "I need you to help me keep it quiet as long as we can. Jesus, we've barely started seeing each other."

"And it's already out of control." Marco sighed. "Look, Gray, I get it. It's annoying that you can't have a relationship without the public knowing all about it. But it's the price of fame. You can't change that. You just have to roll with it." He clasped his hands. "How serious is this thing between the two of you?"

Gray swallowed hard. He'd hated not talking with her for the past couple of days. Weird how quickly he'd gotten used to being with her. It was like his body craved her closeness. "It's serious," he said, his voice low.

Marco nodded. "Okay. How about I arrange for some media training for Maddie? We could fly her to L.A., have her talk to your publicist, work out a way to make it as easy as possible."

"Do we have to?" Gray grimaced.

"If you want to protect her, then yeah. Either we work out a strategy to deal with the media, or they'll come running for you. This way it's under our control."

"I'll talk to her," Gray muttered. Marco was right, he knew it, but it didn't stop him from feeling angry. Hartson's Creek was a whole other world to L.A., and he hated the way his two home towns seemed to be getting closer. For the past few weeks it had felt like the town had wrapped its arms around him and welcomed him home.

Now he felt like he was setting fire to the whole damn place.

～

"Mom?" Maddie called out, glancing inside the bedroom. Her mom was propped up on pillows, her reading glasses perched at the end of her nose. She took them off and looked up, a smile on her face.

"Hello, sweetheart."

"I'm heading out for the evening. Any problems just call me. I'll probably be late."

Her mom's smile faltered. "Should I ask where you're going?"

"Probably not," Maddie admitted.

"Okay. Well, be safe." Her eyes were soft. "Ashleigh invited me over for dinner on Sunday. I thought maybe I could talk to her. See if we can build some bridges." She twisted her glasses in her hands. "There has to be a way for you girls to get along."

"Try not to worry about us," Maddie told her, hating the way her mom sounded so forlorn. "None of this is your fault, and it's not your job to repair things."

"But I do worry. You and Ashleigh are my world. It breaks my heart that you're not speaking to each other."

Another heart broken. Maddie was leaving a trail of them. And all because she didn't want to break her own. Look how that turned out, her chest felt like it was being pulled apart.

"I'm sorry," she whispered.

Her mom attempted a smile. "Go and have a good time doing whatever it is you're doing. You'll work it out. I know you will."

Taking a deep breath, Maddie managed to conjure her own smile. "Thank you. Sleep tight."

She closed the door softly and glanced at her phone again. Her messages with Gray were still on the screen.

I'll pick you up at eight. Wear flats and bring a change of clothes – G.

A change of clothes? Why? Are you planning on throwing me in the creek? – M.

Something like that. I'll see you tonight. – G.

She felt a sense of relief now that the journalist had returned to L.A. and things were going back to normal. As far as she knew, he hadn't contacted Ashleigh – thank God. At least she'd managed to dodge a bullet there.

But more than anything, the relief came from being able to see Gray again. It had only been a couple of days since they were last together, but it felt like so much longer.

At exactly eight, a black car pulled up outside the house.

She grabbed the canvas bag she'd stuffed with a spare pair of jeans and t-shirt before she checked herself in the mirror, fluffing up the back of her hair with her free hand.

As she walked outside, to her surprise, the passenger door opened and Gray climbed out, a smile curling his lips.

"Aren't you driving?" she asked him, bemused.

"I hired a car for the night instead." He reached the steps, his eyes soft as he stopped in front of her. "God, I've missed you." He curled his hand around her waist and pulled her against him. She sighed at the feeling of his strong, lean body pressing into hers. And for the first time in days it felt like she could breathe easy again.

"Where are we going?" she asked as he took the bag from her and slung it over his shoulder.

"It's a surprise. You'll see."

She climbed into the backseat, and he followed, pulling the door closed behind him. As soon as they were buckled in, he grabbed her hand, enfolding it in his own.

"You okay?" he asked her, his gaze catching hers.

"I am now."

He grinned. "My sentiments exactly." Still holding her hands, he leaned forward. "Okay, we're good to go."

The sun was setting over the mountains to the west, casting a warm orange glow across the peaks. The driver switched on some music – a soft country song that had been playing non-stop on the radio for weeks, and she felt her body relax into the soft leather seats.

Gray slid his arm around her, pulling her close until her head rested on his broad shoulder. She felt him press his lips against her hair, then he slid his hands under her chin, angling her head until her face was a whisper away from his.

"Hey," he said softly. She could feel the warmth of his breath against her skin.

"Hey." Her chest contracted at his closeness. At the need

211

she felt shooting through her body.

He cupped her chin with his palm and brushed the sweetest of kisses against her lips. "I've missed you."

Hot sparks exploded in her chest as he kissed her again, his tongue soft against hers. She hooked her arms around his neck, her head tipped enough that she could meet his kisses with her own, and god, it felt good.

Too good.

Only when they broke for air did she remember where they were. In a car with a stranger driving them. She glanced in front to see if he'd been watching.

"It's okay," Gray whispered, his voice caressing her ear. "He's signed an NDA."

She lifted an eyebrow. "Why did he need to sign a confidentiality agreement?"

"Because I can't take a shit without somebody knowing about it." Gray shrugged. "And I wanted you to feel comfortable."

"You've been able to do a lot of things without anybody knowing," she pointed out. "Until you invited a journalist to town."

He grinned. "Mea culpa. But like I told you, that's all taken care of. Tonight we can relax and enjoy ourselves."

"So where are we going?" She looked out of the window again. It was getting darker, the sun only half visible beneath the caps of the mountains. She knew from its position they were heading south, but not to where.

"Actually, we're almost there."

"We are?" she frowned. "But there are only fields."

"When I say *there*, I mean we're at our first destination. This is where the car drops us off."

A minute later she saw an old, weather beaten wooden sign affixed to a metal post. *Sumner Airfield.* "We're going flying?" she asked, as the car turned right and drove through the gateway. Ahead of them were two large metal hangars. A myriad of small planes dotted on the blacktop and grassy field beyond. "At this time of night?"

Gray leaned down to kiss the tender spot between her jaw and neck. "Kinda," he murmured. "Just wait and see."

The car continued along the makeshift road, past the first hangar, then took a left alongside the second, coming to a stop when they reached the far side.

"A helicopter?" A bemused smile lifted her lips.

"Just for a short ride. It's faster than taking a car then a boat."

"A car then a boat," she repeated. "Where the heck are we going?" Her eyes were alight as they met his, a buzz shooting through her body. Nobody had ever done this for her before. Arranged a surprise – and what a damn surprise this was.

"I promised you a kiss in the ocean."

"Will a helicopter get us all the way to the west coast?"

He laughed, and it lit up his eyes. "No. But it'll get us to a pretty little island in the Atlantic, where I can kiss the hell out of you without anybody seeing."

"We're here, Mr. Hartson. Enjoy your evening," the driver said, climbing out of the car to open Maddie's door. She grabbed her bag of spare clothes and followed Gray to the little cabin next to the helipad. After they checked in with the pilot, he gave them a safety talk and told them how to correctly enter and exit the helicopter.

And then they were climbing aboard, Gray helping her up the steps and into one of the back passenger seats. He climbed into the other and they both buckled themselves in and put their headsets on as the pilot directed.

"Are you ready?" Gray asked her.

"I think so." Her heart was pounding, her body full of adrenaline. Gray took her hand, squeezing it tightly as the engine started up and the propellers began to beat. Even with the headphones on the sound was loud, the whomp-whomp of their rhythm matching the beat of her heart.

"Good evening," the pilot's voice echoed through their headphones. "We're just waiting for the rotors to get up to speed and for air traffic control to give us the nod to take off. Then we'll be flying for approximately thirty minutes to Samphire Island. The wind is with us on this leg, so coming back it might take a little longer. Go ahead and sit back, relax, and enjoy the views."

Maddie held her breath as the helicopter lifted vertically. It wasn't anything like flying in an airplane. Instead, it felt as though the ground was falling away beneath them, along with her stomach. She looked out of the window, watching as the world beneath them became smaller, the lights of the houses becoming tiny yellow and white dots.

Then they were flying forward and the sensation made her giddy. She laughed out loud, looking at Gray with sparkling eyes. The way he was staring at her made her breathless. There was a need in his eyes, but a softness, too. One that made her want to crawl her way into his lap and stay there forever.

"What do you think?" he asked.

"It's amazing." Her breath was short. "I thought it would feel like being in a plane, but it doesn't at all."

Twilight was in full force below them, and it made the landscape look desolate and beautiful. As they made their way toward the coast, the mountains giving way to the flats, and then to the dunes, she couldn't help but marvel at the beauty.

"Isn't it wonderful?" she asked Gray.

"Yeah." He grinned. "It is."

"How many times have you flown in a helicopter?"

"A few." He shrugged. "But this is my first time with you."

The way he said it made her skin tingle all over.

But it also made her realize how different his life was from hers. These past few weeks they'd felt like equals. Two inhabitants of Hartson's Creek spending time with each other. Falling for each other. But he wasn't just some guy who lived in town. He was Gray Hartson. He sold out arenas and took helicopters like they were taxis.

"You okay?" he asked her, as though he noticed her change in thoughts.

"Yeah. Just thinking about your life and mine. How different they are."

He reached out to stroke her cheek. "That's why I like you. Why I like this. Watching your face as you experience this flight for the first time. I'm not looking for somebody who likes me because I'm a singer or because I have money. I want you because you like the Gray Hartson who repairs roofs and cuts his hand up."

The tightness in her chest loosened a little. "But it all has to end soon, doesn't it? You'll go back to L.A. and touring, and I'll be here teaching piano and serving at the diner." No more late night visits. No more kisses that become dirty. No more hearing his deep voice in her ear as they make love beneath the stars. God, she was going to miss that.

"It doesn't have to end, Maddie."

"Okay, folks, we'll be landing in a few minutes. If you take a look outside, you'll see the Atlantic Ocean. And up ahead, if you stare real hard, you'll see a lighter dot. That's Samphire Island, your destination."

The dot grew bigger as they got closer, and she slipped her hand into Gray's as the helicopter slowed down and hovered over the helipad, slowly lowering down until the rails hit the ground.

And when the rotors finally stopped, Gray climbed out first, holding her waist as he helped her to the ground. Maddie knew the night was only just beginning.

CHAPTER TWENTY-FOUR

*D*inner was set up on the beach. The white chairs and table were positioned under a canopy of sparkling lights, facing toward the ocean as it ebbed and flowed against the shore. Gray couldn't stop looking at her, despite the beauty around him. At the way her face lit up as she saw the tiny candles lining a path to the water, or the waiter standing next to the table with a bottle of champagne in his hand and a cloth draped over his forearm.

"This is crazy," Maddie told him, shaking her head with a grin. "You know that, right?"

"Maybe we need a little crazy," he said. "It's been a tough few weeks."

"You know, I would have put out for a lot less." She tipped her head to the side. "You don't have to do all this. I'm pretty much a sure thing where you're concerned."

He pulled her against him, closing his eyes as he breathed her in. The floral scents of her shampoo mixed with the salty tang of the ocean, filling him up. "You're never a sure thing," he whispered. "I wish you were."

She tipped her head up to look at him. "Nobody's ever done this for me. Nobody. And you must know I'd go anywhere for you. It has to be written on my face."

His throat felt tight. Not just because this felt so right, but because it was what his soul needed. Somebody who wanted him for *him*. Not because he was Gray the football captain, or Gray the son who managed everything. And definitely not because he was Gray the successful musician.

But because he was Grayson Hartson IV, the kid who cried every night when his mom died, but hid it from his siblings because they needed him to be the strong one. The boy who protected them from their father's wrath. The teenager who escaped to follow his dreams, only to discover they had an edge of a nightmare, too.

And now Maddie was waking him up from those bad dreams. Showing him what life could be like if he could only have her.

Truth was, he wanted her more than he'd ever wanted anything in his life. Including his career.

"I want to kiss you," he said, his voice rough.

"Here on the beach?"

"No. In the ocean." He nodded his head toward the vast darkness. "The way I promised we would."

"Won't it be cold?" she asked, looking down at her jeans. "Is that why I brought a change of clothing?"

"Yeah. I figured we might get a little wet." He held his hand out. "Will you come with me?" The words felt heavy; full of unasked questions. And yet she slid her hand into his without hesitation, filling his heart with warmth. With a grin, he lifted her until she was in his arms, her legs wrapped around his waist, her arms around his neck, and he carried her to the water, loving the way she was laughing against his ear.

He didn't want to stop to take his clothes off, no matter how expensive they were. Didn't care about his socks or the designer jeans his stylist had paid way too much for. Instead, he kicked off his shoes and waded through the water, holding the woman he ached for in his arms, wincing as the cold water soaked the denim.

"Shouldn't we have taken off our clothes?" she asked him.

"Yeah." His voice was gruff. "We can do it now."

"Where will we put them?"

"They'll wash to the shore." He shrugged. "I'm not sure they'll be salvageable though." As if to demonstrate, he pulled her strappy flat sandals off and threw them onto the sand.

He glanced at where the waiter was still standing. "We'll be ready to eat in an hour."

The waiter nodded. "As you wish, sir. I'll be back then." He turned and left.

Then it was just the two of them and the ocean. He gently set Maddie down and pulled his t-shirt off, taking a sharp breath in as the spray hit his bare chest. Rolling it into a wet ball, he threw it until it thumped against the sand. "Score," he said softly.

"Don't get your hand wet," Maddie told him, nodding at the bandage on his left palm."

"Wouldn't dream of it." He winked.

Maddie grinned and pulled her dress off, revealing an ivory lace bra that barely covered her breasts. She followed his lead, throwing it, though her aim was worse than his and it bobbed in the tide.

Before he could take off his jeans, she was diving into the water. He watched as the ripples closed over her, before she surfaced again, swimming out toward the waves. "Come on," she called.

He grinned and unzipped his jeans, having to tug at the soaked denim to peel them from his legs. Then he pushed through the water, closing the distance between them with strong, sure strides.

He grabbed her waist with his good hand and pulled her to him. The water was chest deep here, and he could feel her float against him as she pressed against him. And damn if he didn't have the biggest hard-on as her chest pressed against his. Her arms curled around his neck to keep herself steady, and he cupped her face with his free, injured hand.

"You're beautiful," he whispered, brushing his lips down her neck and tasting the salt there. Her hair was damp, pulled back from her face. She arched her back, and he buried his face into her chest, pulling at her nipple with his lips. She unclipped her bra, throwing it into the water.

"I'll never see that agai… oh…" He sucked her in again, his tongue lapping against her sensitive flesh, and he felt her legs tighten around him. "Gray," she whispered.

"Yeah?"

"I haven't… we haven't got anything." She gasped as he moved to her other breast. "Condoms, I mean."

He laughed. "I guess we'll have to stop ourselves before we get too crazy."

But he wasn't ready yet; nowhere near. Not when she was grinding against him with every lash of his tongue, the water lifting her up and down as it gently ebbed and flowed. She shimmied against him until her core was against his hardness, dipping his head to catch her lips with his. She was clinging to him, her body naturally grinding against his.

Yeah, they didn't have anything, but he still wanted her to come. And when she did, he watched her. Head tipped back and mouth opened with a half-scream, her arms and legs clinging to him like she never wanted to let go.

Christ she was beautiful. He was determined to keep her. No matter the price he had to pay.

~

"THERE'S something I wanted to ask you," Gray said, putting his silverware onto the empty plate in front of him. They'd just eaten an amazing dish of soft shell crab with risotto and a green salad. Maddie could still taste the gorgeous dressing on her tongue.

"What is it?" she asked, looking over at him. The moon was high in the sky, illuminating his face, highlighting his prominent cheekbones and sharp jaw.

"I want you to fly to L.A. with me. Meet with my publicist."

She blinked. "When? Why?"

"Because like I told you before, I don't want this to be the end. I'm falling for you, Maddie. Hell, I think I fell about three weeks ago. But I have to go back to L.A. to record my album, and then I'll need to go on tour to promote it. That means being back in the limelight, and if I'm there, you will be too." He swallowed hard. "If you want to be with me, of course."

Her breath caught in her throat. "Of course I want to."

"You don't sound so sure."

"I'm just afraid," she admitted, looking down at her empty plate.

"What is there to be afraid of?" he asked her. "I'll be with you every step of the way. I won't let anything happen to you."

Her chest was so tight it felt like her heart was being pushed into her throat. "I'm afraid I'm not good enough for you," she told him.

Gray winced. "Why would you think that?"

"I'm just being honest." She shrugged. "Look at you and then look at me. We're worlds apart. And when people see me standing by your side they're going to see the same thing I do. They're going to talk about how you're batting below your average. How I'm pulling you down. I don't want that for you," she said softly. "Or for me."

He frowned. "Who treated you so poorly that you don't see yourself the way everybody else does?" he asked her. "Because you're crazy. Look at you. You're beautiful, you're funny as hell, and you sing and play piano like a goddamned angel. If anybody's batting below their average it's you."

Her eyes stung with tears. "There are things you don't know about me."

"Then tell me," he urged.

Her lip wobbled. He walked around the table and dropped to his knees next to her, his warm eyes catching hers. "There's nothing you can say that won't make me want you, Maddie. Can't you tell how I feel about you?"

"I..."

"I'm in love with you, Maddie. It sounds crazy, I know. It's only been a few weeks, and you're Ashleigh's sister, and all those other things stacked against us. But every time I close my eyes you're there. I wake up smiling every morning because I know I'll get to talk to you. And when I hold you in my arms, it feels like everything is right for the first time in forever. Since my mom died, I guess. You fill the hole in my heart that I didn't want to admit was there. So tell me whatever it is that's making you upset, because I never want to see you cry."

He pulled her against him, until her head was resting against his shoulder. She breathed in a ragged breath, tears spilling from her eyes. He loved her. The words filled her up. And yet there was so much he didn't know about her.

"Have you heard of Brad Rickson?" she asked, her lips pressing against his fresh shirt.

He kissed her damp hair. "No. Who is he? An ex?"

Oh god. Oh god. *Oh god.* She squeezed her eyes tightly shut. "He was at Ansell the same time I was. We dated for a while. And he just got a contract with your record company."

"He has?" Gray's voice was wary. When she opened her eyes again, his were trained on her face.

"Yeah. I should probably remind you who I was before I went to Ansell," Maddie said, forcing herself to meet his gaze. "I was just a kid. A sheltered one, too. The only time I'd been up to New York was for my interview, and I hadn't had time to linger. I was the definition of a small town girl, living in a small town world."

"There's nothing small about you." His voice was gruff.

The ghost of a smile passed her lips. "I guess I felt small. Some of that was growing up in Ashleigh's shadow. I was always *Ashleigh Clark's sister,* you know? Just not as pretty or as popular."

"You want me to tell you how much prettier you are?" he asked, sliding his hands through her hair. "Or I can show you?" He brushed his lips against hers.

She let out a sigh. "Wait. Let me tell you this, then you can decide what you think of me."

His face was serious when he pulled back, as though he understood the gravity of what she needed to say. His eyes were dark, his mouth a thin line. It made her chest contract.

"When I arrived at Ansell, it was the first time in my life that people weren't comparing me to Ashleigh," she told him softly. "And it felt good. Real good. I felt stronger, older, as though people were finally liking me for who I was." She bit her lip. "And that's where Brad came in."

"He saw you for who you were?"

Her voice caught. "I thought so. He was two years older. He'd spent a couple of years playing gigs and supporting bands to earn his tuition, and that age difference was huge to me. He'd been living in New York for years. He played in bars at night, and had a huge group of friends who all seemed so sophisticated." She swallowed hard. "So when he started talking to me in the hallways, it felt like I was special."

From the corner of her eye she could see Gray's hands curling into fists. As though he knew what was coming next. But he said nothing, his expression neutral.

"He was my first," she told him. "I hadn't really had a boyfriend before him. That first night he was gentle and kind, and when I woke up the next morning I was already thinking about how to ask him to come home with me for Spring Break so I could introduce him to my family."

"Did he come with you?"

She shook her head. "He said he was too busy and had to stay in New York." She shrugged. "But I guess the truth was, he didn't want to come. So I came home and spent the whole week dreaming of him, before going back and throwing myself into his arms. I was sleeping at his place most nights by that point. I'd go and watch him at a bar, or join him and his friends at a club. I guess I was trying real hard to be part of his crowd, though I still had this nagging feeling that I didn't fit in. With the girls, especially. They felt a bit out of reach, like they didn't want to engage with me." She pulled her gaze from his. "I drank more than I should've, in attempt to fit in. And tried some drugs, too."

"I know how that feels."

"I know you do," she whispered. "Maybe that's why I feel so connected to you."

"So what happened between you and Brad? What made you leave Ansell?"

"It was one night, not long before the end of the second semester. We'd been together for a while by that point, though he never referred to me as his girlfriend. Not in public, anyway." She bit down on her lip. So many red flags, but she'd been too naïve to see them. Too desperate to be accepted. "He'd been singing with his band and the alcohol had been flowing. One of the girls who hung around with them offered me a pill."

"What kind of pill?"

"The kind that makes everything feel hazy and good. I was buzzing by the time the bar closed. When Brad suggested the girl come home with us for another drink, I agreed, because I didn't want the night to end."

There was a tic in Gray's jaw. She watched as it dipped in and out.

"There was more drinking when we got back to Brad's place. Tequila, I think. He put some music on, was his usual charming self. And then he started kissing the other girl." She licked her dry lips. "Then he told me to kiss her, too."

"Did you?"

"I did. But I didn't like it. And I started to get upset." She looked down at her hands. "You probably think I'm a real prude."

"I don't think that at all. I know you're not. But I know I'd never want to share you with anybody else."

"I started to get hysterical. Accusing him of cheating on me. And Brad tried to calm me down. He took me in the bedroom, kissed me. Told me I was his number one and he'd never want me to do something I didn't want to do. He suggested I get ready for bed while he got rid of the girl. So I did. I showered because I felt weird, then I climbed into bed and waited for him. At some point I must have fallen asleep."

"Did he come to bed with you?" Gray asked.

She nodded. "Yeah. And so did she."

Gray's eyebrow lifted. "Did he make you?" he asked, his teeth gritted. "Did he make you have a threesome?"

"No." Her voice caught. "I woke up to the covers bunched around my feet. And, and they were having sex next to me while I was sleeping. I was so confused at first. Still woozy from the alcohol and drugs. I tried to say something, but the words wouldn't come out." She pressed her lips together. "I tried to move, to do anything, but it was like my whole body was weighted down. I guess I was lucky that he didn't take long to finish."

"The fucker." Gray spat the words out.

"That wasn't the worse thing." She brought her gaze to his.

He frowned. "What else did he do? Did he rape you?"

"No."

"Thank fuck. But I still want to kill him."

"He recorded it. The whole thing. Them having sex next to me while I was sleeping. My reaction when I woke up. All of it." She exhaled slowly. "Though I didn't know about that until I walked into school the next day."

"What happened?" He pulled her against him.

She fought against the urge to pull away, to run, to hide. She wanted to curl up in a ball and block it all out again, the way she had for so many years. To forget about the cruelty she'd witnessed. The pain that had shot through her when she realized he didn't feel the same way she did.

To forget about the way people *laughed*.

"Maddie?"

She blinked and pulled herself out of her thoughts. "It was all a joke. A bet. They were all members of some stupid club. Some of them had to swindle money out of people. Others had to face their worst fears. And Brad..." she sucked in a shaky breath. "Brad had to humiliate a virgin."

"Jesus, Maddie..."

"He uploaded the video to a porn site. Then he printed out fliers with a photo of me and the web address. I was a laughing stock within a couple of hours. Everywhere I went people were watching the video of me sleeping while they had sex."

"Did you report it?"

"To the dean?" she asked. "No. Not at first. Though Ashleigh contacted them as soon as I told her."

"I meant the police."

She shook her head. "The dean wanted to call the police, but I just..." her voice broke. "I couldn't." She blinked back tears. "It was so humiliating. I couldn't stand to be in New York anymore. Ashleigh drove up the moment I called her, and brought me home even though she wanted me to stay and fight for myself." She pressed her lips together. "She saved me." And now they weren't even talking. Her heart hurt at that thought.

"He got away with it," Gray muttered. "And now he's got a recording contract and you're here..." His jaw was tight, his eyes flashing. Maddie curled her fingers around his bicep.

"It's okay," she whispered.

"No, it isn't. I want to fucking kill him." His eyes drilled into hers. "The thought of him touching you. Hurting you. The bastard deserves to be destroyed for ruining your life."

"It's old news," she told him. "I'm over it. And the fact is, even if he'd never done anything to me, and I'd stayed at Ansell, I probably would have come home after graduating. My mom's here as well as Ashleigh and her family. I like my life."

"I have contacts. I can mess him up."

"No." Her voice was firm. "I don't want you to get involved. As I said, it's history. Over and done with. I just want to move on." She shifted in her chair. "But can you see now why it wouldn't work?"

"No." He shook his head. "I can't see that at all. I'm not like that asshole. I'd never hurt you like that. I want to protect you, Maddie. I want you to be with me. I don't want to see you cry like this." He wiped the tears from her cheeks.

"But you can't. You're famous, always in the news. And I can't..." her voice broke. "I can't do that with you. I've been talked about before and I can't stand it."

He cupped her chin with his palm, lifting her face until it was directly in front of his. She could see herself reflected in the depths of his eyes. "Maddie," he whispered. "You're damn beautiful. Since you walked into my life." He smiled. "Or jumped into it, things haven't been the same. I'll never be the same. You're all I think about. Yours is the name on my lips as I fall asleep, and when I wake up it's still there. Whatever it'll take to make this work, I'm ready to do it. Just say the word."

His words took her breath away. She wanted to believe him, she really did. And yeah, she knew he wasn't like Brad. He was a good guy. She'd been around him enough to know that.

"I'm scared," she said again.

"There's nothing to be scared of. I have a great publicist, and she'll help us with everything. We can just be us. You'll fly to LA. I'll fly back here. We can make this work if we want it enough."

Her heart was hammering against her chest. Not just with the memories of her humiliation, but because of the expression on his face. There was need there, and maybe a little bit of love, too. But more than anything, he looked vulnerable, and it touched her soul.

"I want to try," she whispered, and he closed his eyes for a moment. When he opened them again, a wide smile broke out on his lips.

"Thank God," he said. He kissed her like she was the air he needed to breathe, even though when he pulled away he was breathless. "Because I can't imagine being without you.

I'll call Marco and my publicist in the morning and warn them about this. I promise you I'll make it okay."

Maddie sighed against his lips, relief assailing her. He knew and he wasn't rejecting her. Maybe he was right. Things could work out after all.

CHAPTER TWENTY-FIVE

*H*e was in love with Madison Clark. Gray had no doubt about it. He'd loved her before tonight, but to know what she'd dealt with in New York made him admire her even more. Yeah, he had rumors printed about him, and done stupid things that had ended up as headlines in the wrong kind of newspapers. But he'd also had a publicist to deal with that, and fans who'd do anything to show they supported him.

But Maddie... It killed him to think about her being so alone and violated. Of somebody like Brad Rickson using her as a joke. Not caring about the hurt he'd caused.

Gray held her hand in his for the entire ride back in the helicopter, then held her body close against his in the backseat of the car that had brought them home, where they were right now. The driver was pointedly staring ahead through the windshield as Gray ran his finger down Maddie's face and leaned in to kiss her again, her lips tasting salty thanks to her dried tears.

"Can I come in with you?" he asked her, nodding at the bungalow.

"My mom's in there," Maddie said, her eyes wide.

"Yeah, I know. But I don't want to leave you tonight." He waited for her to fight, but instead her eyes met his and she nodded her head.

"Okay. But let me go in first and check that she's asleep." She pulled the passenger door open, then leaned forward to thank the driver.

A smile tugged at Gray's mouth. She was nothing if not polite at all times. Except to him. He loved that about her.

It was two minutes later that he saw her bedroom window open up. She leaned out and beckoned him. Even from behind, he could see the driver's grin.

"I'll head out. Thanks for driving," Gray told him.

"It's been a pleasure. I hope you enjoy the rest of your evening, sir."

Gray glanced at the clock on the dashboard. It showed a quarter after three a.m. "I will."

"I hope Miss Clark does, too. She's a lovely young woman."

"Yeah," Gray said, his throat scratchy. "Yeah, she is."

He climbed out of the car and watched it pull away, then walked over to where Maddie was waiting for him at the window.

"You want me to climb in?" he asked her. "Or will you be letting me in through the front door?"

She shrugged and stepped back, tugging at the curtain. "Climb away. Why break the habits of a lifetime?"

He did as he was told, using his good hand to scale the low sill, his feet landing on the soft cream carpet in her bedroom. She'd kicked her own shoes off and was barefoot. He could see a few grains of sand clinging to her skin. She reached up to touch her hair, wavy and salt-kissed from the ocean. "I should probably shower before bed."

"Stay like that. I like you dirty."

She rolled her eyes. It was like the old, sassy Maddie was back and he liked that. He liked her vulnerability, too. Christ, he liked everything about her. It was crazy how fast he'd fallen for her.

He watched as she changed into her pajama shorts and tank, and tugged a brush through her thick waves, wincing as it hit some knots. "I don't have anything for you to wear," she told him. "Unless you think you can fit into my pajamas."

He looked down at his body. A foot taller and at least sixty pounds heavier than Maddie's. "That wasn't how I planned on getting into your pajamas."

She pulled the blanket back and pointed at the mattress. "Just get in."

"Wait." He pulled his shoes off, then his jeans, and finally his t-shirt, before he climbed into her small bed wearing just his shorts. She followed him in, her legs warm as they brushed against his. There wasn't enough room for them not to. He turned on his side and reached his arm out, and she snuggled into the crook.

"Just so you know, there's no sex happening in here," she told him.

"No?" He grinned.

"Nope. This bed hasn't been christened and it'd like to stay that way." She looked up at him through her thick eyelashes. "You're the first guy that's ever been in here."

"When you say stuff like that, my body takes it as a challenge." He took her hand and slid it down between his thighs. "See?"

She curled her fingers around him and he groaned. "Maddie…"

"Your willpower is weak," she whispered.

"Yeah. It really is." He turned his head on the pillow. "How strong is yours?"

"Like a fortress."

231

He ran a finger down her throat to her chest. "Really?"

Her breath hitched as he reached the swell of her chest. "Yeah."

With the tip of his finger he traced over her breast, down her stomach, and continued until he reached her bare thighs. "So if I did this," he whispered, sliding his hand between her inner thighs, "you wouldn't open them."

She laughed because she already had. "It's just a reflex."

"Yeah. That's what I thought." He moved his hand up until it was an inch away from her core. "So your mind has willpower, but your body doesn't."

With the gentlest of touches, he brushed his thumb against her. Maddie gasped and tilted her head back. Her eyes softened as they met his, and he realized how much he wanted this. *Wanted her.*

"Maddie," he whispered, pressing his lips against her throat. "If you don't want me to do this I'll stop."

He was a gentleman. He knew right from wrong. But more than anything, he knew how important it was for her to be able to say yes or no. For her wishes to be heard. After everything she'd been through, her consent was everything.

"Just touching," she whispered. "Nothing more."

He grinned. "I can live with that." He slid his fingers beneath the soft fabric of her shorts, biting down a groan as they brushed her heat. God he wanted her. Any way he could. His thumb brushed the part of her that made her back arch in response, her skin heat up, and her eyes widen.

He could never get tired of this. Never get tired of her. He loved her.

And it was the scariest, most beautiful thought in the world.

$\sim$

"OH SHIT." Maddie's eyes widened as she realized it was morning, and Gray was still laying next to her in bed. Her skin was hot from being pressed against him all night, her hair a crazy mess from tossing and turning next to him. Just as he'd promised, they'd done nothing more than touching.

She never knew touching could be that hot.

"Gray," she whispered, shaking his shoulder.

"Uh?" He opened one eye, and then closed it again. It took her thirty seconds to realize he hadn't woken at all.

"Gray," she said louder, her face close to his. This time both eyes opened. A slow, sexy smile formed on his lips as he pulled her against his warm, firm chest.

"Morning, beautiful."

"We overslept. And Mom is up," Maddie whispered. She could hear her mom wheeling herself around the kitchen. "You need to go."

He blinked. "She knows about us, right?"

"Yeah. And she's not happy about the arguments between me and Ashleigh because of it."

He sat up, and she tried really hard not to look at the ridges of his chest, or the beautiful ink adorning it. "Then it sounds like a good time to lay on some charm."

"Now?" Her mouth dropped open.

"Why not?" He tucked his finger beneath her chin and closed it again. "And then we should go over to my family's place. Join them for breakfast."

"After that, why don't we take out an ad in *Rock Magazine*?" she teased. "Just to make sure nobody misses out on the news."

He grinned. "That's a good idea. I'll call my publicist."

"Gray!" She laughed. "Stop it." She climbed off the bed, catching her reflection in the mirror. "Ugh, I can't meet your family like this. I'm a mess."

"They already know what you look like," he pointed out. "And you look amazing as always."

"Yeah, they know what I look like. But only as Maddie, their friend and waitress. They'll look at me in a different way now that they know about us." She pulled her lip between her teeth.

"Aunt Gina and Becca love you. You have no worries there."

"But what about your father?" She gave him a worried glance.

"He'll be too busy judging me to worry about you."

Though he said it nonchalantly, there was a catch in his voice. And she knew that feeling all too well. The one where you didn't feel good enough.

"Okay," she said, taking a deep breath in. "We'll do the whole shebang. But let me take a shower and put some makeup on first, okay?"

Twenty minutes later, Maddie walked into the kitchen. Her mom was at the table, leaning over the crossword. She glanced up on hearing Maddie, putting her pen down on the newspaper.

"Good morning."

"Hi, Mom. I… um… we got back late so Gray stayed over." The last few words came out in a hurry, tumbling over each other.

"Hello, Gray," her mom said, her expression ominously neutral. "How are you?"

"I'm good, thank you, Mrs. Clark. How are you?"

"I'm very well. Apart from my daughters fighting like cats." She gave him a wry smile. "I'm hoping you'll help Maddie smooth things over. Now would you like some coffee? There's some in the pot."

"Actually, Mom, we're heading over to Gray's for breakfast," Maddie told her. "But I can make you something to eat first."

"I'm quite capable of making my own toast," she said pointedly. "You don't have to worry about me."

"Okay, then." It still felt weird. Standing in this kitchen next to Gray Hartson. Maddie could feel the warmth of him behind her. "I guess we'll see you later."

"That you will." Her mom picked up her pen and tapped it against her lips. Just as Maddie turned to leave, her eyes meeting Gray's, her mom spoke again. "Oh, Gray, can I have a word with you. In private?"

"Really, Mom?" Maddie let out a sigh.

"It's okay." Gray winked at her. "Sure. What's up, Mrs. Clark?"

"You should probably call me Jenny," she heard her mom say as Maddie walked into the hallway and reluctantly closed the door.

She should feel relieved. They'd made the first step, after all.

But she couldn't help but feel they still had a hundred flights more to scale.

"You okay?" Gray asked as they arrived at his place. Maddie drove them over in her car. She had a couple of hours before her shift at the diner, but she felt better having her car here. An escape route of sorts.

Just in case she needed it.

"What did my mom have to say?" she asked him as they climbed out. He looked so at ease as he slid his arm around her and pulled her against him. As they walked up the path to his father's house, he looked down at her.

"She reminded me that underneath all those wisecracks you have a soft heart."

"I hope you told her I have no heart." She shook her head. It was just like her mom to say something like that.

"I told her your soft heart is one of the reasons I like you." He grinned. "Along with your wisecracks." He steered her around to the back of the house.

"Where are we going?"

"You're family. We go in through the back door."

Breakfast was in full flow in the Hartson house. Through the sparkling glass window Maddie could see Becca holding a slice of toast and gesticulating wildly with it. Aunt Gina was saying something to her with an exasperated smile on her face. And Gray's father was watching them silently, his eyes soft as the two women carried out talking.

"You ready?" Gray asked her.

"What if I say no?" She grinned at him.

"I'd remind you that I had to do it first. And I even agreed to talk to your mom in private."

"Okay, I'm ready. But don't leave me alone with them."

"Wasn't planning on it." He winked and pushed the door open.

Three sets of eyes looked up at them as they walked into the kitchen. Aunt Gina's were full of curiosity. Becca's were wide with excitement. And Mr. Hartson? His seemed... wary.

"Morning," Gray said, his voice easy as he sauntered in. "I've brought Maddie over for some breakfast. Hope that's okay."

Aunt Gina was the first to recover. She stood and smiled widely. "Of course that's okay. Maddie's always welcome here. Come in. Let me grab some coffee."

Becca's eyes were still sparkling. "You can sit here," she said, patting the chair next to her. "And we can all listen as Gray tells us why he didn't come home last night."

"Becca," Aunt Gina said. It wasn't a question, more of a warning.

"Hey, I was worried about him," she protested, a mischievous smile lighting up her face.

"I took Maddie on a date."

Becca turned around on her chair to look at them both. "So you two are definitely dating?" she asked, turning to Maddie. "Aunt Gina told me, but I didn't believe her. And getting Gray to open up about anything is like trying to pry open a rock."

"Shut up," Gray said, sitting in the seat next to Maddie's. He slung his arm over the back of her chair. "We're dating, okay?"

"Oh my god!" Becca said, leaning forward to hug Maddie. "That's amazing. I never would have thought you two would after Ash…" she trailed off as though she thought better of it. "Does that mean you'll be coming home more often?" she asked Gray.

"We're still working things out."

"I always wanted a sister," Becca told Maddie. "You don't know what hell it is to have four brothers."

"I can imagine," Maddie said, her voice deadpan.

"All that testosterone and fighting. And the girlfriends." Becca rolled her eyes. "Present company excepted, of course. Being the sister of the four Heartbreak brothers is a special kind of hell. I must have done something really bad in my previous life."

"You've done a few bad things in *this* life," Aunt Gina pointed out. "Now let's stop with the twenty questions and let our guest have some breakfast. Maddie, would you like some eggs and bacon?" she asked her, standing up to carry the food over.

"That sounds wonderful," Maddie said gratefully, aware of Becca still staring at her and Gray.

"I'll have some bacon, too," Gray said, holding his plate up.

"You can serve yourself, young man," Aunt Gina told him, shaking her head. "You're not a guest and you still have one good hand. Unless that one gets injured, I don't plan on waiting on you." She sighed loudly. "Now Maddie, dear, would you like some orange juice?"

"Yes, please." Maddie bit down a smile at the way Gray's aunt and sister treated him. He didn't seem fazed at all. The only person who hadn't said a word was his father, who was watching all of them intently.

CHAPTER TWENTY-SIX

"*H*ave you read it?" Marco asked over the phone a few days later. Gray was sitting at the dining room table, this month's copy of *Rock Magazine* open in front of him. A courier had brought it this morning – knocking on the door twenty minutes ago and depositing the thick envelope in Gray's hand. He'd immediately brought it into the kitchen, which was mercifully empty, and opened it up, skimming through the pages until he found the one with his photograph splashed across it.

"Yeah, I've read it."

"And Maddie?"

"Not yet. She's working. I'll pick her up and let her read it then." He flicked through the glossy pages once more. "It's not so bad. She knew they'd print something about her time at Ansell. If anything, she's gotten off lighter than I hoped. Thanks for your help with that. I appreciate it."

Something beeped. It had to be Marco's phone. "One minute, Gray…"

"I should probably call the publicity department. They did a good job. And you spoke to the record company about

Brad Rickson, right? Told them I don't want him anywhere near me," Gray continued.

"Yeah, I did. I told them he upset your girlfriend and you don't want to be in the same room as him, even though you wouldn't give me all the gory details." Marcus sighed. "But Gray—"

"If I see him, I'm gonna hit the bastard. You know that, right?"

"Yeah. But that's not important right now." Marco talked fast, in an effort to stop Gray from interrupting him again. "I just got a message. There's a link to a video on Twitter. It's going viral."

"What video?"

"A video of Maddie from when she was at Ansell. A sex video. Do you know about this?"

It was like somebody had punched him in the face. Gray physically recoiled. "Where Brad is having sex with another woman next to her?" he asked, his stomach turning over.

"It looks like it. Christ, this isn't good. Why the hell didn't you tell me about it when you told me about Brad?"

"Because Maddie didn't want anybody to know. It was supposed to be old history." Gray raked his fingers through his hair. "Can you suppress it? Get Twitter to take it down?"

"Yeah, I can try. But it will take time. And somebody else will just post it again. These things are like flies. Every time you think you've got rid of one another appears." He cleared his throat. "I'll need to make some calls. But keep your phone close and I'll let you know what happens."

"I need to find Maddie," Gray said, his stomach churning. The thought of that video being out there would cut her up. Everybody would see it, and it would feel like she was being violated all over again. "Do what you can to make it go away."

"I'll try."

Gray didn't like the way Marco didn't sound very sure.

He pressed his lips together and slid his phone into his pocket, as his sister walked down the stairs

"Becca!" he called out, thanking God it was her day off. "Can you give me a ride into town?"

She scrambled down the stairs. "Sure," she said, tying her hair into a knot. "What's up, getting Maddie withdrawal symptoms?"

"Nope." He turned his phone over so she could see the screen. Becca skimmed the tweets, her eyes widening as she saw the contents.

"Oh shit," she whispered. "Poor, Maddie."

"These are going to kill her. I want to be there when she finds out."

"Okay," Becca said, pulling her keys from the hook on the wall. "Let's go."

MADDIE CLEARED the table a group had recently vacated, piling the plates on top of her arm before grabbing the mugs and glasses, balancing them carefully. She carried them over to the kitchen, using her behind to push the metal doors open, then deposited them in front of the dishwasher.

"They didn't touch their grits," Murphy grumbled, scraping the remnants into the trashcan. "Sometimes I don't know why I bother.

"What's eating you?" she asked him. "You've been in a bad mood all day."

"And you've been unreasonably happy for weeks. What happened to all those sarcastic remarks and the wise cracks?" Murphy asked her. "I hate happy people."

"No you don't."

He looked up at her with raised eyebrows. "I really do. So can you tone it down with that smile?"

She hadn't even realized she was smiling. That seemed to be happening a lot. Since her heart-to-heart with Gray on the beach, and their coming out to their families as a couple, she'd felt light as a feather. Her cheeks were beginning to ache.

"Happy waitresses are good for business," she pointed out. "I'm doing you a favor."

"Hmmph." Murphy slid the plates into the dishwasher. "In my experience, happy waitresses put in their notice. There's a definite correlation."

On a whim, she leaned forward and kissed his cheek. She wasn't sure who was more surprised, Murphy or her. "I'm not leaving," she told him. "I'm just happy. Try to be happy for me, too."

Grabbing the cleaning spray and a cloth, she walked back into the diner to wipe the table down. A group of girls were staring at their phones and giggling at something. She patted her jeans to find her own phone, and realized she'd left it in her jacket pocket, hanging in the kitchen.

The door opened, the bell ringing out, and Jessica Martin walked in with two other made up women.

"Grab a table, I'll bring some menus over," Maddie called out.

"Actually, Maddie," Jessica said, walking up to the counter. "I just came to make sure you were all right."

Maddie's brows pinched together. "I'm fine, thank you. How are you?" She wondered if Ashleigh had been talking to her.

"Well I'm not the one who's gone viral, so I'm doing great." Jessica smiled. "I'm glad you're not letting it bother you. People *are* going to talk, right?"

So the news about her and Gray was out. She knew it would be. "You read the magazine article?"

Jessica shook her head. "What magazine article? I'm

talking about that video of you and your... I don't know. Was he a boyfriend? And the girl, was she your girlfriend? I'm a little sheltered living here in Hartson's Creek. I don't know how those threesomes work." She laughed. "You're a dark horse, you know that?"

Maddie's chest felt tight. She tried to breathe in, but the air wouldn't go down. The door opened again, and Gray walked in, and it felt like everybody in the room turned to look at him.

And then at her.

Their eyes met, and she could see her worry reflected back in his deep blue depths. "Maddie..." he said, swallowing hard.

"I know." Her voice was croaky.

"Hi, Gray." Jessica smiled at him. "Long time no see."

He frowned. "Do I know you?" For a second, Maddie wanted to kiss him.

"I'm Jessica Martin. Formerly Jessica Chilton. You must remember me. I was a cheerleader." She looked affronted.

He shook his head, a frown pinching the skin between his brows. "Maddie, I need to talk to you."

"Oh, I heard you two had a thing going on. I guess it makes sense, right? She's the kind of girl that attracts the bad boys." Jessica shrugged. "I was just telling Maddie what a dark horse she is. I don't think I've ever met anybody who's had a threesome before."

"Judy, was it?" Gray asked. "Can you shut up and leave us alone?"

Her back straightened. "I'm a paying customer. I don't expect to be talked to like that."

"If you'll go sit down and shut the hell up, maybe somebody will come and serve you," Gray said.

Jessica opened her mouth and closed it again, shaking her head as though she was trying to work it out. Ignoring her silent protest, Gray took Maddie's arm and steered her toward the kitchen door.

Murphy looked up from the dishwasher as they entered. "Hey, no customers back here."

Maddie pulled her arm from Gray's hold and pulled the phone from her coat pocket, quickly opening it with her thumb.

"You don't need to look." Gray's voice was low. "It'll make you feel worse."

"I need to know how bad it is." She pulled up Twitter, frowning as that damn bird seemed to freeze on the screen.

"It's bad, Maddie," he said softly. "Real bad. But I'm working on it, okay?"

Twitter finally opened up on her phone, and she found herself typing her own name in. When the results came up, she stared at the screen, trying not to cry.

Never in her worst nightmares had she imagined being splashed over social media like this. Bad didn't even begin to cover it.

GRAY WATCHED as Maddie's face paled and her lips parted, knowing exactly what she was seeing. He'd watched it himself and just the memory of it made him want to get on a plane to L.A. and drag Brad Rickson by his hair down Hollywood Boulevard.

That asshole had it coming.

"Oh god, everybody will see this." Maddie's voice was thin. "Jessica will tell a few people and they'll tell others and everyone in town will know."

"And when they see it, they'll know that you were a victim."

She shook her head. "No. They'll see me as a laughing

stock. I can't do this. I can't go back out there and serve customers who are watching this." She squeezed her eyes shut and a tear escaped. "I just…" Her voice cracked.

Murphy walked over to Maddie, shooting Gray a strange look. "Maddie? You okay?"

She looked up at him, her eyes shining, and shook her head.

He glanced at the screen and frowned. "Is that you?"

Gray watched her hands shake as she passed him the phone. "You'll probably want me to leave," she said. "I understand."

"You want to go home?" Murphy asked her.

"No, I mean you'll want to fire me."

His frown deepened. "Why would I fire my best worker?"

"Do you see what this is, Murph?" she asked him, showing him her phone again. "This is a sex tape. With me in it. And all your customers are going to know what I look like with my clothes off."

"Maddie…"

She gasped in some air, her chest rising and falling rapidly. "I can't deal with this. I can't. I need to go…"

"I'll take you home," Gray said. "Becca's waiting outside."

"I can't go home. Mom doesn't know about this." She covered her mouth with her hand. "Oh god, Mom's going to find out."

She was starting to hyperventilate, her breath coming and going in shallow, ragged breaths. Gray reached out for her, but she recoiled as though his palm would burn her.

He felt helpless. And guilty. Because this was his fault. She'd been living with this secret for years. Nobody in town had known the real reason she'd left Ansell. But now, thanks to him, her name would be on everybody's lips.

"I'll shut the diner," Murphy said, his voice quiet. "You go home, Maddie. Where you belong." He glanced at Gray, then looked back at her. "You want me to drive you?"

"My car's outside. I'll drive myself."

"I'll come with you," Gray said quickly. "We can talk about what to do next. Let me tell Becca, okay?"

Maddie's voice was firm, in spite of her tears. "No. I need to be alone." Her arms were wrapped around her torso, as though she was protecting herself. It felt like she was warding him off.

Christ, he felt useless. He wanted to do something. Anything to take away the hurt expression on her face. Wanted to pull her into his arms and protect her from everything.

"You shouldn't be alone," Murphy said quietly. Gray was warming to him by the minute.

She pulled her jacket on and grabbed her keys from her pocket. "I can't be around people right now. I just need some time to think." She pressed her lips together in a grim smile. "I'll speak to you both later."

"Are you sure?" Gray asked her.

She nodded, and it felt like a stab to his heart. "Yeah, I'm sure." Then she walked out of the door that led to the paved back lot, pulling it softly closed behind her.

"Well, shit," Murphy said when she was gone. "And she was only telling me a few minutes ago how happy she was." He shrugged. "I guess we best go and close up."

THE FIRST THING Gray noticed when they walked out of the kitchen was how many people had entered the diner in the last few minutes. The second was the fiery-eyed blonde standing at the counter, shooting flaming daggers in his direction.

"Ashleigh." He nodded at her.

"Where's Maddie?" she asked, her voice low. "Does she know about the video?"

"Yeah, she knows," he whispered back. Just about everybody in the diner was staring at them.

"Is she in the kitchen? I need to talk to her."

"She just left."

"Where to?"

"Home, I guess." Gray swallowed.

"And you let her go?" Ashleigh's voice rose. The few people who hadn't been looking at them raised their heads to stare. "Jesus, Gray. She must be a complete mess."

"She wouldn't let me come with her. She wanted to be alone."

"Dear god, you're an idiot." She shook her head. "This is all your fault, you know that?"

"Yeah, I do." He curled his good hand into a fist.

"If you hadn't come sauntering back into town and made her fall in love with you, this would never have happened." She sighed heavily. "I promised her nobody would ever find out." Her eyes flashed. "You made me a liar."

"I didn't make you anything," he pointed out. "And does it matter if I did?"

Maddie was in love with him? He put that thought away to think about later.

"No, I guess not."

"Ashleigh. I'm surprised to see you here. I thought you and Maddie weren't talking." Jessica was still in here? Gray put his hands behind his back, because it really wasn't polite to hit a woman.

"She's my sister, Jessica."

"Not much of one. Not after she started sleeping with your ex. I'd kill my sister if she did that." Jessica leaned forward and whispered conspiratorially. "Have you seen the video? Is that why Gray likes her?"

"You know what, Jess?" Ashleigh said, exasperation in her voice. "Why don't you fuck off?"

The whole diner silenced. Enough for Murphy to be heard as he shouted out to tell them he was closing early.

"What did you say?" Jessica blinked.

"You heard me." Ashleigh squared up to her. For a moment, it was like being back in high school, watching the cheerleaders bitch at each other for some imagined slight.

"I'm on your side," Jessica hissed. "Your sister hurt you."

"Yeah, well, I don't need your kind of support. And neither does Maddie." Ashleigh turned to Gray. "I'm going to find my sister. Are you coming?"

"Yeah," he said. "I'm coming."

She grabbed his arm. "Then let's go."

CHAPTER TWENTY-SEVEN

"*N*ice car," he said as he climbed into Ashleigh's silver Mercedes. The interior was pristine, with tan leather seats polished to a shine.

"Thanks." She switched on the ignition. "What kind of car do you have?"

"In L.A? A Prius."

She pulled out of the parking space. "I never knew you cared about the environment."

"I don't like to make things worse than I need to." He shrugged and buckled his seatbelt.

"Could have fooled me."

He lifted an eyebrow. "Touché."

His phone rang as she turned left from the square, heading for the home where Maddie and her mom lived. "I need to take this. It's my manager."

"Sure. Your career always comes first."

He rolled his eyes and put the call on speaker. "Marco."

"I'm at the record company. All hell's breaking loose. We're working on a strategy to reduce the heat of the situation."

"Is Brad Rickson there?"

"No. He's laying low, but I saw his manager in with one of the big chiefs. I don't think they were throwing any parties. Anyway, the reason I called is because I'm with Angie."

"My publicist?"

Ashleigh shook her head.

"Yeah. She's doing what she can to get the video down, but that horse has pretty much bolted. We need to spin the story *now*, the best way we can."

"I'm listening."

"Her car isn't here," Ashleigh said, peering through the windshield. "Stay here, I'm going to check if she's inside." She climbed out of the car and slammed the door loudly.

"Okay," Marco continued talking to Gray. "We're setting up a second interview with *Rock Magazine*, but of course that won't come out until next month. We need something immediate, so Angie's calling around to all the late night TV shows. We're hoping Dan O'Leary might have a spot for you."

"You want me to be interviewed?" He couldn't stand sitting here waiting. With the phone still in his hand, he climbed out. "I can't fly to L.A., I'm needed here."

"You could bring Maddie with you. Make an exclusive about your relationship," Marco suggested. "That would definitely get the gossip spinning."

"It's not gonna happen," Gray growled. "I'm not subjecting Maddie to all that speculation."

"Glad to hear it," Ashleigh said, coming out of the house. "And she's not here. We need to get back in the car."

"Who's that with you?" Marco asked. "Is it Maddie?"

"It's her sister."

"Her sister, as in your ex?" Marco's voice rose up. "Gray, don't make this any worse than it is."

"Can you tell him I can hear every word he says?" Ashleigh said through gritted teeth.

"I'm sorry." Marco sighed. "But really, this is a mess, Gray. One that we need to clear up before the record company gets pissed. I'll book you on a flight tomorrow."

"I'm not coming. I'm not going to sit and spill the beans to Dan O'Leary."

"Yeah, you are," Ashleigh said. "You're going to get on that TV show and clear my sister's name. Damn, Laura hasn't seen her either. Do you think she might have gone to your place?"

"No. Becca would have called if she was there." Gray pressed his lips together. *Where was she?*

"Okay. We need to think of where she might be. Any ideas?"

"Marco, I need to go find Maddie. Can I call you back?"

"Sure. I'll book your tickets while you're looking and arrange for a car to pick you up in the morning."

"Great," he said sarcastically, ending the call. "Do you think she could be driving around still?" he asked Ashleigh.

"Was she crying?"

His heart clenched. "Yeah, she was," he said softly.

"Then no. It's really hard to drive when you're crying." She blew out a mouthful of air. "Ask me how I know."

"Ash…"

She shook her head. "Ignore me. I'm being a bitch again. I just want to find my sister."

"I'm sorry," he told her, his voice soft. "I'm really sorry I broke your heart."

Ashleigh nodded as she backed the car out of the driveway. "Thank you. I think that's all I needed to hear."

"And I have an idea on where to find Maddie."

"Where?" She shifted into drive.

"At the lake."

Ashleigh frowned. "Why the hell would Maddie be there?"

"We went there once. She told me she was never allowed there as a kid. I told her it used to be my favorite place to think."

"Okay." Ashleigh didn't sound so sure. "But I'm parking on the road. I don't want to get the car dirty."

When they pulled up to the turn, there were fresh tire marks in the mud. Gray glanced through the trees and spotted a red car parked to the side. "There's her car."

"Okay." Ashleigh glanced down at her feet. "Ugh. I'm going to have to ruin these shoes."

"I'll go get her."

"No you won't." She shook her head. "This is a sister job. Why don't you head home and I'll have her call you later?"

"Nope. I'm not going anywhere."

"You always were a stubborn asshole."

He grinned. "You remember."

"Well, stay here for a bit. I want to talk to her, sister to sister, okay?"

He looked at her curiously. "I thought you weren't talking."

"Yeah, well things have changed."

"I've got a feeling that beneath your icy demeanor you've got a heart of gold."

"Shut up," Ashleigh said, switching off the ignition. "For that comment, I'm not leaving you with any AC."

"I'll get out. Use nature's cooling. I'm a Prius driver, remember?"

"Whatever." She wrenched the door open. "Just don't get any mud in my car."

"Wouldn't dream of it." He climbed out of the passenger side and watched Ashleigh's ginger steps as she tried to avoid her heels sinking into the mud. He bit down a grin as she stumbled and had to lean on a tree to keep herself upright.

As soon as she was out of sight, he leaned on her car and

sighed. It had been a long day, and it felt like it was only getting started.

~

MADDIE PICKED up a stone and threw it into the lake. She'd turned her phone off. Couldn't bear to look at that damn video again. She'd thought she'd seen the last of it years ago, when Brad had taken it down at the Dean's insistence.

She felt violated. And ashamed. The thought of people in this town seeing it made her want to scream. She picked up another stone and threw it so hard it made her wrist hurt. It completely missed the lake and rebounded off a tree to the left.

"Here you are. Have you ever tried to walk through mud in a pair of stilettos?"

Recognizing the voice, Maddie shifted around and did a double take. Her usually pristine sister was holding a pair of mud-caked shoes in her hands. Her stockinged feet were covered in dirt. And her hair looked like she'd been to battle.

"Ash?"

"Gray thought you might be here." She wrinkled her nose. "I don't like that he was right."

"Why are *you* here?"

"Because I'm worried about you." Ashleigh walked on tiptoes across the grass, then stared down at the log Maddie was sitting on. There was moss on it, and some of the bark was pulling away.

"In for a penny." Ashleigh shrugged and smoothed her skirt down, taking a seat next to Maddie.

"You should get yourself a pair of jeans," Maddie suggested.

"I have a pair. I wear them when we're decorating the house."

"Once a year on Christmas?" Maddie's lips twitched.

"That's right." Ashleigh shrugged. "I didn't like this skirt much. Or these shoes." She leaned into Maddie, bumping her shoulder against her. "How are you doing, kiddo?"

"Are we talking now?"

"It looks like it." Ashleigh tipped her head to the side. "Unless you'd like me to leave?"

"You can stay." Maddie shrugged, trying to be nonchalant. The truth was, she wanted Ashleigh here with her. It felt comforting, like wrapping a warm blanket around her body. "Even though I broke your heart."

Ashleigh snorted. "I might have exaggerated a bit. I was upset with you."

"I got that message. I didn't realize how important Gray was to you."

"He isn't." Ashleigh waved her hand. "It was my ego talking. Nothing else." She laid her head on Maddie's shoulder. "You may have noticed I have quite a big one."

"I didn't."

"And that's why I love you." Ashleigh smiled at her. "Anyway, I got kind of pissed that Gray Hartson was okay with ditching me, yet he wanted you enough to incur everybody's wrath. It hit me where it hurts. Right in my self esteem." She pretended to bend over with pain. "And I took it out at you. I'm sorry."

"It's okay. It doesn't matter."

"Yeah, it does. But I guess we have more important things to deal with now."

"Like how you're going to smuggle me out of town and send me to a deserted island with no Wi-Fi?"

"You don't need to joke with me. I know how much this hurts." Ashleigh slid her arm around Maddie's shoulders. It was like she'd opened a dam. Tears pooled in Maddie's eyes. Angry ones. Hurt ones. Shameful ones. They spilled out and down her cheeks as she thought about that damn recording.

"Everybody will watch it."

"I know." Ashleigh nodded.

"And they'll all see me naked in bed next to those two…" Maddie's voice caught. "They'll laugh at me. The same way Brad and his friends did."

"No they won't." Ashleigh's voice was strong. "Because there's nothing funny about it, Maddie. What he did wasn't just immoral, it was illegal. He recorded you and uploaded it without your consent. None of this is your fault. Not one single bit. People are worried about you. That's all."

"Jessica looked pretty smug about it."

"Yeah, well she's a bitch. And if I hear her saying anything I'll pop her one."

Maddie sniffed. "I don't think I can do this again. I'm not strong enough."

"Yes you are. And there's a guy back at my car wanting to see how strong you are. I had to practically restrain him from coming with me."

"Gray's here?" Maddie frowned.

"I couldn't keep him away." Ashleigh rolled her eyes. "And I tried, believe me. I think that guy might really like you."

Yeah, well the feeling was mutual. Maddie liked him too much. The fear of getting hurt – *again* – pulled at her, making her want to curl in a ball like an armadillo, leaving only her hard armor for the world to see.

Life was easier if you didn't expose yourself to hurt. So much smoother when you let yourself be hard to the world. For one reckless moment, she'd exposed her tender flesh to it, and the knives had stabbed in.

She was an idiot. Because she knew this would happen.

"I want to go home now," she whispered.

Ashleigh took her hand. "Okay."

"And I want to eat my own body weight in ice cream."

"We can do that." Ashleigh nodded.

"And once that's gone, I want to open a bottle of whiskey and drink until everything disappears."

"From what I know of you, that'll only take two shots." Ashleigh stood and pulled Maddie with her. "Come on, let's take you home."

CHAPTER TWENTY-EIGHT

*A*shleigh turned her car onto Mulberry Drive, slamming her foot on the brake and forcing Maddie and Gray to lurch forward. In the passenger seat, Gray automatically braced his hands against the dash, and winced as the pain shot up his injured arm. He was in the middle of typing a message to Becca, asking her to pick up Maddie's car. He'd offered to drive her home, but Ashleigh had argued they'd all be safer in her car. In the end, Gray couldn't be bothered to fight.

"Goddamn."

"Do you see them?" Ashleigh asked, staring straight out of the windshield.

Maddie leaned forward from the backseat. "Who are they all?"

"The press." Gray let his head fall against the seat. "They're fast. Must be local. Nobody could get here from New York or L.A. this quickly."

"Mom's in there," Maddie said. Gray turned to look at her, taking in her worried expression. "We need to go help her."

"I'll call her." Ashleigh leaned over to pull her phone from her purse, opening it up with a swipe of her finger. "Mom?" she said as soon as the call connected. "You okay?"

"I assume you're referring to the circus outside the house. They've tried knocking a few times but I ignored them. " Her voice echoed over the loud speaker. "Is Maddie with you?"

"I'm here and I'm fine," Maddie lied. There was no way she wanted to cause her mom any more worries.

"Reverend Maitland called. Told me not to go online or watch any videos. I told him I have no idea how to surf the world wide web. Anyway, he's coming over and bringing a few friends with him. Said he'd talk to the press for us."

Maddie's eyes met Gray's. They were still watery. But for the first time since she'd come back to the car with Ashleigh, he could see something other than sadness there. Maybe humor. And a little bit of anger. He liked the change more than he could say.

"Ma'am, I'm going to take Maddie somewhere safe," Gray told her.

"Well don't take her to your house. Gina called to say there are folks banging on the door there, too."

"Shit." Gray blew out a mouthful of air. "I'll try to find us a hotel to stay in."

"No." Ashleigh shook her head. "I'll take her to my house. They won't find us there. And if they do, it's on a huge estate with closed gates. Nobody can get anywhere near her. Mom, I'll call you back later."

The thought of Maddie being away from him felt like a constrictor squeezing his chest. But he knew it was right. She wasn't ready for this exposure. He needed to make things right first.

"Okay," he said. "That seems for the best. I fly to L.A. tomorrow, but I'll be back early next week. Hopefully things will have calmed down by then, and we can get back to normal."

"Don't I get a say about this?" Maddie asked, arching an eyebrow.

Gray smiled. "Of course you do. Where do you want to go? If you'd rather go to a hotel, I'll find one."

She sighed. "No, it's okay. I'll go to Ashleigh's."

"You should probably get out of here, Gray," Ashleigh said, turning the car around. "Walk home through the woods. That way nobody will spot you."

"Can I say goodbye to my girl first?"

"Don't push it," Ashleigh muttered. But then she stopped the car, unclipped her seatbelt, and climbed out. "You have one minute, and then I'm coming back in. Don't dirty my car, okay?" She stomped out, ignoring the irony of her feet and shoes caked with dry mud. As soon as the door closed, Gray managed to climb through the gap in the seats until he was next to Maddie.

"You could have come through the door," Maddie told him. He hated the way her voice was so thick with emotion.

"That's not how we do things, is it?" He reached out to wipe away the tears on her cheeks. "Climbing is our thing."

"Like Romeo and Juliet."

"With a less tragic outcome, I hope." His eyes were soft as he smiled at her. "I'm sorry I got you caught up in this mess. You don't deserve it." He pressed his lips against hers. They were soft and swollen and made him ache for her. "I wish I could make it go away."

"So do I," she whispered, her mouth moving against his. "But you can't."

He slid his arm around her back, pulling her against him as he deepened the kiss, loving the way her breath came in tiny pants against his lips. When he pulled away, her eyes were hot and heated, and it was only by force of will that he didn't kiss her again.

"I have to go," he told her. "Before Ashleigh throws a fit."

"She's been so nice today."

"Yeah," he said with a smile. "It's making me nervous."

She laughed. It was quiet and muted, but still a laugh. He'd take it.

"She's okay," she said softly. "She may be a bitch at times, but she's always been there for me when I've needed her."

"Don't make me like her," he warned. "That's a step too far."

The driver's door opened and Ashleigh peered in. "Are you done?" she asked Gray.

His eyes caught Maddie's. "We're not even started."

"Just get out," Ashleigh said with a sigh. "Before the paparazzi catch you in my car."

He kissed the tip of Maddie's nose. "I'll call you later. I'll be in L.A. for two days. Three at the most."

"Where are you going now?"

"Back to my dad's. I need to pack. And I want to make sure they're okay."

"Be careful."

"I can deal with the press. I've been doing it for years. It's you I'm worried about."

"If you're that worried, maybe you can get the hell out of here before we all get mobbed." Ashleigh climbed in and shut the door with a bang.

"I changed my mind," Gray told Maddie. "I do kind of like her. The same way I kind of like Hannibal Lecter."

"Get out, rockstar."

He grinned. He couldn't imagine a time when he wouldn't enjoy messing with Ashleigh. Maybe that was a good thing. Whether Maddie knew it or not, he was planning on being around for a while.

∾

"YOUR FATHER'S IN THE STUDY," Aunt Gina told him as Gray walked through the kitchen door. "You might want to tell him you're home."

Gray let out a mouthful of air. The last thing he needed was another confrontation with his dad. And he knew this *would* be a confrontation. There were cars haphazardly parked up the road, and a group of journalists and photographers milling around the end of the driveway. They hadn't spotted him come home, thanks to the back route through the woods, but it was only a matter of time before they came and knocked at the door again.

"I'll go see him."

"I warned Becca about all those cars out there. She's staying with her friend Ellie tonight," Aunt Gina said, untying the apron she'd been wearing to clean the dishes. "I'm heading over to Jenny Clark's place. We're all taking turns sitting with her."

Another thing he was responsible for. "Should I pay for a hotel room for Maddie's mom until things die down?"

Aunt Gina's face softened. She walked forward and reached up to pat his cheek. "You're a good boy, you know that? But no, Jenny prefers to stay in her house. She knows where everything is there. It's adapted for her. She'll wait them out. She has plenty of time." Her expression turned grim. "And if they try to mess with her, they'll have to get through us."

Gray walked into his father's study a couple of minutes later.

His dad glanced up from the newspaper he'd been reading. "I see you've caused mayhem outside."

Gray leaned against the doorjamb, stuffing his hands in

his pockets. "You don't need to worry. They'll be gone by tomorrow. I'm heading to L.A."

"You're leaving?"

"For a few days. There are some things I need to do."

"Hmm."

"I have an interview. To talk about me and Maddie Clark."

"Your relationships are giving me whiplash. It doesn't seem that long ago that you and Ashleigh were dating."

Gray figured he might as well get used to talking to a hostile audience. "I dated Ashleigh when I was a kid. But Maddie's the woman I've fallen for."

"Right." His dad carefully folded his newspaper, pushing it aside to give Gray his full attention. "And are you planning on breaking this Clark girl's heart, too? One might be seen as a mistake. Two looks like you're targeting the family."

"I'm not planning on hurting her at all. I'm in love with her."

His father's brow lifted. "Ah. That sounds messy."

"I'm not expecting your blessing," Gray told him. "I've learned over the years to live without that. I just want you to know, in case you hear people talking."

"I don't listen to gossip."

"I know that."

His dad pushed himself to standing, wincing as his knees cracked. With his palms flat on his desk, he leaned forward, his eyes catching Gray's. "I know you think I've been hard on you."

"I don't think it, I know it. You busted my ass constantly as a kid. And as an adult. Why do you think I never came home all these years?"

His dad winced. "There's a reason for that. Life's hard, Gray. Damn hard. I wanted you and your brothers to be tough enough to take it. God knows I wish somebody had taught me that."

Gray's heart was clamoring against his ribcage. He thought about all those years he'd been desperate for his father's approval, but instead had gotten his condemnation instead. Yeah, they'd made him hard. Hard enough to face this now.

But at what cost?

"I just wanted your love," Gray told him, his voice thick. "But I know you had none of that left in you. Not after Mom died." He took a deep breath. "But I've come to realize I don't need it. Not any more. I'm not scared of you, Dad. I feel sorry for you."

His dad pressed his lips together and grabbed his cane, leaning heavily on it. "I'm an old man, Grayson. Too old to change and start talking about love and happiness." He walked over to where Gray was standing. "But maybe you should look in the top drawer of my desk. You might learn something."

Gray stepped to the left so his father could walk through the doorway.

"I'm going to sit in the garden," he said. "I expect you'll be gone by the time I come back."

Gray silently watched his father leave. Curious, he walked over to his dad's old mahogany desk, and sat down in the green leather chair he'd just vacated. It was still warm.

He curled the fingers of his good hand beneath the handle and pulled at the drawer, frowning when it stuck. Another tug and it grudgingly opened.

Gray reached inside to pull something out. A CD. He lifted it to his eyes and saw it was one of his. His second album, with his bare, tattooed torso on the front.

There were more CDs in there. Four of them in total. And there were printed programs from his tours – ones that Aunt Gina must have brought back with her. Blinking, he pulled out a large scrapbook and opened it up. The pages were covered with magazine and newspaper articles, and fliers from his shows. Gray turned the pages carefully, his throat scratchy as he read early reviews of his first album, when nobody had known who he was.

And then the last item pasted. His interview with *Rock Magazine*. His dad must have done that this morning.

Tears stung at his eyes. He blinked them away as he closed the scrapbook and carefully replaced it in the drawer. The top of the book snagged at something. A frame. Gray lifted it carefully, so it didn't catch at the scrapbook and turned it over to look at the photograph. It was in color, but faded as though it had been left facing the sun for too long. Still, it was clear enough for Gray to recognize the people standing in the backyard of this very house.

His father looked so young. He couldn't have been much older than Gray was now. And he was standing next to a beautiful young woman. *Gray's mom.* There was a baby in her arms – himself, he presumed – and the two of them were looking down at the little one, smiles lighting up their faces.

He swallowed hard. He'd never seen this photograph before. Never seen it on his father's desk or in his bedroom. Had he hidden it away because the memories were too painful? God knew it hurt Gray to look at it.

His chest was still tight as he pushed the drawer closed and stood to walk out of the study.

His father was too old to change, he'd admitted as much himself, but maybe Gray could live with that. Understand it, even. Because if he'd lost Maddie the way his father had lost his mom, it would kill him.

With that thought, he headed upstairs to pack the essentials he'd need for the flight to L.A. It was time to stand up for the one good thing in his life.

CHAPTER TWENTY-NINE

*M*addie was moping, and she didn't like it one bit. She didn't let things affect her, not any more. She had trampoline skin, problems bounced off her and on to somebody else. And the things that didn't? Well, she usually had a sarcastic retort that made it look as though it didn't hurt.

But this video and all the comments people were making about it? They hurt her to the core. Some people were saying she was a gold-digger, first setting her eyes on Brad Rickson and then on Gray Hartson. Others were making fun of her, asking how she could sleep through two people having sex next to her.

And yeah, there were kind words, too. People saying how despicable it was that Brad recorded his cheating on her while she was sleeping. Others calling for him to be prosecuted for sex crimes.

Either way, all of it made her want to hide away from the world. To unzip herself from this body and climb into a dark corner until the gossip died down.

That's if it ever died down. Hartson's Creek was a small

town. People here gossiped the same way they breathed in oxygen.

"Grace wants you to read her a story," Ashleigh said as she walked into the family room. "That's if you're up for it."

"Of course I am." Maddie put her phone down resolutely. "I'd love to read to her."

"When you come back down, we can open a bottle of wine and eat that ice cream you were talking about. And watch something on Netflix."

"Are you sure I'm not causing you any problems by being here?" Maddie asked her. "I can't imagine this is what you had planned for this evening."

"Honey, you're my sister. Nothing is more important than making sure you're okay right now."

It was strange how easily they'd fell out and made up again. It had been like that ever since they were little girls. Maybe blood did run thicker than water. Because Maddie felt love for her sister wash over her.

She felt something else, too. The strength she'd been searching for all day. It hadn't disappeared forever, it was just hiding for a while. Licking its wounds while it thought about its next move. She felt her spine straighten. Not enough for it to be visibly noticeable, but it was there.

She was sick of moping and being the victim. That wasn't her. Not any more.

"Can I get a raincheck for the movie?" she asked her sister. "Because I have something else to do first."

"What?" Ashleigh smiled, bemused.

"I need to book a ticket. I'm going to L.A. to meet Gray."

"Okay, so let's go over this one more time," Angie, his PR consultant said, looking down at the notes she'd made on her phone. "We've agreed that you'll talk about the upcoming album, your hand, and of course about you and Maddie, but there's to be no mention of Brad Rickson and his involvement in the tape. Not while the record company is still consulting their lawyers."

"And if Dan O'Leary asks me about him?"

"He's agreed not to. It's only a five minute segment. When it's complete, you'll perform *Along the River*." She smiled at him. "Without your guitar, of course."

"We've got a great lead guitarist to play for you," Marco told him. "Alex Drummond. You know him, right?"

"I've toured with him."

"Excellent. You guys will have some rehearsal time before the show starts. You need to be at the studio by six."

"And before that, you'll meet Rich Charles from *Rock Magazine*," Angie told him. "He's joining you for an early dinner. That gives us an hour. Shall we go through some questions again?" she asked, smiling brightly. "I could record us and we can watch you back if that helps?"

No, it wouldn't help. Not one little bit.

The fact is, he didn't want to be here. He wanted to be in a little town about two-and-a-half thousand miles away, leaning on the counter of a diner that served the worst eggs in the country. He wanted to be watching the pretty woman behind it. To be catching her eye.

He wanted what he had. Now that he was back in L.A., he felt the loss keenly.

It hadn't helped that when he arrived at LAX last night he'd been greeted by a throng of paparazzi. Flash bulbs had momentarily blinded him as he pushed his way through to the exit, aware of the bodyguard the record company had hired standing right behind him. Gray wasn't a small man, not at six-three, but the protective giant had dwarfed him.

And he hated that he needed that protection.

He checked his phone to see if Maddie had replied to the text he'd sent earlier, but the message was still unread. He frowned, then tapped out a message to Becca asking if everything was okay in Hartson's Creek.

Her reply came back fast. *Yeah. Most of the press have gone. Murphy started threatening to cook them breakfast – I think that's what finally scattered them.*

"You okay?" Marco asked him.

Gray sighed. "Yeah, I'm okay. I just wish this would go away. That the press would leave me alone."

"It's the price you pay," Marco reminded him. "It's never worried you before."

"Maybe I've changed."

Marco forced a smile. "Let's hope you haven't changed *too* much. Your fans like you the way you are. By tomorrow you'll be yesterday's news. Just go on the O'Leary show, say what we agreed, and Angie will do the rest."

And then what? That was the question. Ever since that video had gone viral, he'd had a griping pain in the pit of his stomach. He only had to think of Maddie's face when she looked at her phone to know how devastated she was at her secret getting out. Even if the press stopped talking about it, the good folks of Hartson's Creek wouldn't. Thanks to him, Maddie was going to have to live with that.

There was another thought going through his head. One that made that gripe turn into actual pain. What if this was all too much for her? What if she decided she didn't want to be in the spotlight? That she'd rather keep under the radar than be with him?

He gritted his teeth at the thought of it. These few weeks with her, they'd been life-changing. She'd shown him another way of living. One that didn't involve constant touring and paparazzi and meaningless relationships.

Maddie was the real deal, and she was the only one who saw into his soul.

Losing her could kill him.

Marco's phone buzzed. "Your car's here," he told Gray. "We'll head over to the restaurant a little early. It'll give us a chance to catch up."

Gray said goodbye to Angie and followed Marco out of the conference room. The hallway was wide, the walls covered in posters and golden discs, and Gray raised an eyebrow when he saw his latest one there.

"Gray," a voice called. "Can I talk to you?"

He looked up to see a woman of around thirty walking toward him. Her hair was cut short and dyed platinum. With her drainpipe jeans and skin-tight black band tee, she fit right in around here.

"Not now, Rae," Marco said. Then under his breath, he muttered to Gray, "That's Brad Rickson's manager."

"It won't take long, Marco. Brad would like to talk to Gray for a moment." She raised her eyebrows. "To apologize."

"I've got nothing to say to him," Gray told her, fire rising up inside him. "And it isn't me he needs to apologize to."

"He'd like to set up a meeting with Maddie, too." Rae's smile was conciliatory. "He's aware of how much he messed up when he was a kid and he's disgusted by it all. He's as upset as you are that it's leaked. It had to be somebody from the school they both went to."

"That's not a good idea," Marco said firmly. "Thank you, but no."

"It was years ago," Rae protested as they passed her by. "Are you really going to let his career be ruined over this? It was a prank gone wrong. A bad judgment. Haven't we all made those? Come on, at least talk to him. Man to man."

Gray whipped around, his eyes blazing. "He's not a fucking man, he's an asshole. And I don't deal with assholes, full stop. If you're his manager, then I advise you to keep him away from me, unless you want to manage a dead singer."

"Gray," Marco murmured, patting his arm. "Keep calm."

"He ruined Maddie's life, did you know that?" Gray told her. "She left Ansell because of him. Abandoned her musical career. So don't ask me to feel sorry that his career is ruined. He deserves so much more than that."

"Everything okay?" Liam, his security detail, asked, coming out of the elevator. "The car's still waiting down there and the coast is clear."

"We're coming now," Marco assured him, steering Gray down the hallway.

"Call me if you change your mind," Rae shouted out at their retreating backs. "Marco has my number."

"We're not calling her," Gray muttered as they walked into the open elevator. "Not now and not ever."

"Of course we're not." Marco nodded. "Come on, let's go talk to some journalists. Start setting the record straight."

IT HAD BEEN LESS than two months since Gray sang in front of an audience like this, but it felt like a lifetime spanned between then and now. He felt bare without his guitar. He leaned into the microphone, his good hand curling around the stem as he looked out at the crowd.

They were on his side. He knew that from the moment they'd applauded wildly as soon as Dan O'Leary had called his name. They'd cheered again when he told them that Brad Rickson was an asshole, although Dan had apologized profusely for Gray's language.

"It's the only thing I can think of at the moment that won't get you kicked off air," Gray had told him. "And I don't want that to happen."

The audience had laughed, and he'd known he had them. He wondered if Maddie was watching the show at Ashleigh's house. He hoped she was.

It had been Angie's suggestion that he sing one of his most popular songs. "Now's not the time to be trying out your new stuff," she told him. "You want the fans to connect with you right away; both the ones in the audience and the ones at home. Give them something they can sing along to. Help them bond with you."

There was only one song he really wanted to sing. The one he'd sung in front of her. And that night at the Moonlight Bar he hadn't even realized how he felt about her. Hadn't understood that every word he sang was for her.

But now he knew.

The guitarist strummed the intro, and the audience began clapping again. He looked out at them, and then at the camera, willing Maddie to be looking back at him.

Then he felt the adrenaline surge. It was like a drug rushing through his veins. His heart started beating to the rhythm of the drummer, and all those thoughts, those worries, they dissolved into the air, the music taking over.

"Remember when we were kids?" He kept his eyes on the camera.

His voice was deep and smooth. Somebody had once told him he could sing the panties off a nun. He'd laughed, but right now he wanted to sing into her heart. If that made him soft he didn't care.

"And everything we did? The days we spent at school right by the river."

He could hear the backup singers right with him, their harmonies melting into his.

"The day that love died. And everybody cried. We held each other tight by the river."

God, he wanted to hold her again. To feel the softness of

271

her chest against his hard planes. To stroke her hair and feel its silky tendrils twisting between his fingers. With every word he sang, his heart ached because now he knew what those words meant.

He knew what love was. And he wanted to sing it to the world.

When the song came to an end, the audience sprung to their feet and clapped wildly, whistles echoing through the studio. Dan O'Leary was clapping, too, a huge smile on his face as he walked over to thank Gray. A moment later, he turned to face the camera and segued into the commercial break.

Then they were off-air and it was over. The adrenaline remained, though, making Gray's movements a little jerky.

"You were amazing. The audience loved you," Dan told him, shaking his hand. "Come back soon, okay?"

"That sounds good." Gray nodded.

"And for what it's worth, I've met Brad Rickson and he *is* an asshole." Dan gave him a wry smile. "I hope he gets what's coming to him."

Gray didn't linger in the studio. After thanking the band and the production staff, Liam hustled him and Marco toward the stage door. As it opened, he could see people everywhere. Fans crowding around, desperate to get a look at him. When they saw him walk out, they began to chant his name.

"There's too many people," Liam said to Marco. "We'll need to get him straight to the car."

"No." Gray shook his head. "I always make time for my fans."

Marco shrugged. "It's up to you. Ten minutes, okay? And if there's any trouble we get out of here."

Gray spoke to as many of them as he could, posing for selfies, signing posters. When they got too close, Liam would shuffle between them, pushing them back. Gray's cheeks were aching from smiling, and his hand was throbbing like a bitch. Still, he continued to make his way through, thanking them for all their support and for being there.

It was overwhelming. Maybe that's why he almost missed her standing there in the street..

She was hanging at the back, an amused grin on her face as he looked up at her. Her warm eyes met his, it felt like he was being enveloped in a blanket of good feelings.

"Maddie?"

"Hey." She grinned at him. The first thing he noticed was that the red rims around her eyes were gone. Where her mouth had been tight with worry the last time they were together, there now was an ease.

And damn if he didn't want to kiss those lips.

"What are you doing here?"

She shrugged, still smiling. "I kind of missed you."

Thank Christ. "I kind of missed you, too." His voice was rough. Not just from the singing. There was a lump in his throat he couldn't quite clear.

"Gray! Can I talk to you?"

His smile disappeared when he saw Brad Rickson walking toward them. His first instinct was to step in front of her, to shield her from the asshole. He looked around to see where Liam was.

Thank god, he was right behind them.

A murmur came from the crowd. From the corner of his eye, Gray could see them lifting their phones to record the scene.

"Liam, we need to go," he muttered.

"I'm on it."

"What's going on?" Maddie asked, grabbing his arm. She must have seen Brad right after, because Gray heard her gasp.

273

"It's okay. We're leaving. You don't have to talk to him."

"Is that Maddie?" Brad asked, pushing his way toward them. "Maddie, I need to talk to you. You need to tell everyone it's a misunderstanding."

"Get out of here," Gray said, his voice ominously quiet. "Don't say a word to her."

"She's a fucking freak." Brad's voice rose up. "Everybody at school said so. She's nothing. Nobody. So why the hell is she ruining my career?"

Gray's hands curled into fists. "Get out," he growled. "Before I fucking slay you."

"Let's get you out of here." Liam put his hand on Gray's arm, but he shrugged him off.

"Get Maddie out. I'm okay."

"I'm not going anywhere," Maddie told him. "Not without you."

"Jesus, she's doing it again. She was fucking clingy with me, too." Brad shook his head. "I hope she's a better lay now than she was when I was with her."

He stepped forward, his good arm pulling back to give his punch enough impact. But before his hand could connect with Brad's jaw, Maddie was stepping in front of him. Gray had to stagger back to avoid hitting her.

Then Brad was stumbling backward, a shocked expression on his face. It was only when Maddie cursed and cradled her fist that Gray realized she'd hit Brad herself.

There were phones everywhere, being held up and pointed at the three of them. Liam stepped between Maddie and Brad, who was standing completely still, as though he was dazed. "Miss Clark, we need to get you and Mr. Hartson out of here."

Maddie nodded. She looked pretty dazed herself. "Okay."

Liam hustled the three of them through the crowd, then opened the door of the black town car that was waiting at the end of the street. Maddie climbed in first, followed by Gray and Marco. Liam walked around to get into the front seat.

"Okay," Liam told the driver. "We can go." He turned to look at Maddie. "Unless the lady wants to take another swing at Mr. Rickson."

CHAPTER THIRTY

The corners of Gray's eyes crinkled up as he grinned at her. "I've been messaging you all day. Now I know why you didn't reply."

"I replied when I arrived in LAX, but you were probably in the studio by then," she told him. She was still shocked from seeing Brad again. From hitting him. It was like she was in some kind of dream.

It hurt to move her hand. She winced when she tried.

"Let me take a look," Gray murmured, reaching for her hand. He touched it gently with his own good one. "Does it hurt?"

"Yeah. Like a bitch." She raised her eyebrows.

"You should have let me hit him."

"And had you ruin your remaining good hand? I don't think so."

His eyes were soft and warm. "I'd have done it for you."

"I know you would've. But I'm glad I hit him. He had it coming. Has for years."

Gray's lips twitched. "You should have seen his face. It was a freaking picture."

She tried – and failed – to swallow down her laugh. "I saw it."

"Well you'll be pleased to hear it's been recorded for posterity," Marco said, not sounding amused at all. "It's all over social media. So much for stopping this story in its tracks."

Marco's phone began to buzz and he let out a sigh. "That's Angie. She's going to be pissed."

As he answered the phone, Gray gently folded his fingers around Maddie's aching hand. "We should take you to the hospital," he told her.

"Nothing's broken. I can move it. There'll just be a bruise," she whispered.

He lifted it up and brushed his lips against her palm. "Better safe than sorry."

"I'll call a doctor to come to your house," Marco said, covering his phone with his hand. "Probably best to stay out of the public eye for now." He shook his head and went back to his conversation.

It took half an hour to get to Gray's sprawling home, overlooking the Malibu coast. Even at this time of night, the L.A. traffic was nose to tail. Maddie blinked as the car swung through the open electric gates, her eyes widening as she took in the low-level white stuccoed house. It was modern and sleek and nothing like the houses in Hartson's Creek. She couldn't help but feel a little intimidated by it.

Liam went in first to check the house. Two minutes later, he came back out of the front door and leaned into the car. "Everything's clear. You both have a good evening."

"And try not to hit anybody else tonight, okay? Unless it's Gray, in which case you have my full approval." Marco grinned at Maddie.

Gray laughed and shook his head.

They climbed out of the car and onto Gray's graveled driveway.

The first thing she noticed was the sound of the waves crashing against the sand below. She could smell the salty tang of the ocean, along with the sweet fragrance of the jasmine lining the pathway. Gray slung her bag over his shoulder and slid his arm around her, leading her up the steps.

They walked inside and the driver started the engine again, driving back out through the gates, taking Liam and Marco with him. Maddie was surprised at how quiet it was up here. Once the sound of the car had disappeared there was nothing except the ocean and her heartbeat.

"So this is me." Gray led her into a huge hallway. The walls were painted white, the floor a sandstone tile. In the center was a round sofa, the seats facing outward, upholstered in a light gray velvet that caught the lights as he turned them on.

"It's different to home," Maddie said, trying not to be overwhelmed by the size of everything.

Gray laughed. "You could say that. Let's head to the kitchen. Are you hungry?"

She shook her head. "No. Not really."

"I'll grab us a couple bottles of water. Then I'll show you around the place."

It felt like every room was more impressive than the last. The furniture was big – custom made, according to Gray – and the whitewashed walls were covered in paintings and posters. But they did nothing to dull the echo of their footsteps as they walked through the doorways of the rooms. There was something else, too. Maddie frowned, trying to place what was missing.

"Where's all your stuff?" she finally asked him.

"What stuff?"

She bit her lip, thinking of her own bedroom strewn with photographs and mementos, clothes and cosmetics. And of course her music. That was everywhere.

But Gray's place felt like an elegant hotel room. Beautifully furnished and full of style, and yet somehow soulless.

"Your things. Your clothes. Your shoes. Magazines or books or things you leave on the table because you're tired and can't be bothered to clean up."

He blinked. "I guess the maid puts everything away. I'm not here that often. A few weeks at a time. And when I'm here, I just want to relax, you know? Stare out at the ocean, play my guitar. I don't have a lot of things."

"Oh."

He smiled at her. "It's a big house for one person. I bought it a few years ago, thinking I'd eventually settle down and find someone to live in here with me."

"It's very beautiful," she told him, ignoring the tightness in her chest. "For the right person, it would make a wonderful home."

They'd made it to the living room. She followed him to the huge sliding glass doors that overlooked the beach. Even at night she could see how amazing the view was. No wonder he'd fallen in love with it.

And yet… it wasn't home.

Not to her.

"You don't like it," he said, his voice casual.

"I didn't say that. It's just not…" she trailed off and took a deep breath. "It seems so impersonal."

His eyes softened. "It's okay," he told her. "I feel the same. It's like living on the set of a movie or something. It's not real life."

He'd captured it exactly. Being here felt like being on vacation. Perfect to spend a few days, but after that, she'd yearn for home.

He turned to her and cupped her face with his warm palm. She closed her eyes and breathed him in.

"I bought this place because I had something to prove," he said softly, leaning in to brush his lips against hers. "To my dad, more than anybody. And he doesn't even know it exists. I wanted everybody who saw it to know I'd made it. That I'm someone. But at the end of the day it's just bricks and mortar."

Her eyes caught his. "I know you have to spend a lot of time here. And L.A. is an amazing place. But Hartson's Creek is home. For me at least."

He kissed her again. Firmer and surer this time. In spite of her exhaustion, and the throbbing ache in her hand, she could feel her body respond to him. She pressed her chest against his, curled her good hand around his neck and kissed him harder.

Gray moaned into her lips and a jolt of pleasure shot through her.

"Baby, home is wherever you are," he told her, his mouth moving against hers. "Hartson's Creek, London, Paris. I don't give a shit. I just want you in my arms."

"You say that now, but what about your job?"

"I'm always traveling, you know that. Maybe sometimes you'll travel with me and sometimes you won't. Eventually, we'll have to rethink things when we have kids."

Her lips curled. "We're having kids?"

"Yeah. I'm thinking four boys."

She laughed. "Because that worked out so well for you."

He ran his finger along the sharp line of her cheek. "Boys, girls, I don't really care. I just want a few of them. And you, playing the piano and keeping us all in order. I like the idea of that a lot."

She was grinning now. The picture he was painting was pulling at her heart.

"And on Sundays, we'll go to church and make Reverend Maitland happy. Then we'll take the kids to Murphy's and tell them to avoid the eggs."

"You've got it all planned out."

"I've had a while to think about things," he told her. "Maybe Hartson's Creek is in my blood. The same way it's in yours. God knows I've tried to out run it, and I thought I'd done it, too. But then I went home and found my heart. Found a way to breathe again." He pressed his brow against hers, their lashes touching. "Thanks to you."

"Where would we live?" she asked him, not ready to give up the picture yet.

"We'd find a piece of land. Build a big house and have a studio attached. You can teach piano. Maybe write songs, too. When I'm not touring I'll record my albums there. Maybe even produce for a few others. And at the end of each day we'll sit on a couple of Adirondack chairs with a beer and stare at the lightning bugs."

God, she wanted that. More than she'd ever realized. "What about the paparazzi?"

"They'll move on because we'll be boring as hell." He grinned. "There's not much money in a rockstar living happily ever after." He tipped his head to the side, his eyes scanning her face. "Of course, that means you'll probably have to hang up your boxing gloves."

She raised her brows. "I can do that. It was only for one night."

"That's good, because you have a mean right hook."

"You'd do well to remember it."

"Baby, I will." He kissed her jaw, her throat, the little dip at the base of her neck. She held her breath as her nipples peaked beneath her thin t-shirt. "And I mean every word of it. I want the happily ever after, the white picket fence. The Brady Bunch family who sings together." His eyes were intent as he lifted his head from her chest. "I want you, Madison Clark. Will you have me?"

Her body ached with need. For him. His vision of the future. The family he wanted them to make. She could see the truth in his eyes as the corner of his lips curled up into that sexy smile she could never resist.

"Yeah, Gray Hartson. I'll have you."

THE STORY of Maddie hitting Brad Rickson dominated social media for almost twenty-four hours. It even got it's own hashtag – #suckerpunched. But then a national politician was caught on camera with a Hollywood actress and nobody was talking about Maddie and Gray anymore.

Gray couldn't help but feel grateful that someone else had taken their place in the Twittersphere as they landed in Baltimore airport. It meant that their transfer from the plane to the car waiting for them outside was almost seamless. Only a couple of teenage girls noticed them.

"I guess we're already yesterday's news," he said as the car drove down the highway toward Hartson's Creek.

"Thank goodness." Maddie leaned her head against his shoulder. Her hand was bandaged tightly, thanks to the doctor who'd arrived at Gray's house two nights before. He'd told her to rest it up for a few days, and apply cold compresses if it ached any more. Gray laughed every time he looked at their matching injuries. "Maybe they'll leave us alone for a while now."

"Here's hoping." He kissed the skin on her brow. It was impossible to describe how warm he felt right now, driving toward his father's house with the woman he loved next to him. The emptiness was gone, replaced by her. Maddie

Clark. The woman he intended to spend the rest of his life with.

There was a reception line waiting for them when they arrived at his dad's house an hour later. Becca was there, grinning, with her fists held up as though she was about to fight. Next to her was Ashleigh, dressed to the nines in what looked like a brand spanking new pair of shoes and silk skirt suit, along with Maddie's mom, and Aunt Gina. Gray swallowed hard when he looked up to see his dad standing at the top of the steps that led to the front door, his back ramrod straight, his face almost impassive.

Almost because Gray swore he could see a hint of a smile there before he turned and walked back into the house.

"I guess this is Hartson's Creek's version of paparazzi," he murmured as the car came to a halt.

"They look innocent, but they'll break you in thirty seconds," Maddie agreed, her eyes bright with happiness. "We should go face the music."

"Yeah we should." He turned her to face him, then pressed the sweetest kiss to her lips. He wasn't in any rush to get out and talk to them. Not when he could be kissing Madison Clark to his heart's content.

"Gray?"

"Mmm?" His words vibrated against her lips.

"I think they're watching."

"Let 'em." He kissed her again. "They need to get used to it. Because I intend to kiss you a lot."

"Sounds terrible." She kissed him back breathlessly.

He laughed. "That's why I love you. You know how to stroke my ego."

"Your ego doesn't need stroking. It's big enough." Her voice dipped, her eyes softening. "I love you, too, Gray Hartson. Even though everything about us shouldn't work."

"But it does," he told her, his heart growing about ten

sizes bigger. She loved him and it lit up his world like a firework. He could never get enough of hearing it.

"Yeah, it does." She leaned forward to kiss him again. "Now let's go and face the inquisition. They're starting to get restless."

Sure enough, Becca was bearing down on them, along with Ashleigh and Aunt Gina.

"Okay," he agreed, his eyes bright with love. "Let's do it."

*M*oney didn't just talk, it worked its ass off for you, Maddie thought as she stared up at the house. It had taken just under eight months to build. From the moment they put in the plans to the zoning committee, to the day the last contractor drove away, his orange van kicking up a cloud of dust as he disappeared into the distance.

And now it wasn't just a house, it was a home. *Their home.* The one they would live in and work in. The one where her mom would eventually move into the specially built annex to the left of the main house, that was adapted to her needs.

There was a huge music studio at the end of the grassy yard. Along with the recording studio for Gray, it housed a separate music room for Maddie. There, she could teach the students she'd kept on, and work on writing her own music. She'd written two of the songs on Gray's latest album, and they sounded great. Sometimes she had to pinch herself to believe it.

And when it was just the two of them working at the

studio, the overstuffed leather sofa in Gray's office was the perfect place for them to reconnect.

Yeah, that *might* have happened that morning. So sue her. He was her boyfriend and he was hot. Some things were too good to pass up.

"What time is it?" Gray asked, his shadow falling over her as he embraced her from behind.

"Almost four," Maddie said, leaning her head back on his chest. He leaned down to kiss her neck and she felt it all over again. Those shivers, that need. Would they ever go away? She grinned as she pictured them being the kind of parents who drove their kids mad with too much affection. "People should start arriving by six. Your brother called to say they'd landed."

"Which brother?" He curled his hand around her waist, sliding his lips along the curve of her shoulder.

"Tanner. He's picking up Logan and Cameron, remember?"

He grinned against her skin. "I remember. I was just wondering which one of them would think to call. I should've known it was Tanner."

In the past few months, Maddie had gotten to know Gray's brothers better. They'd taken her under their wings, teased her the same way they teased Becca when they video-called. Challenged her to fist fights when they met up in real life. It was hard to not fall for *all* the Heartbreak Brothers. They were strong and warm, and if you were family, they protected you to the death. She liked them being part of her life.

Even Ashleigh had grudgingly admitted they were okay. Which was high praise from her.

"So, family here tonight, and then a big party tomorrow," Gray said, sliding his hands down her hips. She loved the way he always had to touch her when they were close. As though he was half-afraid she wasn't real. "And after that, we get the place to ourselves again."

"Until you start recording in two weeks," she reminded him. "And then the band is staying with us."

He looked up, wrinkling his nose. "Do you think I could postpone it? I want to spend some time with my girl."

"You've spent nothing but time with me." But she grinned anyway because she knew how he felt. "I came with you to L.A. for the album, then you stayed here with me so I could work with my students. And then we both went to Mexico because you needed the break."

"Maybe I should rethink this producing thing," he murmured. "Become a house husband instead."

"You'd get bored in a minute," she said, raising an eyebrow.

"No I wouldn't."

She grinned. "Yeah, you would. You couldn't even sit still for five minutes in Mexico. You ended up writing four songs. And when this place was being built, you kept insisting on helping the contractors. Let's face it, Gray, you're a guy who doesn't like sitting around doing nothing."

"I'd do it with you," he told her, his lips curling into a smile. *That smile.* The one that always made her body shiver.

She slid her hand into his. "Then come and sit with me now. Tell me about your day. Then we can go and get ready for our families. You know Aunt Gina is always early."

"And your mom and Ashleigh are always late."

She grinned. "And your brothers usually get the wrong day completely." It was amazing how easily he'd slotted into her world, the same way she'd fit perfectly into his. As though there was a Maddie and Gray shaped space in each of their lives, just waiting to be filled. Some weekends they really did go to church and then on to see Murphy – who'd finally come to terms with her quitting her job. And others were in L.A., spending time with Gray's music friends and talking with his record label. She'd even managed to sell a few of her songs to them directly. It was a source of pride that it wasn't only his money that had gone into building the home they were sharing together.

"You know, I've got a better idea," Gray said, pulling her up the steps to the house before swinging her into his arms. "We've got an hour before anybody arrives, and a huge bed that's missing us. We should go check on it."

"Yeah, we should." Maddie nodded. "I'd hate for an inanimate piece of furniture to feel lonely."

He slid his hands down her back, his palms warming her through her thin sundress. "There's only one way to make it feel better."

"Sleep in it?"

He pulled her against him tight, until she was in no doubt about the way she affected him. "What I had in mind doesn't include sleeping."

She arched an eyebrow, loving every minute. "What does it include?"

"Let me show you." He backed her up until she was through the door and in the kitchen, his arms still holding her hips. "It won't take long."

"Famous last words." But she loved it anyway. Loved being in his arms. Loved being kissed by him. Loved the way he always wanted to be with her, on her, *inside* her.

Because that's what she wanted, too.

OKAY, so it had taken a little longer than he'd planned. But it had been worth every minute of worshipping her body. Gray let his head fall back on his pillow as Maddie curled her body into his, her head nestled into his crook.

Even after all these months he couldn't get enough of her. He honestly thought he never would. They'd be old and decrepit and he'd still slowly shuffle her up to bed so he could take her all over again.

"What are you thinking about?" Maddie asked.

"You getting old and wrinkly."

"Eww." She turned to look at him. "That's horrible."

"Nope." He grinned. "I was thinking how sexy you'll be then. All that extra skin for me to kiss."

She rolled her eyes. "Did you start drinking early?"

"This is all me, babe. No alcohol needed. You're enough of a drug." His eyes sparkled as they met hers. He could see the love he had for her reflected back in them, and it made him want her all over again.

"We should get up. Take a shower." She rolled onto her side to check the clock on the table next to the bed.

That's when the front door slammed. She whipped her head back, her eyes wide as a voice called up the stairs.

"Gray, you in here?"

"Tanner," Gray mouthed. Maddie's mouth dropped open, and he had to bite down a laugh.

"Where's the beer?" That was either Logan or Cam. Gray still couldn't tell their voices apart.

"Stop opening every cupboard, Cam." Okay, that was *definitely* Logan. "You should wait to be invited."

"They're early," Maddie whispered.

"Yep."

"And I'm naked."

"I noticed." His voice was low and appreciative.

"You need to go down and stop them from coming up." Maddie jumped out of bed. "Tell them I'm showering because… because… I've spent all day unpacking."

"Sure." He gave her a crooked smile. "They'll believe that."

289

He climbed off the mattress and grabbed his clothes. "I'll wash up real fast and go down to say hi."

She covered her face with her palms. "I can't believe I let you talk me into this."

He slowly peeled her fingers away. "Babe?"

"Yes?"

"They're my brothers. They're not going to care what we've been doing. They might make a few jokes to see you blush, but they love you. So, go take that shower and come down to say hello, because they'll be happy to see you."

She took a deep breath, her eyes meeting his. "Okay."

God, she was amazing. He'd do anything for her, he really would. She didn't just fight her own demons, she helped him fight his, too. She was his person, the one he'd been searching for forever, and he wouldn't have it any other way.

WHEN HE MADE IT DOWNSTAIRS, his brothers had already made themselves at home. It made his heart swell to see the three of them sitting around his kitchen island, drinking beers that Cam had discovered in the refrigerator.

"Hey." He grinned at them as he walked in. "Is there a bottle for me?"

"Hey, bro. Of course. There's always beer for you." Cam slid an opened bottle down the counter, and Gray caught it with an open palm, beer sloshing over his skin.

"How was your trip?"

"It was good. Except for Cam's snoring," Logan told him.

"I don't snore."

"Yeah, bro, you do. Why do you think I used to stay in my girlfriend's dorm when we were at college?"

Tanner shook his head, his eyes meeting Gray's. "Your house is beautiful. You guys did a great job."

"Thanks." Gray took a sip of beer. "I'll show you around when Maddie comes down."

"Where is she?" Cam asked, looking around as though she was crouching in the corner.

"Taking a shower."

Logan laughed. "Did we interrupt something?"

"The oldest Heartbreak brother strikes again." Cam lifted his bottle up.

"Guys, pipe down. She's been working all day and wanted to clean up before you arrived." Gray shook his head. "You had to be early for once."

"Don't tell me we interrupted you before the end," Tanner said, laughing. "Cam, I told you we should have waited for somebody to open the door."

"No way." Cam grinned. "Remember the time Gray caught me with Ellie Maynard in the summer house? This is payback time."

"You were twelve," Gray told him. "And Ellie was Logan's girl. And the summer house wasn't yours either."

"I'm a twin." Cam shrugged. "I was born to share."

Gray opened his mouth to reply when a loud knock came from the back door. "Hold that thought." He walked over to open it, a grin spreading across his face when he saw his little sister standing there.

"Becca. You're the only one in this family who has manners, do you know that?" he asked, ushering her in. "See, guys, this is how to be polite. You knock, wait for somebody to answer, *then* walk in when invited."

Becca grinned at him. "Now that you've invited me in once I'll probably let myself in from now on, like a vampire." She hugged him then ran over to where her other brothers were sitting, letting them hug her and rag on her and everything else the Hartson family always did. "Thanks," she said to Tanner when he opened her a beer. "And by the way, guess who's back in town?"

"Shady?" Cam suggested.

"Shut up. I'm talking to Tanner."

Cam pretended to be shot in the chest, grasping his pecs as he keeled to the side.

"I'll bite," Tanner said, smiling at his little sister. "Who's back?"

"Savannah Reid."

For an almost imperceptible moment, Tanner's eyes widened. Then he took a mouthful of beer and carefully rearranged his expression. "She is?" he asked, his voice nonchalant.

"Who's Savannah Reid?" Gray asked.

"She was called Van at school," Becca told him.

Gray blinked. "Van as in Tanner's best friend, Van?"

Becca grinned. "Yep. I saw her at the diner yesterday. She didn't say much but I get the impression she's back for good."

Tanner emptied his bottle and put it on the table, saying nothing.

"Little Van is back," Cam said, grinning. "Damn, she was a fireball. Anything we could do, she could do better. Skim stones, play football, she even won a few fights." They all joined in with stories of their childhood. All except Tanner. Gray noticed his brother staring into the distance, his expression thoughtful.

"You okay?" he asked Tanner.

"Yeah, I'm good. I think I'll get another beer. You want one?"

"Still drinking this one." Gray held up his bottle.

"Has the party started already?" Maddie asked, walking down the stairs into the huge kitchen. "I thought it was tomorrow."

"Maddie's here," Becca squealed, running over to hug her. "Thank god, I was getting choked by all the testosterone."

After greeting his brothers with hugs, Maddie slid her arm around Gray's waist and kissed his cheek. "Everything okay?" she murmured.

"More than okay." He turned to kiss her lips. Every word was true. He was surrounded by his family. The ones he was born with and the one he was making, and he couldn't think of anything more perfect. Cameron opened another beer and passed it to her. Gray pulled her into his lap, the breakfast stool standing steadfast against their weight.

He curled his arms around her and breathed in the fresh scent of her shampoo, feeling like he'd finally made it home.

As far as Gray was concerned, there was no place he'd rather be.

THE END

DEAR READER

Thank you so much for reading Maddie and Gray's story. If you enjoyed it and you get a chance, I'd be so grateful if you can leave a review. And don't forget to keep an eye out for **STILL THE ONE,** the second book in the series.

To learn more, you can sign up for my newsletter here: http://www.subscribepage.com/e4u8i8

I can't wait to share more stories with you.

Yours,

Carrie xx

ABOUT THE AUTHOR

Carrie Elks writes contemporary romance with a sizzling edge. Her first book, *Fix You*, has been translated into eight languages and made a surprise appearance on *Big Brother* in Brazil. Luckily for her, it wasn't voted out.

Carrie lives with her husband, two lovely children and a larger-than-life black pug called Plato. When she isn't writing or reading, she can be found baking, drinking an occasional (!) glass of wine, or chatting on social media.

You can find Carrie in all these places
www.carrieelks.com
carrie.elks@mail.com

ALSO BY CARRIE ELKS

THE HEARTBREAK BROTHERS SERIES

Take Me Home

Still The One

A Better Man

ANGEL SANDS SERIES

Let Me Burn

She's Like the Wind

Sweet Little Lies

Just A Kiss

Baby I'm Yours

Pieces Of Us

Chasing The Sun

THE SHAKESPEARE SISTERS SERIES

Summer's Lease

A Winter's Tale

Absent in the Spring

By Virtue Fall

THE LOVE IN LONDON SERIES

Coming Down

Broken Chords

Canada Square

STANDALONE

Fix You

ACKNOWLEDGMENTS

First thanks always go to my lovely family. Ash, Ella, Olly and Plato the pug. I love you guys.

So many thanks and much love to Meire Dias, my agent and my friend. Your unstinting support is amazing. To Flavia, Hannah and Jackie at the Bookcase Agency, thank you for all you do. I'm so proud to be represented by you.

My editor Rose David and my proofreader, Mich, always work tirelessly to make my words shine. Thank you for all you do.

Najla Qamber is a kick-ass designer, and she hit this cover out of the park. You're amazing, lady!

Bloggers have always been such an important part of my book journey. Thanks to each and every one of you who shows me support in so many ways – sharing covers and release days, promoting sales, reading and reviewing books.

You're the engine that keeps the book world going, and I appreciate you so much.

Finally, to my lovely facebook group members (The Water Cooler - COME AND JOIN US!), thank you! We have so much fun – you make Facebook a great place to be. You help with ideas, inspiration and most of all you put a smile on my face. Thanks for being so amazing.